Dear
Lily

BOOKS BY DREW DAVIES

The Shape of Us

DREW
DAVIES

Dear Lily

Bookouture

Published by Bookouture in 2019

An imprint of StoryFire Ltd.

Carmelite House
50 Victoria Embankment
London EC4Y 0DZ

www.bookouture.com

ISBN: 978-1-78681-728-0
eBook ISBN: 978-1-78681-727-3

To my sisters, Ellie, Amber and Holly.

LETTER ONE

Friday, 6 April

~~Dear Lily,~~

No, that's way too formal and composed.

<u>Help! Lily!</u>

Better, but doesn't quite communicate the profoundness (profundity? profundification?) of this mess I'm in.

OH GOD, LILY, I THINK I'VE RUINED MY LIFE!!

Perfect.

Lil – seriously – what have I done? Wrenching myself away from everything I know, and everyone dear to me. I never even stopped to think about the consequences on YOU either – losing your only sibling, abandoned by your much-wiser and (very slightly) older sister.

'Oh, eff off!' I can hear you saying with perfect clarity. 'What wisdom?'

But there are things, Lil. I can always tell when milk is about to go bad, for one – I don't even need to smell it, I just shake the carton. If that's not wisdom, I don't know what is. And I've always been your agony aunt, ~~meddling~~ listening to your problems, especially romantic ones. I was also a great buffer in your infamous shouting matches with Mum – so see, you will miss me.

What's that? you say. Maybe I should come home immediately?

No, actually that doesn't sound like you at all. You've always loved the idea of leaving everything behind and starting over. You'd relish this. Maybe that's why I've done it – to impress you. Impressed yet? Can I leave now?

'Sheesh – give it a chance, lady!' is what you'd actually say. 'It might be fun.'

Fine. I'm in Denmark; the happiest place on Earth, I'm told. And I'm miserable.

Back home, before I left, I'd been so busy – preparing things at work, packing my stuff, going to all those farewell drinks, saying goodbye to you, and Mum and Dad, avoiding my not-boyfriend Robby – I never had a moment to stop and process the fact that I was leaving London. But then, with all my worldly possessions gone from the flat, it finally hit home. Someone (me apparently, although I'd like to see the tapes) had bought a one-way ticket to a strange country I've never even visited before.

WHAT WAS I THINKING?

Okay, breathe.

Yesterday was my last day in the UK office – sending off eleventh-hour emails and doing everything that I'd procrastinated over for the past eight weeks in a crazed, sweaty rush. This included some last-minute social media stalking of my new subordinates (probably shouldn't call them that – colleagues, they're my new Danish colleagues. Probably shouldn't be online stalking them either…) – two guys… and a lady. I know, crazy, huh?, another woman in medical technology (or 'med tech' ~~as the cool kids call it~~)? I wonder if my management style will translate to females (and by management style, I mean vague threats and couched suggestions of more deodorant, because – well, geeky boys smell). The younger of my two male subordinates – Jakob is his name – doesn't look like the sort of person who smells bad though, in fact, I'm a little in love with him already. Jakob's blond, with a lovely smile, and a freckle on his lower lip that I thought was a mark on my screen until I spent a good thirty seconds trying to remove it with a licked thumb. Must remember not to do that in person when I meet him.

My London team had already thrown me a boozy farewell party the night before, so it was pretty awkward seeing everyone again, especially considering how many shots of sambuca I'd put away. 'Still here?' they all said the next morning, at least twice. 'Came back for more cake, did you?' Haha, everyone, hilarious – like I'm not going to help myself to a modest slice of the banana loaf sitting unattended in the breakout room (Full disclosure: I had two massive slices – slabs the size of doorstops – but only as a form of silent protest against the cake-shamers).

After I'd said my goodbyes for the umpteenth time, I raced back home to take meter readings, and get into a long argument with Royal Mail about the forwarding of my post (mostly travel brochure junk mail, but hey, maybe one day I'll want to take that camel ride in the Sahara) and then it was 7.30 p.m., and all I'd consumed all day was two slices of cake (albeit astronomically giant slices) and about fifteen cigarettes (due to stress), so I was already feeling shaky when the power cut out. And it was there, in my dark, empty, increasingly cold flat, that I began to have the tiniest of misgivings. I knew nothing about Denmark. I hadn't even Googled it properly, preferring to live (as I'm sure you'll agree) in a protective bubble of total self-denial.

It was at this point that I started to blame myself. Not <u>me</u> me – I'm an absolute delight – I mean <u>her</u>, the other Joy. The Organised Joy who schedules early-morning yoga classes on the weekend, or spontaneously buys self-help books online, or decides to move to a brand new country when her current one is still (mostly) perfectly adequate – the Joy you're always telling to chill out. But it's always <u>me</u>, this Joy, who has to cancel the yoga, or ~~read return~~ ignore those self-help books, and it's <u>me</u> who is now being displaced – being made a refugee, if you will – by my own good intentions. Okay, maybe conflating my decision to move to a Scandinavian country with the terrible plight of legitimate refugees is over-stepping the mark, but the truth remains, Lil – Organised Joy had really messed stuff up. You should have seen me, walking around my eerily furniture-less flat, checking I'd filled all the holes in the walls properly so I'd get my deposit back, blinking back the tears and trying not to have an existential crisis. I stood in the dark bathroom questioning my decision. I stared into the mirror like a weirdo, lamenting the trim I had on my fringe (too choppy, it doesn't sit right), while also regretting not taking off more from the length, so my hair didn't touch my shoulders. Although I do like the colour – 'Medium Chocolate Brown' to get rid of the random grey. My eyes were swollen, but at least they didn't look wrinkly in the gloom. My face has always looked so child-like, with cheeks that people want to pinch, but I'm getting old, Lil. It's happening.

Since I'm painting you a picture, I should probably reveal I was holding Harville too. That's right – I've kidnapped your beloved childhood teddy bear from Mum and Dad's, and I'm taking him with me. Sorry, you don't use him anymore – he's my emotional support animal now. If you want him back, you'll just have to come and visit (yes, I am blackmailing you).

Oh, and then Mum texted: 'Darling, can you be sure your leaving isn't a way of punishing your father and I? x'

I love how she phrases things, so it's impossible to respond. I sent back a passive-aggressive kissy face emoji, and then a few minutes later, I caved and sent the appeasing, 'I'll visit all the time, I promise.' You'd have been proud of me, Lil, not rising to the bait.

I'd planned on returning some Tupperware to my neighbour Gladys next door and saying goodbye, but she was out (at eighty-nine, Gladys almost has a better social life than I do), so I left the Tupperware on her doorstep, with a blue vase of mine she'd always liked, watered her plants one last time, and wandered back. Inside, I wrapped a sleeping bag around my shoulders and sat outside on the front step with Harville to smoke what I'd decided would definitely be my last ever cigarette – and then one more cigarette, to really hammer home the point. Midway through my third, Robby texted.

'Guess you're really going through with it,' he wrote. 'Bon voyage, I suppose…' Gee, thanks, Robby, that is definitely one of the more depressing messages in the history of human existence. (Yes, I know I'm always a bit mean to Robby. He's lovely and sweet really, but I feel understandably irritated when I think I wasted six whole years of my life trying to make it work with him.) I finished my fourth very-last-ever cigarette and was mentally composing an indignant reply to his message when I heard sirens in the distance, a wailing end-of-the-world cacophony (spelling?). This is pretty much a daily occurrence in London so I barely notice the noise anymore. But I realised I didn't even know what an ambulance or a police car or a fire engine would sound like in Denmark, and so I spent fifteen minutes frantically searching 'Danish ambulance sounds' and 'Danish emergency number' with zero reception on my phone, feeling panicky, until I started to shiver from the cold and shuffled inside to sleep in a messy heap on the floor – but not before Harville suggested one final, last cigarette for good luck (he can be quite a pusher sometimes).

I'd hoped I might feel better in the morning, but when have I ever felt better waking at 4 a.m.? No, I felt wild and totally unprepared when my alarm went off. Somehow, I managed to arrive at the train station, board my train, check my luggage in at the airport, and get through security, but I was in such a manic daze, it was a miracle to find I'd arrived in the right seat, on the right plane, at roughly the right time. As one of the cabin crew passed me the inflight magazine, I tried to smile, but the skin on my face felt like aluminium foil pulled tight by a winch. I sat, swaying slightly, as the crew did their safety demonstration, and I wondered if maybe I should put my hand up and ask to be let off, but then the lights dimmed and the engine roared, and I thought, that's it then. No turning back now. <u>Bon voyage, I suppose.</u>

After we'd taken off, and the lights came on again, I began to cry. Not a big production – conservative even, considering what I'm capable of – but I was in an aisle seat, and I could sense that the couple next to me wanted to get up and maybe go to the loo or something, but they didn't dare ask this crazy stricken girl, soundlessly weeping in seat 21C, to move, and I didn't want to stand up and show everyone my puffy eyes, so we all just sat there, pretending it wasn't happening. Eventually, I stopped blubbering. The male of the couple chivalrously offered me a tissue, and I decided to pull myself together and take stock:

I am a woman in her mid-thirties (yelp!), who hasn't been in a serious relationship for a decade (my on-again, off-again relationship with Robby doesn't count). Everyone my age is either married, has kids, or both – and anyway, they've all moved out of London, so I never see them. I make relatively good money as a project manager at a medical software company, and sometimes I even like my job, but I've been in the same office for eight years, don't have any savings and I'm still a million miles away from owning a house. I've never taken any real risks in my life and so when something came up at work, a role at the Danish office, I didn't exactly jump at the chance, but I lunged in its general direction. And the Universe conspired to make it happen, even with my (many) acts of self-sabotage. I haven't been happy in London for a long time. Some reasons you know, some you don't (I won't go into it here…) so I wanted to try something new, and the Danes are famous for living happy lives – they win happiness awards from the United Nations all the time – that must rub off on you, right? If I…

I was really getting into a groove with all this self-talk, when the pilot announced we'd be starting our descent in ten minutes. Arriving? We'd only just taken off! (I might have become engrossed in the inflight magazine for a good forty-five minutes – did you know Britney Spears has twenty-two perfumes, Lil? My favourite being Fantasy The Naughty Remix, a 'truly unforgettable scent' – which is not always a good thing, Brit). How could a life-changing flight take only a measly hour and a half? My Danish phrasebook remained unopened.

I must have appeared rattled again, because the nice chap next to me offered up a pre-emptive tissue – but then the hostesses were whisking away the magazines, collecting the rubbish, and making us put down the armrests for some reason, and I kept craning my neck to see if I could catch a glimpse of my new homeland through the window (I couldn't), and the lights dimmed again and we made a bumpy landing and then everyone was unbuckling their seatbelts and making a mad dash for their bags in the overhead compartments, and inside I was screaming, 'I'm not ready! Do another lap around the tarmac!', but we were shunted out of the plane, into the cold spring air, and there it was: Denmark. Well, the Copenhagen airport bit of it, grey and dull and overcast – so very much like London then.

We shuffled through passport control – the attendant was surprisingly smiley to everyone, they usually have such poker faces – and then it was a short six-mile hike to collect our bags at a terminal that smelled like farts (from the nearby toilets) and hotdogs (from the nearby hotdog stand). Yes, there was a hotdog stand near the bag carousel. I'm not sure what I was expecting in terms of my first exposure to Danish cuisine, but hotdogs were not high on the list (for research purposes, I did eat one).

After I'd corralled my suitcases and finished my (chewy) hotdog, I zig-zagged my bags towards the exit. I've always hated the moment when everyone watches you arrive through the sliding doors – I get so anxious. All those hopeful, expectant faces, and then the shadow of disappointment when they realise you're not their beloved Aunt Tilly, or their son Duncan back from Afghanistan. Walking through the exit this time, I notice several people (adults and children) holding little red flags with white crosses on them, which I guessed to be the Danish flag (I'd thought it was blue, but that might be Sweden's – shows how much I know about the country I've decided to move to). The flags were charming, especially so early in the morning (some of the people were even half-heartedly waving them for extra effect), and it made the waiting crowd much less intimidating and actually pretty welcoming. Good work, Danes, I thought, you've won this round (I just Googled 'Danish flags airport', and it seems they do this out of a mixture of national pride and just because it looks nice). I did my usual trick of avoiding everyone's eye-line, while also trying to find my driver (I know – super fancy. It was organised by my work before you start lecturing me about being part of the Bourgoisie (sp?) elite) and eventually, I spotted a man holding an iPad (futuristic!) with 'Taranaki' written on it, so I trundled over to him, smiled expectantly and said, 'Hello'.

Without smiling, he said a word that I didn't understand, but which sounded a lot like 'Eeyore,' and so I assumed meant 'hello' in Danish – although he didn't look very Danish.

'Hello,' I said again.

He repeated, 'Eeyore?' but with more of an upwards inflection, and now, I might not be a cunning linguist, but I do recognise that as a sign the person is trying to communicate a question, so I did what any British person would do in the situation and immediately apologised.

'I'm sorry?' I said nervously, and then our man with the iPad repeated, more slowly this time – as if I am deaf or particularly stupid (a valid read considering the evidence) – 'Eeeeeyooooooi?' and pointed at me.

'I don't understand,' I replied, and began to look around in a panic, hoping someone else might translate for us, but they were all too busy waving their little flags to notice.

Finally, I said, 'That's me,' and pointed to his iPad.

'You are Eeyore?' the man asked, surprising me with his grasp of English.

'No, I'm Joy,' I said, and then it dawned on me, he <u>was</u> saying Joy, only put through a heavy accent filter. <u>I am Eeyore!</u> Oh, how we laughed – well, I laughed. He just looked slightly annoyed. Ice broken at least, and communication restored (partially), he helped take my suitcases to his taxi, and I got into the back. The driver's English wasn't great – he was Serbian, he told me – but he already knew where I was staying, so that was a relief. As we drove, there was a general smartness and order to the buildings which felt decidedly un-British (well, un-East London-ish, at least) and soon we'd reached what I guessed was the outer suburbs, and the people walking round did seem taller like everyone says they are, and blonder and better dressed. In the run-up to leaving, everyone had teased me about how short I was going to be compared to the Danes, but I wasn't particularly worried. Being five feet four, I've lived my whole life with the world taller – it would be strange if everyone was shorter than me. But I hadn't considered living in a world of giants. What if they mistook me for a small child? Or if the bathroom sinks were all too high, and I couldn't wash my hands? Would I be able to buy clothes that fit? And what if all the men had massive willies (and not in a good way) so I could never have sex again? The panic attack lasted about three minutes, during which I chugged an antidepressant (I'm medicating again, did I mention?).

I was staying in an area called Frederiksberg (spelling?), and finally, the taxi pulled up to a residential block next to a large red brick church with a rose window, I think it's called, which seemed bulkier and more monastic than the ones we have at home. The driver removed my luggage from the boot, and I wanted to tip him, but I only had big bills, so I decided to give him a compliment instead.

'Thank you – your driving was very smooth,' I said.

'What?'

'Your driving,' I said louder, as if he was now deaf, 'no bumps!'

I shook his hand meekly, and dragged my suitcases away from an oncoming swarm of cyclists. I think the driver probably understood what I meant. On a molecular level.

The Danish office had sent over three Airbnbs to choose from, and I'd picked the one closest to the language school (where I'm doing an intensive five-day Danish course next week) without really looking at the details, so I wasn't sure what to expect. A man buzzed me in and told me to come up to the fourth floor. There was no elevator, so I lugged my cases up four flights of stairs, where I was met by Viggo – my first bona fide Danish person! He wasn't a whole lot taller than me, which was reassuring, and he had blond hair and a stubbly beard, like a lesser Bee Gee brother. He also seemed a bit standoffish, but that might have been in comparison to all the polite fakery we normally do in England, all the gushing and frozen grins, the bobbing and blushing, and 'Oh gosh, really?' and the rest. Viggo made statements impassively, and moved on to the next one without asking how my journey was, or mentioning the weather, or noting that I was still panting heavily (what, me out of shape?). I was surprised to learn I was staying in the large canary-coloured room we were currently standing in, which included a living space – with its own sofa, armchair and coffee table, the desk and computer – as well as a bedroom area, with a double bed. 'But where will you be?' I asked nervously, not wanting to share a communal space, especially not with a strange man, however nice he seemed. 'With my parents,' Viggo said, maybe sensing my nervousness, 'an hour's drive away.' Phew, I thought.

The next surprise was Minnie, the cat. Minnie was small and white, with a black patch on her back, and admittedly, was very cute, but you know how I feel about pets. 'She won't be a problem?' Viggo asked, and I should have lied and said I was allergic or something, but I got caught up in my polite don't-make-a-fuss Englishness, and simply shook my head instead. Next, Viggo gave me a tour of the rest of the apartment: a very detailed account of the kitchen ('This jar is for almonds. This for walnuts'), the bathroom, and a peek into his flatmate's room (a Portuguese PhD student, 'who is out a lot – you will never see her').

Viggo put a few things in a bag, and I felt bad about kicking him out of his own home, but he seemed nonplussed. After he'd gone, I sat down on the bed, and Minnie jumped onto my lap. I patted her noncommittally for a moment or two, and then I noticed the definite smell of man musk emanating from the bed, so I opened a window, and looked out onto the street for a while – the red brick church opposite, a little supermarket on the corner, blocks of five-storey flats (some with turret roofs) – watching all the people, cars and the many bikes come and go. Children on bikes too. One boy with a blue helmet, comically big for him, wobbling behind his mother. She didn't even turn around, she just cycled more slowly until he caught up. When they'd gone from view, I tried to see all the English words I could find, 'Elite' on the supermarket, 'filter' on a van, but everything else was in Danish. It was so surreal to be physically in Copenhagen, and I felt sad again, and tired and hungry (I should have had two hotdogs) and lonely, so much so that I actually picked up the cat and hugged her to my chest and said, 'Oh, Minnie, what have I done?' Minnie scrambled her legs wildly, which felt like a fair response. After I'd let her down again and brushed off all the white cat hair from my jumper, I thought about making a cup of tea, but I didn't have any milk or teabags, and there were only alien cups in the kitchen covered in other people's germs. Instead, I had a cigarette out of the window (I might have bought a cheeky carton of them at duty free – whoops!) and checked my phone –

Mum wishing me a safe flight, someone from the UK office with a pain-in-the-ass request (even though I'm technically on holiday until I start at the Danish office in a week), and of course, one from Robby, simply asking, 'You there yet?' (I didn't reply). After I stubbed out the cigarette, I released Harville from his suitcase prison, and then borrowed several sheets of paper from the printer by Viggo's computer, found a pen in my bag, and sat down at the desk to write you this letter, and reading it over now, it does seem miserable and whiny, and I really do know what you'd say if you were here. Once you'd finished rolling your eyes, you'd give me a big hug (probably scraping my cheek with your nose stud) and say, 'Listen, Joy, if you come back right now, you'll never hear the end of it from Mum. This is your chance for some kind of freedom. It's what we always talked about as teenagers, our own autonomous lives, without her pulling the strings all the time. In a way, you're doing this for both of us.' But that's easy for you to say, Lil – you're still back there, surrounded by everything that's familiar to you – and anyway, there's a lot you haven't been through over the past few years, things you've unknowingly sidestepped. And yes, I am being wilfully mysterious, and no, I'm won't elaborate now – not in my current mental state (you're probably thinking this is some classic Joy over-dramatics too, but it's not, I'm afraid. It does warrant the dramatics. I really wish it didn't).

Maybe I could get up and leave the apartment right now, hail a taxi back to the airport, and get on the first flight home again. Would that be so very bad? Would anyone really care?

Oh, bollocks, I'm getting tears on Viggo's nice wooden desk. Stupid tears.

I am brave. I am good. I haven't made a terrible decision. <u>Have I??</u>

Your woebegone sister,

xxxxx Joy

P.S. Bit late now, but I hope you can read my handwriting x

NIGHT RAMBLINGS

Much later the same.

Hi Lil,

Still here. Can't sleep. Dad's fault.

(Just yawned so vigorously, almost fell off my chair.)

Okay, so earlier tonight, Dad called. I was still in a bad state, and I considered ignoring it – especially as Mum sometimes likes to swipe his phone to catch me out for screening her earlier attempts – but if Dad does bother ringing, it's often because something important has happened, so I panicked and picked up.

'Doll!' he said. 'You made it safe and sound?'

I realised I really needed to hear his kiwi vowels then, and the scared little child in me relaxed considerably (remember how Dad used to come and tuck us in as kids, late from work? He'd have that charcoal smell of whisky on his breath, and he'd always tell us to 'sleep tight and don't let the <u>bid</u> bugs bite'. It was literally years before I twigged he'd been saying BED bugs).

'Yes, Dad, all in one piece. Has something happened? Did Mum make you call?'

'Nothing's wrong, doll – just checking in with my eldest and ugliest. Did all your luggage arrive okay?'

'It's only a short-haul flight, Dad. No major mishaps.'

'Good, good. And what's the new temporary pad like?'

'It's fine – the owner was very nice, he even said I could use his bicycle, which of course I never…'

I trailed off, realising my mistake.

'Who did you say this guy was?' he asked, a growl in his voice.

'Dad, he's the owner of the Airbnb. He'll be staying with his parents the whole time I'm here.'

'That's what he's told you at least. But he has keys and can come and go when he pleases, I'm guessing?'

'Don't worry, he was very sweet.'

'They always are, doll.'

'There's another woman here, a Portuguese PhD student, so you see, I'm quite safe.'

'Have you met her yet?'

'Not exactly.'

'She could be in on it too for all you know.'

'I'm not going to be human trafficked, Dad. Not in Denmark. I should never have let you watch that documentary.'

'Is there a way you can barricade your bedroom door? I'm being serious here, doll. Just for peace of mind.'

'Goodbye, Dad, I love you. But goodbye.'

I do love him though. I hope I wasn't too abrupt. I have to remember that him checking on every detail is the way he shows he cares. He's just making sure the bid bugs don't bite…

Although, yes, maybe I did get a little spooked after that. I considered how I might actually barricade myself in, but then I decided to sit Harville on a chair facing the bedroom door to protect me, because nothing puts off human traffickers like an adorable (albeit slightly moth-eaten) teddy bear, right?

Speaking of, the longer I'm around Harville, the stranger I think it is you've kept him all these years. You are the least senti-mental person I know, Lil, chronically so. Plus, you've always given away your old stuff – clothes, books, bras (there must be at least three sets of bosoms being supported by Lily-hand-me-downs as

I write this). Yet, Harville prevailed. Makes me feel slightly guilty for pinching him (well, borrowing him – I promise you can have him back the moment you come for a visit).

He does remind me of that time – you must have been five or six – when you arrived home in floods of tears because the neighbour found you pulling petals off her prize roses. When she caught you red-handed, you lied and told her Harville had done it, so the woman replied, 'Well, bad little teddy bears go straight to hell.' To a five-or six-year-old! (When Mum found out, she gave the neighbour a proper Persian-mother talking to, replete with Farsi insults, which always meant she was very worked up.)

You came inside, wailing about how Harville was going 'straight down to hell', but after you'd explained what happened, I told you confidently in my big sister bullshittery way, 'No, he won't, Lil.'

'But the lady said…'

'Harville is a brown bear, and when they die, they become polar bears, and polar bears can't go to hell because it's too hot for them.'

As an eight- or nine-year-old, I was thinking on my feet – and that was the best I could come up with at short notice.

You almost bought the story too, except you must have gone to look at one of Dad's encyclopaedias, because half an hour later you came back, in even greater floods of tears, you could barely form the words: 'They don't become polars! They don't become polars!' And Mum had no idea what you were talking about, but I did, and I knew a piece of your innocence had been destroyed forever.

But, that's showbiz, baby.

'Right there!' That's what my therapist Margaret would say about the last line – I'm disassociating through humour again (also surprise, I'm seeing a therapist). She'd say, 'Every time you get close to finishing an emotional memory you undercut it with another joke. Don't tell me another joke, tell me who YOU are.' I never know what to say, Lil. Aren't we the sum of all our experiences (mine just happen to be hilarious)? I'm a teasy big sister, that's who I've always been. I have big tease energy. But if I'm over here, and you're not around to tease anymore, maybe I do have to rethink?

Anyway, I did start eating badly again for a while. Not anywhere near as problematic as my teenage years, thank God. I wasn't starving myself this time, but I would binge eat, and three times I made myself sick. I caught it relatively early, before things got too out of hand. 'Your coping mechanisms need refining,' is how Margaret phrased it. Well, they're definitely refined now. You could put them through a sieve. Joke!

'Yes, that's funny, Joy. But how do you feel? Connect with your emotion. What's underneath the impulse for humour?'

Trying to make you laugh. Keeping sane. Making sense of this crazy world. Not crawling into a ball on the floor. I don't see how a little comedy can be a bad thing?

Sorry to heap all this on you, Lil. I know this is very fragmented. Sorry I didn't tell you before either, about the eating stuff, but I knew you'd worry. Actually, being all the way over here does make some of these things easier to say to you. Maybe that's the silver lining of homesickness.

It's late. I'm going to try and sleep again. I have to take over Harville's watch-duties soon anyway so he can get some rest.

Love you xxxx

P.S. Just made the connection between the rose incident with the neighbour and you hating the smell of overly-pungent flowers…

LETTER TWO

Dearest Lily,

I know you always cringe when I call you 'Lily' instead of 'Lil' (Sidebar: what were our parents' thinking, calling us Lily and Joy?? Of course, they blame my name on a deathbed wish from Dad's crazy grandma, and you're named after the New Zealand Rock Lily, for some strange botanical reason, but we've had to suffer the ironic consequences <u>for years</u>: me, on antidepressants since I was fifteen, and you, dry heaving at the mere whiff of a lily (and of course, everyone buying them for you, as they're your namesake) – but humour me, it's been a tough week.

My dearest, dearest Lil.

I wasn't being dramatic when I said I hadn't prepared for moving here. Surely, I'd done a little research? Or asked a few questions? (The answer is no, and no – and please don't call me Shirley. Classic Dad joke!) I was too scared I'd change my mind, or worried I'd fall into old patterns. But I've really outdone myself this time, I really have.

After my previous letter (the long one, not the shorter late-night rambling one. I think we can both pretend that one doesn't exist), I didn't leave for the airport, obviously – but I did mope all by myself for <u>the entire weekend</u>. My original plan was to arrive in Copenhagen on Friday morning so I could have a long weekend to settle in before the language school on Monday – maybe see a few sights, take a brisk walk or, I don't know, go watch 'Hamlet' or something – but of course, it's me we're talking about, so I wallowed in bed instead, and it's not even my own bed this time, clutching Harville and sobbing, while intermittently watching Disney films. I haven't even met the Portuguese flatmate yet – she always gets home so late! Does she even know I'm here, and not Viggo? If I died, would I slowly decompose, or be quietly eaten by Minnie?

Obviously, after spending two days in bed eating peanut butter ~~sandwiches~~ from the jar with my fingers, I was extremely motivated to start off the new week in the best possible way. But when I opened my eyes on Monday morning – and this is the absolute God's honest truth – my throat was sore. It was, Lil! Hand on heart! There was visible swelling! Don't shake your head at me. When have you ever known me to be a hypochondriac? Okay, sure, those are good examples – I'd forgotten the time at Girl Guide camp when I thought I had lupus. But that was the old me – I'm now the sort of adventurous person who moves to a far-flung country. I take risks! Anyway, by my medical estimations, it was pretty clear I was coming down with pneumonia – the fact I'd woken up twenty minutes before Danish School started (at a very unreasonable 9 a.m.) was in no way related. Luckily, I had my new teacher's number, so I sent Else a message explaining that I was suffering with a temperature caused by possible bronchial lesions. Else, bless her, was so lovely and sweet in her response, I felt instantly relieved – and perhaps a tiny bit guilty. Off the hook, however, I crawled back into the musty bed and watched three hours of 'America's Next Top Model'.

At about lunchtime, however, I began to feel a tad more guilty about not going to class. My throat did seem a lot better after several cups of tea, and maybe – just possibly – the soreness was not caused by a bacterial infection, but due to the fact I'd left the window open overnight. Or the 600 cigarettes I'd smoked. I guess we'll never know for sure. As I started to improve physically though, I rapidly deteriorated mentally. The new office would fire me, I reasoned, because I couldn't speak any Danish, and I would have to go back to England in disgrace – no one would ever hire me again, and I'd be alone and homeless forever. As I plunged further into the abyss, a new thought emerged like a life raft – maybe wine would make the situation better? Yes, wine! Of course! What better panacea to soothe my many ailments? On a Monday? Before you've even had lunch? And red wine was good for the throat, no? NO? I grabbed my coat and passport and marched across the road – avoiding the millions of cyclists – to the supermarket's wine section, as one does at 12.20 p.m. on a Monday. Super casual. Nothing to see here. No red flags. I spent a lot of time reading the labels, because I wanted the other customers to know I was a discerning connoisseur of wine, who was buying this for a fancy dinner party – full of diplomats and professors and the like – and not some weirdo alcoholic. After choosing a moderately expensive bottle ('I hear this is an excellent year,' I garbled to no one in particular), I presented it to the cashier, along with a bag of salted cashews (the upmarket cousin to the humble peanut) and some liquorice. Astoundingly, I was not required to present my passport – the cashier in no way confused as to whether this was a youthful underage person or an (almost) middle-aged woman before them. I wanted to sprint home – but that's when the bikes will get ya! – so I picked my way back to the apartment carefully. Checking the flatmate was out, I rummaged around the kitchen until I found a bottle opener and a tumbler, before following Minnie into my bedroom, slamming the door shut and jumping under the sheets. You might ask – Joy, isn't it difficult to open a bottle of wine while you're sitting in bed? And I would respond – <u>not if you use your teeth, it isn't!</u> Minnie came over and gave the filled glass a sniff, and did that snuffly sneezy thing animals do when they're being judgemental dicks, but I was like, 'More for me then, Minnie!' and happily took a huge swig. Ah, wine. My throat felt better already. 'Cheers, sweetie!' I screamed at the empty room, raising my glass in a toast, startling Minnie and almost sloshing wine onto the bedspread. Everyone knows the first glass is always the best, it's so full of potential. Spirits are lifted, and there's practically a whole bottle left to go! It's only when you've drained the glass in record time, and you realise the bottle is actually half empty, and it's only 12.53 p.m. (11.53 a.m. in London), that there's a moment of pause. But you push through, because that's how we do it in Denmark, baby! Halfway through the second glass, however, I began to feel pretty homesick and I was shouting so belligerently at the screen during more 'Next Top Model' (things like, 'Oh, you're so young and pretty and thin, yes – you have ALL the problems!') that Minnie retreated to the other side of the room. 'Go on, everyone leaves me!' I yelled at the cat, who was now licking her undercarriage on the sofa. I was not in a good place, and I wanted to call you, or even Mum and Dad – God, I even considered ringing Robby – but I realised I needed to do this on my own terms. I was debating the health benefits of buying a second bottle of wine… when I felt sleepy, and zonked out – fully drooling on the pillow – until 3 p.m. When I woke again, I was groggy, with a headache and a whole heap of remorse. I apologised to Minnie for the things I'd drunkenly yelled at her – and hid the empty wine bottle at the bottom of the rubbish bin, punishing myself with two hours of 'How to Learn Danish' videos, weeping occasionally. I'd learnt my lesson though. That night, I planned to go to bed early, lay out my clothes, and Google map how to get to the school, so all I had to do the next morning was show up. Just show up. I could leave straight away if I hated it (how could anyone hate someone who seemed as lovely as Else though?) – and do you want to know something incredible, Lil? After so much procrastination and self-flagellation and remorse, I went to bed at a reasonable hour and woke up early(ish), and I put on those clothes, and waved goodbye to Minnie, and I left the apartment before the phantom flatmate was even up!

TUESDAY

There were bicycles <u>everywhere</u>, and it was disorientating to be outside so early. It was a cold, crisp morning, but sunny for the first time, and I felt something emerge in my chest. Optimism? Hope? Heartburn from all the cashews?

The Danish school is literally five minutes' walk away and seems to be on the same grounds as a high school, because there were lots of teenagers hanging around the buildings, but not the menacing ones you see in London, these were blonde cherubs who all looked as if they were part of a choir. I wanted to pinch their cheeks, even the couple of goth ones (and by goth, I mean the blonde teenagers wearing black beanies). After I'd cooed and mentally patted enough of them on their sandy-coloured heads (the ones that were sitting down at least – they were all giants to me, of course), I made my way to my designated classroom. Walking over the threshold, I felt jubilant – after three and a half days I was no longer in bed! Small victories are victories too… The classroom was organised into a horseshoe of desks around a whiteboard – Danish flags pinned up across the walls – and as I was the first to arrive (being the dedicated student I am. Monday doesn't count), I had my pick of chairs, so I sat in the furthest seat, by the window. My fellow students began to drift in, about ten in total – a red-faced chap in his fifties sitting right next to me. He gave me a cursory nod, before pulling out two notebooks, three pens, a pencil, a pencil sharpener, an eraser and <u>a calculator</u>. Way to make me feel unprepared. Else swept into the classroom next, in a pair of stylish black jeans and a dark grey cashmere sweater

– she was everything I'd imagined her to be; beautiful blue eyes, shoulder-length blonde hair (no side-plait like in 'Frozen', but you can't have everything) and dimpled cheeks. The moment Else spotted me, she clasped her hands to her chest and said, 'Joy!' with such warmth (and in the English pronunciation, not the 'Eeyore' Danish version), it was as if we were long-lost friends – and my heart actually skipped a beat. When Else surveyed the rest of the classroom, however, her expression darkened. 'We had fifteen people yesterday,' she announced, downhearted, as if personally responsible for the absentees, and I felt terrible for missing the previous day's lessons and vowed never to skip even a second of class for the rest of the week (loud clap of thunder).

Our first task was to go around the group and introduce ourselves in English, and then again in Danish. By my turn, I simply parroted back what everyone else had said – which sounded like 'Mi Noun Air [Insert Name]'– and Else clapped her hands and said, 'You have been practising, Joy!' – and I felt a total fraud, because I hadn't, but I also wanted to please her in any way possible, so I just smiled and thought to myself, maybe this whole Danish thing won't be so hard? Perhaps I was a natural linguist? (Ignoring my inability to learn the Maori version of the New Zealand national anthem, even with maximum enthusiasm over the years from Dad.) Unfortunately, that would be the first and only time Else would praise me in class. So began a gruelling lesson on 'common everyday words', where I seemed to comprehend nothing. No, not nothing, Lil – next to nothing, which is worse. I would understand a glimmer of something and then, emboldened, use it in all the wrong ways, so that I was not only confusing myself, but frustrating the rest of the class too. It didn't help that Danish is actively hostile to learn, and makes you do the stupidest things to your mouth, only for Else to scrunch up her beautiful face in disappointment. For example, it's deceptive – Danish looks completely different to how it sounds. I know you might say, isn't that true of every foreign language, Joy? But with Danish, it feels personal. Take the word 'fløde', which means cream. I took one look at it and said, 'flord', channelling my inner Swedish chef from 'The Muppet Show'. But, ah – no. The 'd' is silent (you usually don't say the last part of the word), so it's really 'fleur', but to really sell it correctly, you have to make a sound like you're gagging on your own tongue. Try it now, Lil, I'll wait. See? Isn't that unreasonable? And that's just for cream. Remember how we used to find it hilarious to try and say 'glue' in a Scouse accent? Well, that's basically what Danish sounds like. There were moments when it seemed like the whole class was being rage-strangled by an invisible force, Else demanding, 'More, more!' (she is quite the taskmaster). After an hour and a half of these oral contortions, we stopped for a break, and I followed my fellow students outside, where I was surprised to find almost everyone smoked. As I joined them (I wasn't planning to have any more cigarettes, as punishment for my unproductive weekend, but it pays to be sociable, right?), I caught up with all the smoker gossip; to pass the module, we would be sitting an exam on Friday (eek!). As the course was free for most people (it's paid for by the government), commitment was low, which explained all the dropouts. 'Everyone speaks English here anyway,' said a young, lanky Frenchmen called Jean-Pierre, stubbing his cigarette butt on the sole of his shoe in a very French way. 'If you talk Danish to the Danish, they stare at you like cows.' The group had already turned on a Hungarian woman in the class (who was not a smoker) because she asked too many questions, but I was pleased they all seemed to like Else, the consensus being she was tough, but fair – and had our best interests at heart. Smoke break over, we returned for another hour of ~~dry-retching~~ tongue placement exercises, and the learning of twelve key phrases we could use in our jobs, or in general life, to spark up conversation and show the natives we were at least making a bloody effort:

1. Hello, my name is Joy
2. I am English
3. I live in Frederiksberg
4. I am thirty-five years old
5. I have one younger sister
6. I have no brothers
7. I work in the medical technology industry
8. My favourite colour is emerald
9. I enjoy reading (which is technically a lie – I mean I enjoy reading, but I barely do it anymore)
10. I am single
11. I have no pets
12. I have no children.

Ouch! Those last three stung.

Else instructed us to practise our phrases in partners, and so the red-faced man beside me (called Geoff, he's Canadian) said, 'Hope you're better at this than I am.' To which I replied politely, 'I don't think so, I'm afraid.' To which he responded, 'Should have turned up yesterday then.' Cheek! Calling me out on my absenteeism! I was sick (possibly). I instantly recoiled from Geoff, and everything he did annoyed me; his breath, his odour, his Canadian accent, how all his stuff encroached into my space, how he said, 'behooved' (which has to be a fantastical made-up North American word). Geoff became public enemy number one.

Minnie looked relatively pleased to see me when I returned home, or maybe she hadn't been fed, so I gave her some cat biscuits just in case (Sidebar: I really dislike the sound of a cat crunching, it grosses me out – all that crunch crunch crunch, and seeing their pointy teeth and gums and the grimace, and the bits of biscuit flying everywhere, grim) and then I flopped onto the bed, waking four hours later, fully clothed, with Minnie curled up on my lower back, purring. After a dinner of cashews (I really have to start eating better), I tried working on my homework, but I got sleepy again and crashed out, still not having met my flatmate. We've wiped away each other's crumbs, fed and watered the same cat, yet not physically interacted. Modern life right there.

WEDNESDAY

Day two of school (technically, day three, but my day two) got off to a bad start, as I overslept again – not helped by the fact I woke in the middle of the night and watched 'Friends' episodes until 4 a.m. I burst into class an hour late, apologising profusely – there were only seven other people in the class now, two Spaniards and a Pakistani man were absent, and I sat down on the closest available chair, realising too late it was right beside Geoff. Dang! Else was a bit frosty with me initially, but warmed up, laughing when I tried to say, 'What time is it?' in Danish for the eighteenth time, saying, 'Oh, Joy, you will be the ruin of me,' which for some reason, I took as a compliment.

After lunch, we were all given a book called 'Where is Bo?', which is ostensibly written like a 'Peter and Jane' Ladybird book, except... it's not.

Here's the blurb:

Anne and Ole are nervous. Their six-year-old son has gone to the kiosk to buy rolls, but he did not come home. They are looking for him, but cannot find him. Finally, they call the police. Where is Bo?

You might be wondering, is Bo at the supermarket? He is not. Or at the playground? Nope. Why did parents send a six-year-old to buy bread by himself? Also, a valid question, Lil. He'll be found, safe and sound, though – right? Bo, you made us worry! – the final image, the family all hugging. Wrong again, there's no hugging, because Bo never comes home. Bo never comes home, BECAUSE BO IS DEAD.

As you might expect, there was hushed silence in the classroom after this reveal.

During the smoke break, we all rallied against the inappropriateness of the book (I felt slightly disloyal to Else) and the impending exam. We'd bonded enough by now that everyone discussed their reasons for doing the language course (even the non-smokers joined us outside). JP, the Frenchman, had moved over to be with his Danish girlfriend, and played bass in a band. He also showed us some of his tattoos and his tongue and nipple ring. Boring Geoff was married to a Danish woman who'd been homesick living in Canada, so they'd moved here 'to try it out' for a year. Kwento, from Nigeria, worked for an oil company. The two Sri Lankan women emigrated to be with their families and were kitchen staff in a restaurant. Hanna, the Hungarian woman who annoyed everyone, was part Danish, had divorced her husband, and wanted a fresh start. She was living an hour's journey outside of Copenhagen, and seemed full of unbridled hope. 'This country will embrace us,' she said, but JP was more cynical; 'Everyone is rude here,' and that coming from a Frenchman! I asked him what he meant, and he shrugged and said, 'They think they're better than us.' Surely not, I thought. What about lovely, patient Else? But I felt bummed out for the rest of the afternoon (the morbid book didn't help either) and left early, fibbing and saying I had an appointment – Else was so trusting. Poor trusting Else. I didn't want to go back to the flat, but I was too nervous to go anywhere new, so I walked around for a bit (bicycle near-misses = two), starting to feel a familiar black cloud forming, and I know I have to snap myself out of that, super quick – so I called Mum, hoping her low tolerance for moping would come in useful this once.

She sounded distracted when she answered. 'Oh, here is my daughter calling at last,' she began, and I rolled my eyes silently.

Always with the guilt. Mum was about to teach a class, so we didn't speak long, ironically, considering how many messages she's left begging me to call. That's always the way with her, she's like a siren – the moment you get close, your ship crashes on the rocks. Mum made me promise to ring Dad, and told me the university had offered her another contract, so they were going to stay in Brighton for the foreseeable. 'What about Lil?' I almost said. 'She'll be all alone in London,' but I kept quiet, figuring you might actually prefer it. Still, made me sad – feels like everyone's abandoned you. Being long distance is so bloody hard.

Mum fired off a lot of questions in quick succession: What was my accommodation like? Had I made any friends? Was I eating well? I told her about Minnie, and perhaps it was my description – or Mum not paying attention – but she seemed to believe Minnie was an actual human. 'Does she know any men to set you up with?' Mum asked (she always has her priorities right). 'Don't know, I'll ask,' I replied flatly. 'Good girl,' she said, and I could hear her students filing into class, so I let her go. I tried calling Dad next (it's times like this, I want to call you, but you've always been useless speaking on the phone, even at the best of times). Now that Dad is (semi-) retired, he's decided to build furniture or repair furniture or sand furniture or something – anyway, there was lots of noise, and it wasn't a great connection, so I gave up eventually and went home to trawl through Jakob's Instagram.

You heard me. I've been shamelessly poring over every last photo of my imminent colleague. Not that there's a huge amount of him to see – Jakob's 'gram is mostly progress pictures of some big home renovation he's doing – there might be an exposed hand holding a power tool in one pic (not that kind), or a pink ankle revealed as Jakob squats by a new skirting board. But if you look <u>very</u> carefully, I mean really zoom in, you can sometimes catch Jakob's full body reflected in another surface – a mirror, or a particularly shiny cabinet, perhaps. Using this technique, I've confirmed Jakob likes to wear shorts and a toolbelt when he's DIYing. That's the good news. The bad news is a young woman is sometimes taking the photos – I can also see her in the reflections – but in a way I'm relieved Jakob has a girlfriend, as he's less of a temptation/distraction (although, I write this with one hand, while checking his Instagram for the fifteenth time today on my phone with the other…).

THURSDAY

It was the last day before the exam, and Else was stricter with us – I think she really wanted us to do well (JP said it's just because the school doesn't get paid if we don't pass the module, but he's always super cynical). Else ran drills, and winced whenever I spoke. 'Play with the words in your mouth,' she instructed, and I tried, but – ugh! – learning a language is tough. Towards the end of the day, Else gave us a pep talk about how language was a flame, and we had to keep it burning inside us, not only for the exam, but every day, until it was roaring in our hearts – it was more beautiful the way she phrased it, and we all clapped afterwards, and Else blushed those beautiful dimpled cheeks. I felt vindicated, because it proved Else wanted us to be better people, not just pass the module so the school could get its money – although she didn't follow up her speech with a rousing rendition of 'Let it Go' from 'Frozen', which felt like a missed opportunity.

After our last ever cigarette break, Geoff came over and gifted me a jar of winter berry jam he'd made – he called it 'jelly' (how did he know I loved condiments?) – as good luck for the exam. I instantly felt guilty about making fun of his red complexion and his B.O., especially when I stink of fag smoke. When I gave him a hug, he said, 'You remind me of my first wife,' and choked up a bit. I'd really underestimated that smelly, sweaty pink-faced man.

That night, I finally met the flatmate! She came home earlier than usual, while I was making myself a snack (ham slices on rye bread with mustard – yes, I'm eating meat again, I'm afraid – but at least it's an upgrade from cashews), and I was pretty sheepish, with mustard all over my fingers, but she was very nice, and asked how my stay was going, and how I was enjoying Copenhagen (the three or four streets I've seen so far have been great!).

I promised myself an early night again for the exam, so I made sure to be in bed by 11 p.m., with the computer off, Minnie locked in the kitchen – and I was just moisturising my hands (not a euphemism), when my phone bleeped.

It was a message from Robby, 'You can't just run away from your life, you know. And the people who care about you. It's not right.'

After aggressively rubbing in the hand lotion, I texted back, 'The people who really care about you support your decisions.'

Twenty minutes later, he replied, 'Yeah, I guess. Miss you.'

And I don't know, I was expecting more of a fight – the way he gave up made me both infuriated and sad. That's one of the reasons why I left Robby. His heart was in the right place, but there was never any follow through. Oof, I sound like Mum. As a result, my mind went into overdrive – my brain was so busy coming up with reasons why he'd wasted all my best years, chiefly by being too nice and accommodating when we should have broken up eons ago. I suppose I was waiting to see if I fell in love with him – eventually – whether I'd wake up one morning and realise, 'You were here all along!' But however much I wanted that to happen, it never did. Sorry, Robby. I'd open my eyes and see him drooling on his pillow and think, 'Great, you again' – and then I'd feel guilty for being so horrible, and the day would stretch out before me, one big fat shrug (except for the moments of panic when I began calculating how long I'd need to actually meet the man of my dreams, and get married, and buy a home, and especially to start a family…). As a result, I couldn't get to sleep until well after 2 a.m.

FRIDAY

When I woke, I realised I'd turned off my alarm, and there were only twenty minutes until the exam. I could have made it, if I'd thrown on my clothes and run, but I didn't, Lil, I just lay in bed – paralysed by the fear of failure in a world where I was all alone and everything was unfamiliar – missing the test altogether. Sometimes, when you don't know if you're making the right choices, even embracing a bad one makes you feel powerful. For a short time, at least.

And that's how I stayed most of this weekend, in bed, more or less. I considered calling Margaret the therapist (I'm still seeing her internationally via the magic of FaceTime), but I couldn't even manage that, my only achievement being this letter.

I start my new job tomorrow, Lil. It's the big leagues. If I mess up, there will be real consequences. I can't mess up.

AHHH! Loud sirens – freaked me out! Minnie shot out of here like a rocket. I'm not sure whether they're from a police car or an ambulance, but they don't sound hugely different from the sirens at home – it's sort of comforting. And DO YOU KNOW WHAT? I'm sick of feeling sorry for myself. Now I have some adrenaline pumping, I'm going to leave the apartment while there's still some daylight, as Minnie is my witness. And I'll go – I don't know where – I'll find a McDonald's. Because there's always a McDonald's somewhere. And I'll walk, or I'll take a cab if I have to – and then I'll order a coffee, and maybe a hot apple pie, and

I'll sit and eat my Danish McDonald's, and look out the window like a regular person, and it's baby steps – I realise that – but I don't mind aiming low. At least I'm taking even some responsibility for my frickin' life. At least I'll be out of the house, starting to live.

I'M REALLY DOING THIS, LIL.

I HAVE MY COAT ON!

WISH ME LUCK.

Yours, terrified,

x Joy

LETTER THREE

Middle of the Night (19th?)

I know you're on record saying the most boring thing a person can do is talk about their dreams, and you'd rather 'claw out your own eyes' than listen to another one of mine, but pop on your mittens, sis, because I've just had a doozy...

Remember that game we made up as kids, called Vampire? It was basically tag mixed with hide-and-seek, where the 'in' person was a vampire. Our twist on the formula was adding the gate alongside our house. The vampire couldn't go through the gate, in either direction, but everyone else could run through it north to south, so you'd be safe for a moment, before realising the vampire was coming around the length of the house to get you. They were delicious, those moments, when the vampire almost caught you, and you nipped through the gate, standing there victorious, the invisible force field of the gate protecting you, until you realised you better start running.

In this dream, I was on a team with you, and Jakob was there too – he was wearing regular clothes, and not his shorts and toolbelt combo, unfortunately – his girlfriend had come along as well (yay...), and the girl you used to date, the one you met at Social Worker school, she had red hair. Adalyn, I think her name was? Let's go with Adalyn... She would always tell sad stories about neglected children and make me tear up constantly.

So, in the dream, we were all huddled together by one of the bushes, trying to work out a strategy. Of course, you'd taken it upon yourself to be chief tactician, with these big complicated plans, full of dummy runs, and bird signals, and a moment where we would simultaneously dash out from the bushes and make a break for the gate, but I could tell everyone else was a bit lost, and you were getting frustrated, because your plan was the best, if only everyone listened and followed it to the letter!

'I've an idea,' I said, 'let's split into pairs,' and I grabbed your arm and ran off (I chose you over Jakob, I just realised – you're welcome) to hide behind the trunk of that scratchy lemon tree.

'Lil,' I said when we got there, 'I'll protect you, okay?'

You guffawed, <u>me</u> protect <u>you</u>?

But I was insistent. 'I know this game. It's about timing. When I say run, run.'

'What if you don't run fast enough?' you asked, because admittedly, I am not the fastest runner.

'That doesn't matter. Timing, remember?'

Your eyes were fixed on the gate.

'Lil? You'll wait until I say?'

And you looked at me then, with kindness in your eyes, but also a whole load of condescension. Which riled me, because <u>I</u> was the big sister. Yes, our experiences might have been very different (you realising you were gay, or coping with your dyslexia at school, me worried about body image issues, and contraception when I was older), but I sometimes gave good advice. And the truth is, I often <u>let</u> you boss me around, not because your ideas were better, necessarily, but because it was easier that way.

Of course, you weren't going to wait behind the lemon tree until I told you – you sprinted off, just as the vampire approached.

'Lil!' I yelled, but it was too late, and the vampire was chasing you down the other side of the house. That left the gate exposed, so I darted away from the lemon tree, and rushed towards it, and I could hear yelling, so I turned, and the vampire was right behind me, and it was a real vampire now, its face all twisted and dark, and I ran towards the gate as fast as my stubby legs could carry me, sensing the monster's outstretched hand behind me. I made it through just in time, and I turned triumphantly, but now I could see that the vampire's face was <u>yours</u>, you must have been tagged – and with a snarl, you turned and ran off. In the growing darkness of the garden, I could still hear the voices of everyone playing, squealing, calling to each other, laughing, but I couldn't see anyone, and I felt left out and scared – the game had gone on without me and no one had noticed.

LETTER FOUR

Saturday, 28 April

Hi Lil,

First, I want to apologise. Those previous letters must have read like some crazy shut-in person's insane babbling. I guess I wanted to externalise what was going on and, to be fair, the process of writing everything down (in such minute, and I can only imagine, tedious detail) did help – but it was a lot to dump on you, and I know you were probably worried – and I wanted to tell you I'm much better. I'm gainfully employed! I have my own bedroom! I heat up food before I eat it now, like a high society lady or something!

Wow, so much has changed since my last letter two weeks ago. I feel like a completely different person, I really do.

Obviously, the biggest news is that I've started my new job. The DMTech offices are in a five-storey converted warehouse on the waterfront near the centre of Copenhagen, in an area called Teglholmen, which used to be docks. Everything about the office is super-modernised and whizzy, from electronic shutters that turn with the sun to give the best possible lighting, to our sit/standing desks which transform at the push of a button (mine had to be adjusted, as the lowest setting still required me to stand on an apple crate if I wanted to reach the keyboard).

My first day was pretty intense – I was introduced to my team of three, all Danish: Nansi, who is quiet and introspective, and I think might be pregnant, but in that early stage when you're never sure and it's not polite to ask, and no one mentioned it, so I didn't either; Hagen (who I must never call Häagen-Dazs), who is older than everyone else, mid-forties, I think, and tall, even by Danish standards – the sort of man who wears army surplus clothing, is into survivalism and brews his own beer; and of course Jakob, who I was very nervous to meet in the flesh, after all my virtual ogling, but who is very nice, and less cocky than I imagined he would be from his photos – tall, but not excessively (and not a wrench or hammer to be seen). He's actually quite shy (well, he finds it difficult to maintain eye-contact with me at least), which shouldn't be a surprise. I mean, Jakob does work in MedTech, so he's obviously a big nerd underneath all of his perpetual five o'clock designer stubble and piercing cobalt blue eyes. They were all very welcoming, in that laid-back noncommittal Danish way I'm getting accustomed to, and both men didn't noticeably balk at the idea of a woman bossing them around – so all up, a promising start.

Everyone at the office (and in Copenhagen in general) seems much healthier as a rule. Schlubby was the norm at the London office – especially considering the work we do, which ties you to a computer for the most part. Here, everyone cycles to work, rain or shine. People take the stairs. They compare stats on gadgets and gizmos – steps taken, miles covered, heights traversed. It's very disorientating. They all dress much better too. And their English is impeccable – thank goodness.

I mentioned this to Max from HR, who wears cool designer glasses and who I think might be gay, but he only shrugged.

'Don't people exercise in England?' he asked.

Not really, I thought, unless you count lifting a heavy pint at the end of the week. I mean, there were always a few fitness freaks, turning up to work in sweat-soaked leggings, but they were the exception to the rule.

Now I'm the outlier. Who knows, maybe I'll start training for a triathlon soon? (Waits for Lily to finish laughing.)

Culturally, the office is different too. We're encouraged to use break-out areas and not be confined to our desks. Unusual places I've worked so far include: a suspended swing chair, a sleep pod, a nook and a 'thinking room' (or the padded cell, as I like to call it, where they won't hear your screams of rage when the document you've been working on for the past three days crashes and you realise it's not properly saved). I have a brand-new, top-of-the-line computer, which for the first week, I was mostly using to analyse the progress of my team, who are working on a new software that will help patients who have had a laryngectomy recover their speech more quickly. But I know this is all evil 'Big Pharma' talk to you, so here's the most exciting thing – there's free food! At 12 p.m., someone – usually Hagen – will stand up and say, 'Vi spiser!', which means, 'We're eating', and then we all shuffle down to the canteen to have lunch together. Oh, Lil, the food! The menu changes every day, and you can have anything you like, and there's always dessert, which is obviously dangerous. My team and I sit together, and chat – they mostly speak in English, which is very kind, but switch back to Danish occasionally, and then get carried away and have to stop and translate everything they've said. I've not had to use a single word of Danish yet – not even 'I am single. I have no pets. I have no children…'

Max from HR checks in every couple of days to see how I'm doing, and other random people pop by to ask how I'm settling in too – not like when you start a new job in the UK and everyone ignores you, there it's basically trial by awkwardness. A nice woman in her fifties, whose name I can never grasp, drops by regularly and chats with me for fifteen minutes, and I'm not sure yet how she fits into the overall structure of the company – she doesn't have a wedding ring, so maybe she feels a kinship with me – but I like that everyone is so hospitable (sidebar: I had imagined people here would find it strange that I was in my thirties and single, but no one has batted an eyelid).

Now, let's talk about the office hotties. If I'm brutally honest, the London team was never the prettiest bunch, but here it's all chiselled jaws, bulging arms, and firm pecs (and that's just the women!). I walk around in a constant crushed-out state – it's a miracle I get any work done. It also makes me slightly self-conscious – in the UK, I felt I was a solid 6.5/10, but have I slid down to a 5? Or a 4? I've caught a few men looking at me, but they might just be wondering who this pygmy person is, wandering around the canteen, and why she keeps helping herself to another portion of dessert.

I'm still not sure if I could feasibly date someone over six foot. All my boyfriends have been relatively short (taller than me, but shorter than most) with some quirky detail I fixated on – Robby's sticking-out ears, or that Irish guy I dated with the pronounced Adam's apple (I loved watching him swallow, it was fascinating). I appreciate the beauty of Danish men, but the attraction is the same as the way I was drawn to ponies when I was younger – I don't want to kiss them; I want to brush their lovely hair, pat their butts, and make sure they have plenty of hay.

My other big news is I've moved out of Viggo's Airbnb apartment and into my own proper flat. Max from HR helped organise everything before I'd even arrived in Denmark – a woman called Greta, who works in our communications department, had a spare room, so now it's officially mine. And the best news is it's twenty minutes' walk away from the office, in an area called Vesterbro, which is super trendy – pretty much the Soho of Copenhagen. Talk about landing on your feet! Everyone is very impressed with the location when I tell them. Greta's flat – well, technically, my flat now too – is on the second floor, and everything is painted white and is extra minimalistic – my room is super cute, and has a wardrobe and a double bed, and a bookshelf for my one book (the Danish phrasebook, still in pristine condition) and Harville – most of my stuff is arriving next week. We have a fully stocked kitchen and a living room, with a million throw pillows – the only downside is, there's no shower or bath in the actual flat, you have to use the communal ones downstairs, which apparently is quite common in some of the older buildings over here. There's also a shared laundry room, with its own Twitter account, so you can see which washing machines are free or not!

Greta is a little difficult to read, and I can tell she likes things a certain way, but I prefer a person who keeps things ordered and tidy. Maybe it will rub off on me? And it's a good thing I can't smoke inside, because it will make me smoke less (or even better, quit like you've been nagging me to do for years).

The road I'm living on, Istedgade, is a very colourful street – at one end, there's the main central train station, and hotels interspersed with sex shops and strip clubs. At the halfway point, things start to get fancier, with antique stores and clothing boutiques. That's where we're located, just above a coffee shop, which is bustling during the day, and near a burger joint, which is hopping at night. The best thing about the area is some of the stand-out names – there's a fine establishment called Skank, and another one called Spunk Bar. Chortle.

Of course, moving out of Viggo's place meant one major sacrifice – Minnie. No, I didn't kill her, that's not what I mean. Despite all my natural inclinations, I grew rather attached to that demanding diminutive feline. It was especially tough when it dawned on me I would never see her again, and I even considered asking Viggo if I could drop by from time to time to visit, but I knew that was silly. What Minnie and I had was special, yes, intimate even, but it's time for the next phase of my life. One that doesn't include finding random cat hair on my cashews (thankfully).

Oh, and some crazy news – remember how I missed the Danish exam? A couple of days afterwards, I received a notification saying that I'd actually passed module 1 and could start module 2 whenever I liked. I was stunned. I mean, I'm happy obviously, and it was probably an administrative error, but I can't help thinking that maybe JP was right, and Else really was on the take. My whole worldview is at risk of collapsing in on itself.

And you'll never guess – but sweaty Canadian Geoff has invited me over to dinner at his house. How sweet is that? Well, I hope it's sweet, and he's not being creepy – he didn't seem creepy, and his wife will be there too, but you know me – now I'm terrified they're swingers and they'll want to instigate a three-way over dessert. Or maybe I am dessert. Anyway, I have zero friends yet, so I'll probably say yes.

Thanks again for being my rock and my sounding board, and sorry for all the rambling, depressive letters before.

And look, this one is under sixty pages!

Extra love,

Your much-happier sis,

Joy x

LETTER FIVE

Sunday, 29 April

Oh, Lil.

That last letter is a total fabrication!

It's 3 a.m. the next night and I can't sleep, and everything I said before was subterfuge, and smoke and mirrors, and a big fat lie. I didn't want you to worry, and I thought if I created a version of my life that seemed happy and normal, it might manifest into reality. But I can't go on like that – I have to get the truth out. We've always told each other everything, so we can't start keeping secrets now.

Where to start?

Oh my God – work. I've been there two weeks now, and I don't know what the hell I'm doing. There are so many productivity systems and learning them all is making me so unproductive.

And my team…

Is Nansi pregnant?? IS SHE?? I mean, you'd at least mention it once, wouldn't you? Sometimes I think maybe she has a wheat intolerance and she's bloated because she ate too much bread? Or she's just good-old-fashioned fat? Employment laws are pretty sensitive around pregnancy (and fatness, to be honest) and you have to tread carefully, but why doesn't Nansi come out and say something? Also, I keep catching her playing one of those gem-connect games on her phone, and I'll have to reprimand her soon if it continues, but I don't want to be mean to a (potentially) pregnant woman.

And Hagen keeps asking me so many questions – about the political climate in Britain, and the Falkland Islands, and the rock of bloody Gibraltar, and our crumbling welfare system – and I don't know what to say. He always seems surprised when I don't have good answers, as if it's my personal failing or maybe a symptom of our inferior education system, and he makes this disappointed 'hmmm' sound, and I want to clip him around the ears. He was horrified I couldn't speak any Persian OR Maori (well, nothing I wanted to say out loud to a group of my colleagues, in any case).

And Jakob. Where do I begin? At first I thought he was actively trying to undermine me. He'd say things like, 'Did you mean to put the columns in the wrong order?' and of course I didn't, but he sits there, not saying anything, with this wry mocking look in his eyes, as I flail around giving excuses. He must know by now that long pauses make me squirm, but he does it anyway. And my lips were cracked, because they always get dry in the winter, and drinking wine doesn't help, and I could absolutely tell he was judging me.

There's something else about Jakob too, something I most probably shouldn't tell you, Lil – for privacy, legal and well, ethical, reasons. I have to get this off my chest, though, and it might as well be to you – especially as you're a trained counsellor-type person and social worker who's heard plenty of shocking things in your job. You see, because I'm Jakob's manager, I have to know certain things about him. One of those things is that once a week he gets signed off to go to a therapist. There's no shame in that, of course (I have FaceTime Margaret, after all), but I happened to notice that this therapist specialises in addiction, and now I can't stop my brain thinking what Jakob might be addicted to. The obvious answer would be DIY. He and Hagen can talk about different types of screwdrivers for <u>hours</u>, Googling screwdrivers, bringing in screwdrivers to fondle and caress. I've even memorised what screwdriver is in Danish, it's 'skruetrækker' – which sounds like 'screwdriver' if it were yelled by an angry troll with a bad headache under a bridge.

His addiction is probably not DIY, in reality. What else then? Drugs doesn't seem likely, and Jakob's talked several times about having a drink over the weekend, which he wouldn't do if he was an alcoholic. My best guess is gambling, because when he's trying to prove a point, he always says, 'I bet you a million kroner,' and sometimes he takes a long time in the loo, and now each time I imagine him frantically calling bookies and placing bets on racehorses, or compulsively playing poker on his phone like Robby used to. I wonder if Jakob's girlfriend knows? God, I'm so unprofessionally nosy. But what if he loses all his money at a casino, and can't keep his job? I need him on this project. And also to ~~lust after~~ look at platonically. No one ever considers the effects of gambling addition on project managers!

And, oh Christ – the lunches! We all sit together every single blinking time, and we exhausted the light chit-chat the first week, and then Hagen started on his 'Question Time' grillings, and so one day, I told them I was going to nip out to get a sandwich instead of joining them. All I wanted was twenty minutes alone to collect my thoughts. But in the afternoon, Max – from HR – made a visit to see if everything was all right, and I knew exactly what that meant – you don't skip the lunches. But I get so claustrophobic, and I want to throw myself into a vat of soup or smash my face into a quiche so I don't have to answer another question about Britain's relationship with the European Union. And Jakob always strokes his stubble and says things in Danish that I don't understand, and everyone laughs, and I want to murder him.

The lunches wouldn't be so bad if I was coping better at my job. I have total imposter syndrome. I think I was expected to bring some secret UK effectiveness with me, because everyone keeps asking, 'How did you do it in London?' – but to be honest, our process was to make a lot of costly mistakes and then overcome them by working extra-long hours. There was no magic bullet, it was just hard graft. Everyone here has one foot out the door by 4 p.m. I mentioned to my team that we might have to increase our output to reach the first deadline, and you'd think I'd asked them to walk over hot coals. I don't know what I'm supposed to do – it's my job to keep everything on schedule.

Also, I don't know who my boss is. I know that sounds ridiculous, but it's true – I have no idea who I'm reporting to. It's an open-plan office, there are no private offices, no one has their job descriptions on their desks, and I have no clue what anyone does outside of my immediate team. That nice woman who keeps coming up to me and asking how things are going – is she my boss? IS SHE? I can't ask Max, because I know he's watching me now, and possibly reporting any mistakes I make to the invisible higher-ups and I can't ask anyone who reports to me, without looking like a complete fool. I can't even Google the woman or look her up on LinkedIn, because I don't know how to spell her name (I've already asked Nansi how to pronounce it three times). So, every few days, I have a similar chatty conversation with the woman, but really, I want to scream, <u>Are you my superior?</u> Tell me what to do! Grade my performance! Anything!

Lil – I hate Greta, my new flatmate and colleague. I know that's harsh, but it's the truth. I actively hate her. She's so pernickety and judgemental, and work or home – there's no escape. We have a dishwasher, but I decided to handwash a few things, and afterwards, there was a knock at my bedroom door, and it was Greta, and she beckoned me to follow her back to the kitchen, and then she explained that I hadn't rinsed the suds off properly, and I had to stand and watch as she showed me <u>how to rinse a glass under cold water</u>. Also, apparently, I was using her favourite

cup all the time, so that's now out of bounds. And everything
in the flat is white, even the sofa and the cushions and the rugs
(what sort of masochist has WHITE RUGS?) and I'm terrified
I'm going to get them dirty. The other day I forgot to extinguish
the candles in the living room before I went to sleep, and Greta
emailed me AT WORK about it. When I see her at lunch, she
never smiles, and she sits with all these other female PR and
communications types in their blouses and expensive-looking
mohair jumpers, and I know they're talking about me and the
goddamn candles.

I shouldn't complain really, because I'm lucky my place is
central – but my bedroom is so noisy at night. The burger place
downstairs gets very busy Thursday to Saturday, but Friday is
the worst. Everyone has big booming Viking voices, and in the
morning, there are empty beer bottles on the street everywhere,
and I've listened to the conversations (the ones in English I can
understand) and they seem good-natured enough and there are no
actual fights, but it's as if they don't know how loud their voices
can get, and I want to stick my head out of the window and yell
at them it's 2 a.m. and to keep it bloody down, but I don't want
to be that crazy foreigner, so instead, I lie awake, miserable, and
also a bit sad that it's not me down there, having fun with my
friends on the weekend.

And why doesn't the flat have its own shower? What is this,
1863? It's freezing cold every day, and I have to go outside, and
there are unisex showers, and I always forget my conditioner,
and you know how I'm scared of catching ringworm. Just when
you've finished showering, and you're back in the warm flat,
you realise you don't have any clean clothes for the morning, so
you have to go downstairs again to the laundry room this time,
only to find all the machines are busy, so you go back up to your
room and wait and refresh the laundry Twitter obsessively until
it's 10 p.m., and you give up and decide to wear the least smelly

thing (which has a slight mayonnaise stain), and go to bed, but not before checking <u>for a third time</u> that all the candles are well and truly out.

Plus, Mum and Dad have been really weird lately. I know they're always weird – I mean, weirder than normal.

Here are a few select text messages from Mum:

'Please tell your father about asbestos.' (Sure, Mum, just a general overview, or shall I prepare a PowerPoint presentation?)

'My colleague's new precious baby girl. The curls of hair! This could be yours if you wanted it.' (Is she selling, Mum? Also of note, text sent with no accompanying photo.)

'Do you have my green serving bowl? I think you borrowed it and never gave it back.' (Untrue, and what if I did, does she want me to mail it to her?)

'We visited your sister today, she misses you, when are you seeing her next?' (Um, I'm in another country, remember, Mum? And you'd never actually admit you were missing me, I call bollocks.)

'There is sawdust all over the house, I may send your father to liver with you soon [sic].' (Fine, as long as he remembers to rinse the dishes properly.)

Speaking of, here's an extract of the call with Dad yesterday:

Dad: Hi, doll
Me: Hi, Dad
Dad: Hi, cherry blossom
Me: (okay, that's a new one) Hi… sunflower… blossom?
Dad: (right off the bat) Have they deported you yet?
Me: (laughing uncomfortably) Not so far.
Dad: How are you finding it though? You eating properly?
Me: I'm doing fine, Dad.
Dad: That's good to hear, doll. You're so far away, I can't pay for a taxi to come get you if anything goes tits up.

Me: I'm coping, Dad. Really, I'm okay.

Dad: Good, good. You watch the rugby?

Me: I never watch the rugby, Dad, you know that.

Dad: You might have started. Now you're in 'Denmark' (said with a weird Eastern European accent).

Me: How's Mum?

Dad: Yeah, good as gold.

Me: And are you finding things to do?

Dad: (distractedly) I'm keeping busy. Did you say you watched the game?

It went on like that <u>forever</u>. I swear, they both have early onset dementia (I shouldn't say things like that, but what if they do, Lil? I'm not looking after them, you're on your own, kiddo.)

But the thing I'm least proud of?

I've been messaging Robby. Ugh!

He preys on my weaknesses! Honestly, I think he senses when I'm at my lowest ebb and swoops in for the kill. Here's the worst part – I may have inadvertently invited him to come to Copenhagen. I tried to backtrack as soon as I realised, but he's already talking about booking a flight with Norwegian Airlines and coming over for a couple of days. And there is a small part of me that would like to see a friendly face. Even his stupid friendly face (I wish you'd come over. What if I buy you a first-class ticket? Caveat: a first-class Ryanair ticket, which means they don't drop-kick your luggage down the runway. Seriously though, it's very unreasonable – I've been here for literally weeks, and you've not visited once).

While I'm getting everything off my chest, I might as well tell you how Robby and I left everything before I came over to Denmark (Spoilers: not well).

As you know, we've always been chronically on-again, off-again our whole relationship, mostly due to the fact that Robby works such unsociable hours as a bar manager. In the early days, it was fun – I would hang out on a barstool and feel like I was Scarlett Johansson in 'Lost in Translation', and Robby would get me free caipirinhas (remember my caipirinha years?), and I'd meet friends there, and you, of course. But then I got sick of going, and it meant I was alone most nights, and if Robby did come back to mine, he always stank of booze and fag smoke, and in my weakest moments, I was jealous he'd cheat on me with one of those dippy girls who were always hanging around.

And Robby didn't really understand my job either. He tried to, bless him – I'd find him reading articles about MedTech on his phone, but he'd bring up stuff randomly and nonsensically, and it only showed the limitations of our relationship.

Pretty soon a pattern emerged, where we'd break up for a few months, and then I'd drop by the bar after work (drinks), and we'd end up going back to his, and we'd have this amazing weekend together – he'd call in sick, and we'd eat cereal in bed with that awful long-life milk, because he never had any proper food in the house – and the cycle would start all over.

But we couldn't go on weekends away, because he always had to work, and I don't know how I feel about children, and I'm sure Robby would make a great dad, but he's been talking about finishing his degree since I first met him, and what if I did get pregnant? Would he still work evenings? If so, how would we bring up the child together? Plus, he was enabling my smoking (and my bed cereal eating). And I used to find random notes with women's phone numbers on in his pockets when I was ~~kindly washing his clothes~~ snooping. That doesn't mean he acted on them, but still. Mum and Dad were never hugely keen on Robby, and I know you like him, and he is sweet, but it just wasn't enough.

. Moving countries seemed like a humane way of breaking up. But now I've invited him over – it's going to get messy again.

Maybe he won't come. This was his response when I told him I was leaving the UK:

Me: I've decided to move to Denmark.
Robby: (laughs)
Me: I'm serious.
Robby (laughs harder)
Me: Robby, look at me.
Robby: (stops laughing) You're joking?
Me: You know I want to travel more.
Robby: You hate travelling.
Me: I don't.
Robby: You complained the whole time we were in Dorset for that wedding. You hate packing, you hate sleeping on a foreign mattress, you don't like it when the pillows are too big and they give you neck ache, travelling gives you constipation, you couldn't understand the accents in <u>Dorset</u> and they were speaking English…
Me: I've changed. I mean, I will change. I plan to change.
Robby: I'll believe it when I see it. Now, I have to go to work and flirt with unscrupulous women.

Okay, maybe he didn't say that last part. But Robby just sort of let me go. He didn't try to stop me, there was never any grand gesture (not that I wanted him to propose or anything). Oh God – what if he comes over here and proposes to me? He would never, <u>would he</u>? My blood just ran cold, that's not a great sign. But I'm weak – what if I said yes? I might do it in the moment, I might. Especially if there was champagne involved. And I'm so lonely, Lil, I'd marry anyone if they asked me. I'd marry one of Greta's candles she's always lighting. Or the laundry Twitter, if it was sentient. I'd even marry sweaty Geoff! Oh God, I'm imagining Robby going down on one knee, and it would be an ugly ring,

I just know it (remember that hideous quartz stone he used to wear in his ear before I told him it was a deal breaker?). I would run away, I would. Robby would bend down to tie his shoelace, and I'd be halfway to Sweden. God, what do I do, Lil?

Oh, and I just had a panic dream about Minnie – and is it wrong that I want a kitten, even though I don't officially like cats?

I could really do with a hug, Lil. Send me one? Back of a postcard will do…

X Joy

P.S. Great, we're back to another whiny, tear-stained, million-paged letter – you're welcome.

P.P.S. <u>And</u> the weather here is worse than London. It's colder, wetter, greyer…

EXTRA BIT

~~Addendenum~~ ~~Addendum?~~ Extra bit.

I forgot to tell you the most mortifying part – at lunch the other day, Nansi and Hagen had already finished, so it was only Jakob and I left at the table. There's always this energy between us, like I want to pinch him, and I'm always afraid he's found some long, curly hair on my eyebrow, or a pimple coming up – he looks at me too hard, if you know what I mean, it's intrusive.

Jakob had opened a sachet of sugar and was tipping the contents into a small pile on his plate.

'Have you been keeping up with my house improvements?' he asked, and at first, I thought he must be talking to someone on another table, but when I looked up there was nobody else.

'Your house improvements?' I repeated, hesitantly. 'The ones you talk about with Hagen?' (All the bloody time, I thought, but did not say.)

'Yes, but are you following still on Instagram?' he asked.

My body tensed. Jakob gave a little smirk, and I knew, I KNEW my online stalking had been rumbled, but how? And would I get in trouble? But mostly, HOW?

Jakob waited for me to respond, but I kept absolutely frozen, and so eventually, he continued, '…after you sent the flames to one of my Instagram stories?'

Still frozen, I tried to process what he meant. What flames? Was it something Danish? My mind raced.

'I didn't know if you liked my new kitchen,' Jakob added with a laugh, 'or you were telling me to burn it.' And Lil, I shrugged. I do it all the time over here. I'm constantly shrugging, making out I don't understand. It's the easiest trick in the book when you're a foreigner. Moments later, in a hastily made trip to the loo, I discovered I'd accidentally sent a flame emoji to one of Jakob's stories! The flame emoji creates a fire animation on the screen. So yes, it looks like I was suggesting he burn his new kitchen to the ground.

And what if he IS seeing a therapist because he's an arsonist? Have I inadvertently given Jakob some signal I want to go light fires with him now? I'd probably do it as well – just because it's less embarrassing than telling him the truth, that I've been scouring his social media for weeks for the flash of an exposed thigh.

Finding people attractive in another country is very complicated, Lil.

Ugh.

LETTER SIX

Saturday, 5 May

Lily! My little sister,

I'm not long back from the soirée tonight, and it's late and I'm a little tipsy (hiccup), but I wanted to write to my favourite sister. You! Yay, you win! (technically, you're my only sister, but shhhh).

Just let me get some water. Need to stay hydrated! Hydration first!

Right, I'm back, and I didn't wake up mean Greta, so that's a bonus.

Update – I went to Geoff's tonight for dinner, and I was worried it might be awkward, but Geoff is like a different person when he's not in a classroom. He was relaxed and even looked handsome in a smart striped shirt when he opened the door, and he hugged me, but I decided it was in a friendly way, and not in the 'I want to mash your boobs against my chest' way that some men have. So that was nice.

I'm just going to have some more water.

Where was I? Oh yeah. Geoff's apartment was really lovely, lots of mood lighting, and then I met his wife, Sara, and I was surprised because she seemed so normal and attractive (no offence, Geoff – well, maybe some offence). Anyway, Sara was so sweet. She's Danish and speaks English with a very slight Canadian accent. Really, she's one of the friendliest people I've met, and super sharp – I instantly felt she was one of 'our people' – and after I'd taken off my boots and coat, we went into the living room to join the others; a woman called Megan in her forties, who had good posture, and a younger Italian guy called Angelo, who was only few inches taller than me when he stood up to shake my hand. Then Sara brought me some wine, and I thought, this is it! I'm having hygge! (you know, the Danish word that means cosy or something). Or doing hygge! I'm not sure how you use the term correctly. Hygge was happening, at least! And there were candles, but not oppressive ones like Greta's – because I was in no way responsible for them. I found out Megan worked as a consultant for a bank, and Angelo was finishing his Masters in something, I forget what – and I assumed they were a couple, even though there was an age gap, because Geoff and Sara have an age gap – it was an age gap dinner party! Because of this, I sort of took Angelo out of the love equation in my mind, and maybe I was less guarded and more relaxed as a result, without trying to impress anyone.

'How are you liking Copenhagen?' Angelo asked me.

'It's great,' I replied, although this was a bit of a lie, considering how much I'm struggling. 'It's like London, but everyone's taller, more attractive, there's better transport, it's prettier and you don't have to worry about getting stabbed, or someone on a moped stealing your purse and then stabbing you.'

'Are there really such a lot of stabbings in London?' Angelo asked, looking horror-struck.

'Not always,' I said, taking a big gulp of my wine. 'Sometimes they throw acid instead.'

'I had no idea,' he said. 'We have a lot of killings in Sicily too, where I'm from.' He shook his head sadly. 'What is it about life on small islands which brings such violence?'

I struggled for something to say, instead watching Angelo's face as he processed the grief in his statement. A handsome face, like a Roman statue.

After we finished our drinks, Sara invited us into a dining room, where everything was beautifully laid out, there was even a centrepiece with wood, and dried flowers and leaves, and I could tell how much Sara and Geoff loved each other by the way they held each other's hand. I was surprised to learn they'd met while Geoff was still married to his second wife – they had an affair (scandalous!) – and I couldn't imagine Geoff being so clandestine and ripping off his clothes in a cheap motel or something. But there you go, love happens. And I'm usually pretty judgemental about relationships that start from ~~infidility~~ cheating, because I think – look at the precedent the cheater has set – but they've been together for seven years, and they seem very much in love. So, what do I know?

After I'd had another glass of wine, I started pressing Angelo about Tuscany, because it's a place I've always been romantically drawn to, and I knew nothing about Sicily (Disclaimer: I was perhaps trying to be flirty without being too flirty – because I thought Megan was Angelo's girlfriend).

'I've never been,' he said, about Tuscany.

'Never?' I replied, incredulously, because how could you not? It's Tuscany. You're Italian. Get. Your. Shit. Together. Angelo. 'Do you know anything about it?' I asked.

'They have a good football team called Fiorentina in Florence, in the – how do you say – Premiership League?'

'I mean, are there beautiful, dilapidated houses everywhere?' I said. 'Does everyone drink lovely wines with each meal?'

'Yes, the wine is very good. But the food, not so much. Expensive. It's full of tourists too. You know – la Torre di Pisa,' Angelo mimed supporting a wine bottle's weight at an angle.

'But I bet it's magical,' I prompted, although it felt like I was trying to get blood from an Italian stone.

'You like magic?' he asked, some excitement in his eyes finally.

'Of course,' I replied. Magic and destiny and meeting cute boys when you least expect them.

'Have you read "Harry Potter"?'

I scrunched up my nose and shook my head (remember the pact we made to never read the books or see the films because of your school nemesis, that girl Harmony? She used to tease you for not liking girly stuff, and then all the 'cool' kids in your class started reading them, and Harmony made everyone call her Hermione, and You. Hated. It. So much so, you made me promise never to touch the books in any form. Also, they didn't have enough brown characters for your liking. To top it off, Mum hated the books too, and basically banned them from the house in case they swayed her daughters away from sensible futures in science or medicine. 'They are the devil's work,' she'd say, whenever it came on the news. 'All those children standing in a line at midnight to buy a book – it's an evil cult!').

'You've not read <u>any</u> "Harry Potter"?' Angelo asked, wide-eyed.

'It's not really my thing,' I replied, and I swear Angelo winced.

'How do you know if you've never read them?'

'I can just tell,' I replied, trying to think of a way to bring the conversation back around to Tuscany. 'It's basically "Star Wars", but set in a boarding school. You know, there's a chosen one, good versus a terrible evil, the baddie uses magic to lift people up by their necks. But in "Harry Potter", it's all sticks and broomsticks, instead of robots and lightsabers. It's just a very low-tech "Star Wars", where all they have is boring sticks. And I don't even like "Star Wars".'

Angelo looked like he was about to make a firm rebuttal, but then dinner was served, and the food was amazing (duck, and I don't usually like duck). At some point during the meal, I realised Angelo and Megan weren't actually a couple – they just both knew Sara through the university. And Geoff and I chatted about the Danish course, and the exam, and my passing without attending – and I thought he might be funny about it, because I pegged Geoff as a stickler for the rules, but he only chuckled and said, 'Fair play,' and I liked him even more.

After we'd finished dinner, we had dessert and coffees, and then Geoff suggested we move on to a bar around the corner. I was a bit drunk and slightly wobbly at this point, and I didn't really feel like leaving the warm, safe, candle-lit interior of the flat, especially as I'd eaten so much, but then we were all putting on our shoes, and Angelo helped me down the stairs, which was chivalrous of him, and I suddenly thought – what if I've been set up on a blind date? Were Megan and I brought along for Angelo to choose from? Two old maids? It was entirely possible, but I tried to put it out of my mind, although I did appreciate that Angelo walked the whole way with me to the bar, even if it was only an attempt to convince me to read the first 'Harry Potter' book.

Inside the bar, it was busy and smoky (you can still smoke inside here – can you believe it? And I thought Danes were supposed to be super health-conscious!), and we ordered a big round of drinks – well, I did, because that's part of my British cultural heritage – and I laughed at Angelo, because he wanted an appletini, and then I bought us all shots of this herby spirit they have over here called Akvavit, and afterwards I got the biggest surprise, because the band came on, and you'll never guess who was playing bass? Everyone's favourite lanky Frenchman with a tongue ring – Jean-Pierre (from our Danish class)! He was really good too, and we all sort of danced where we were standing by the bar, doing that bobby shuffly dance, and at some point I was grooving with Sara, who could really move, and then with Geoff, who really couldn't, and then Angelo, and after we'd stopped dancing, he took my hand, and I thought, I really do quite like Copenhagen.

When the band finished their set, JP bounded over and introduced us to his girlfriend and said he'd passed the exam too, and was starting module 2 in a few weeks (I'm obviously not doing it, dropout that I am). He looked at me with Angelo, and gave me a 'wink wink, nudge nudge', and I told him, 'We only met tonight,' and JP shook his head and replied, 'You English girls move fast,' and I laughed because he called me a girl, and then Geoff and Sara and Megan said they were leaving (Sara confirmed Megan was definitely not Angelo's girlfriend), and Angelo told me he could walk me home if I liked, and I kind of wanted to stay and be a groupie and hang out with the band and smoke cigarettes, but I'm pleased I didn't overall, because Angelo and I had a little snog outside the burger place under my flat (full disclosure: I bought a burger, and I forgot to talk in a whisper. In fact, I think I spoke pretty loudly. Oh God, I've become everything I most despise in this world. I'm one of the late night bellow-y burger people), and Angelo gave me his number.

'How old are you?' I asked, my mouth full of burger.

'A quarter of a century,' he replied.

'Yes, but how old?' I said (I was drunk! I can't do maths).

TWENTY-FIVE, LIL. And then he asked me how old I was, and I took another big bite of my burger and tried to smile coquettishly, which isn't easy when you have ketchup dribbling down your chin. Angelo doesn't smoke, so I was terrified I tasted like an ashtray and burger meat, but he said I didn't, and kissed me again to prove it.

'I have enjoyed my evening with you,' Angelo said, rather formally, like he was about to bow.

'And no one got stabbed,' I said. 'See, if this was London, we'd have lost a lot of blood by now.'

'In Sicily too,' Angelo said, and kissed me again. 'I have never talked so much about violence on a first date. Usually, the book says don't talk about knives if you like a woman.'

'The book?'

'You know… the dating book.'

'There's a dating book in Italy?'

'No, it's… it's not a real book. It is a metaphor.'

I was teasing.

'So this is a first date?'

'Perhaps.'

Should I invite him up? I thought. But no, Angelo was an old-school romantic. After snogging him again, I came upstairs as quietly as I could, and it took me twenty minutes to find the right door key, and now my belly is so full of burger and other food and wine (and butterflies), I'm going to have cramps tomorrow, I can just tell, but it'll be Saturday and I have the whole weekend, and I really, really miss you, and I wish we were kids again, and shared the same room and slept in bunkbeds, and I could tell you all about my night first-hand.

Love you, love you.

Sleep now.

Your drunken blister,

Joy Kisses

P.S. Lil, whyy did youuuu... anyway... that's just making me saddd

MESSAGE FROM LILY

Hey Joy, I'm in your bedroom looking at all the books you've 'borrowed' from me (oh, there's my Katherine Mansfield collection) & killing time while you're at the shop getting idontknowwhat – peanut butter? This is hard for me to say, but you were right before. I did bite your head off. It wasn't fair that I compared you to Mum. You are only trying to help. I guess I'm bummed over this breakup, because I really liked youknowwho. And you liked her too. See, your opinion does matter. I find it hard to say things like this to your face, and so I get passive-aggressive instead. It's my womanly pride. I also have an image to protect, so I'm going to stick this confession into one of your books here, and pretend nothing happened, but in the future, if you ever say, 'Lil, why do you always have to be right?' I'll direct you to find this, so you'll see just how wrong you are. Lil wins. Kidding xL

LETTER SEVEN

Monday, 4 June

Hi Lil,

I found your note in one of my books. I'd never seen it before. Made me smile, and then sad – because I miss you – and then smile again. And then sad. You probably see the pattern. I'm trying to remember when this was, and who you'd broken up with. Which girlfriend of yours did I like? I want to say Tabitha, the swim instructor? See you can put pen to paper, when you want to… I also recall you writing all those letters for Amnesty International when you were a teenager, trying to free that blogger in Iran (successfully, I might add).

Anyway, it's been a while. You probably appreciated the break, but I'm back and ready to start oversharing again.

Can you believe it's been a whole month? I'm practically a native. I eat topless sandwiches, and drink strong mud-like coffee, and wear head-to-toe black. And here's the biggest shocker… Lil, I ride bicycles. Yep, those spinning suicide contraptions – I have ~~mastered~~ ~~tamed~~ not fallen off them (yet).

But before I get into my #cyclinglife, there's something I need to clear up. I hope you're sitting down, because this will absolutely blow your mind:

<u>Not every Danish person is blonde.</u>

Crazy, right? When I arrived in Copenhagen, everyone <u>seemed</u> blonde, because the blondies grab your attention, but after several weeks, your eyes start to adjust, and you realise many Danes have mousy-brown hair. Let that sink in for a moment. And compared to other Scandinavians – like the Swedes, whose blondeness can make your teeth ache – Danes are on the hazier end of the spectrum.

Another surprise is that the British, on the whole, seem relatively liked over here. It might have something to do with 'The Crown' and 'Downton Abbey', or how much the Danes respect their own royalty, or the fact that we haven't drunkenly infiltrated Denmark in the same way Brits have in the rest of Europe – and vomited on everyone's shoes, and picked a drunken fight with a seagull, and fallen asleep on the side of the road, naked – but being from the UK is even slightly respectable over here. Also, Danes love to practise their English. I've lost count of the times a male barista has peered over the counter at me, only for their gorgeous, square-jawed face to bloom into a smile once I've stuttered out a few words. At first, I thought they were flirting, and I'd blush and get even more tongue-tied, but then I realised they were just working on their pronunciation. Geoff's Sara (my new best friend) says that Danish service people are infamous for being rude – waiters are particularly bad – but I've found the opposite to be true, everyone seems much friendlier than all the po-faced Londoners.

Now I've started to get my bearings, I'm realising Copenhagen is a relatively small city, and everything becomes vastly more accessible on a bike (just to reiterate, I've ridden on multiple bicycles! Me… Joy!). There's the city centre – which is all shops and department stores, and Tivoli, which is this famous traditional amusement park – and the Carlsberg factory, the Royal Palace, lots of lakes and canals, but the most insane part of Copenhagen is called Christiania. It's famous for being run by hippies, selling drugs (mostly marijuana) at a place called Pusher Street, and making special tricycles with a box at the front for pushing passengers in called, unsurprisingly, 'Christiania bikes'.

Bikes! You see, you can't escape them in Copenhagen. And the reason I've been on all these bike rides, and seen so much of the city? It's starting to get slightly warmer and sunnier for one – a lot of the Danish men are already wearing shorts, although it's practically minus ten and still far too cold for that, silly men. No, the main, <u>main</u> reason – and I can't believe I've gone all coy, but this is the first time I've formalised it in writing – is because I seem to have wangled myself a boyfriend again.

No, not Robby. God, no! (Who hasn't come and visited me yet – thank goodness.)

Angelo – the Italian I met at Geoff and Sara's – he might not know anything useful or interesting about Tuscany, but he does know how to win an English girl's heart. Actually, I'm not sure if my heart is won – not yet perhaps, it's early days. But, Lil, I think I like him. And my liking him, and him liking me, all happened so organically, with none of my usual underminings. Really, I don't think I've done one thing wrong (so far).

That first night, Angelo gave me his number, so the next day I sent a text message thanking him for getting me home safely (but really thanking him for the lovely snog and hinting I would like another), and so we started chatting, and before long, he'd invited me for a walk along the canals on the Sunday. Well, I assumed it was a walk, because I wore a longish skirt, and my most sensible boots, but when he arrived at my flat (looking very cute, it has to be said – he has a cowlick on his left temple, making his curly dark hair even more disobediently cuter), he was wheeling two bicycles – his bike, and one he'd rented especially for me. Angelo must have seen the panic in my eyes, because he spent a lot of time making soothing noises, and adjusting the seat to the perfect height, and showing me how to use the brakes, and promising to go extra slow, as all the while I recited the statistical probabilities of death and injury, and explained the medical reasons for my poor balance (due to all those inner ear infections I had as a child. What, it's true – you were there). I was still extremely unwilling, but Angelo has this steely pragmatism about him, and suggested I simply try getting on the bike, and if I didn't like it we could stop, and so against all my better judgement I found myself, moments later, careening down Istedgade on two flimsy wheels. I was terrified, Lil – I thought I'd fall off instantly and land on my ass, and all the trendy Danish people would point and laugh, but after a couple of hairy moments, I realised it feels quite nice with the wind on your face – and you do move much faster than walking – and of course, I've ridden bicycles before, but not for a very long time, and there's something connected to childhood about it – you and I cycling around our neighbourhood as kids, the freedom and feeling of invincibility, knowing we were travelling farther and farther away from Mum's clutches – and I'm still very much a ~~realist~~ fatalist, but here's the thing – everyone obeys the road rules over here. Every. Single. Person. They uniformly stop at amber lights. No one runs a red light. In fact, they all ride like old grannys – and it's wonderful – and there are bike lanes everywhere, and you feel a strength in numbers with so many bicycles, and I like the rules, I do, they make me feel safe.

During our maiden voyage, Angelo cycled next to me encouragingly – being on the wrong side of the road is terrifying, and turning left is terrifying, and whenever another cyclist dinged their bell I would scream, but the sun came out, and I felt the wind in my hair, and the joyous feeling of my legs working (actual exercise), and watching Angelo's calves bulge as he pedalled, and everyone was being so courteous.

'No, you go first,' I said with a big smile to a woman slightly behind me with three children squatting in her cargo box.

When we finally stopped cycling, my legs were shaking, but I was also jubilant, and you forget how much of an aphrodisiac risking life and limb is, because Angelo wasn't quite prepared for the way I threw myself at him once we'd made it safely back to my flat. On our first proper date too, what a hussy! (Note: 'hussy' said in jest. You've drummed enough sex-positivity into me, okay, Lil?)

Not only does Angelo love cycling, he also runs. And goes to the gym. In fact, he never stops moving. If Angelo is by a step, chances are he'll be doing an elevated lunge. He's constantly on the hunt for things to do chin-ups on – tree branches, bits of exposed pipe, the top of the window frame in our living room, much to Greta's chagrin. Angelo is also into parkour, which is basically a death wish, and means he'll be standing beside you one moment, and then off scaling a water tower the next. To top it all off, he's finishing his Masters in human nutrition at the University of Copenhagen, so he's also an expert in food. Not intimidating at all. But you should see his body, Lil. He's a small, perfectly formed Adonis. There are parts of him that are so pointy and ripped, he seems almost insectoid-like. The other night, when he stayed over, I had to move over in bed because his bony hip was poking into my side. I've never dated someone so fit (or young). It's very disconcerting. At first, I was self-conscious and worried that we kept going on bike rides because he thought I was a flabby fatty, and he was trying to get me into better shape, but he swears black and blue he likes my body type (that's what he calls it, my 'body type' – so romantic), and I'm slowly beginning to believe him.

Angelo is a fantastic lover, and without being too graphic, sorry, sis, he absolutely worships my body (I mean, Robby wasn't terrible either, except for all the leg yanking. I don't know if you get this in your line of work – but men have a tendency to articulate your legs like they're manually resetting a large clock). There's one major drawback of having an athletic lover with lots of stamina, however – I've always been a one-and-done gal, whereas now, just when I think we've properly finished and I'm drifting off to sleep or thinking about making a sandwich, Angelo rouses, and it's all back on again. Sometimes I have to pry him off, because I'm dehydrated, or his abs are being too knobbly.

Of course, I'm constantly over-analysing everything. Can a person have too much sex? Should I really have thrown myself into a new relationship, straight out the gate after moving countries? Did I simply gravitate towards the first person I saw who was short and brown enough, like me? (Over here, Italian basically constitutes 'ethnically radical'.) Is Angelo doing the same? And should we both be dating someone closer to our own ages? Margaret, my FaceTime therapist, unhelpfully says I should be aware of any old patterns emerging, but not get too caught up on the small stuff. But what if the small stuff is old patterns emerging? What then, FaceTime Margaret, huh?

At the very least, it seems to have improved my general demeanour. Yesterday, at work, Jakob asked, 'What's that on your face?' (He's always coming over to my desk and loitering in my personal space, but because he smells nice, I don't especially mind).

'Oh,' I stammered, reaching for a tissue, 'probably mayonnaise from lunch…'

'No, you don't have a frown. And your lips are curling up at the sides. Are you sick?' (Jakob is a real comedian.)

'Maybe it's because I'm dating someone,' I said, point-blank, not sure if you're supposed to talk about personal things like that in the workplace here, but wanting to shock him a bit. Jakob visibly recoiled, so I took that as a sign I had overstepped the mark and didn't mention it to anyone else in the office. Whoops!

Apart from cycling everywhere, and avoiding Angelo's bony bits, we mostly hang out at his flat (he lives with two guys, both students, near the university) and sometimes at mine – although Angelo isn't the biggest fan of Greta either (the other day, she came home with a framed poster that read 'Good Vibes Only', which sounds more like a military command coming from her, rather than anything inspirational). Angelo has been making a concerted effort to get me to read 'Harry Potter' – he's like a zealot, worried I won't go to magic heaven if I don't consume it somehow – so I suggested a compromise. I'd consent to watching the first 'Harry Potter' film, but only if he'd see my favourite movie, 'Under the Tuscan Sun', with me (he was hesitant, because he feels the 'Potter' books are the purest form of the work and should be experienced first).

The problem is, it's almost impossible for Angelo to watch anything, because he has a very fast metabolism, and falls asleep instantly. He has borderline narcolepsy. Yesterday, I popped to the laundry room downstairs, and when I came back, he was perched on a stool, with his head in his hands, out cold. How is that even physically possible to fall asleep seated? And I am not prepared to sit through baby Daniel Radcliffe, baby Emma Watson and the ginger one being baby witches and wizards, if Angelo can't even make it through the opening credits (although when he's asleep, at least I can stop trying to channel my inner Sophia Loren – it's hard to be sexy when you're constantly sucking in your stomach and trying to recline in a way that doesn't cause anything to bulge unpleasantly).

Dating Angelo also makes my conspicuous consumption of booze and cigarettes a lot more conspicuous. Angelo drinks in that very European way, which means not at all really – he can take or leave it, and even if he does have a tipple, he'll nurse it all night, taking tiny, ineffective sips. I drink like a fish in comparison. I'll bring a nice bottle of wine over to his place on a Friday night, and present it to him pointedly, only for him to put it in the fridge and promptly forget about it. And then I think, if I bring up the wine, does that make me sound desperate? So I bite my tongue, but I'm so highly strung – because I had a busy week, and I want to relax, and I still don't know if Nansi is pregnant or not, and it's Friday night after all – until finally I engineer the opening of Angelo's fridge, so I can exclaim, 'Oh, we forgot the wine!' in a tone I hope does not convey desperation, and Angelo looks surprised, but takes it upon himself to open the bottle with a great flourish, only to pour two thimble-sized glasses, which I spend the next thirty minutes furiously trying not to chug.

Don't get me started on the cigarettes. I need to quit, I really do – and meeting Angelo is a real kick up the pants – but there are so many moving parts in my life right now, I need some constants. And smoking happens to be one of those constants. It's not an excuse, it's a fact. Anyway, Angelo knew I was a smoker – I must have smoked at least fifty cigarettes the night we met – and it's not like he says I have to quit – both his parents and his older brother still smoke – but it would be nice not to have the feeling of utter failure as I stand outside on his balcony puffing away, and then afterwards, when I have to brush my teeth and soak myself in perfume and chew gum and use breath freshener and beat myself with rosary beads – it's a lot. But everyone in Copenhagen smokes, Lil – everyone. It's a cancer-fest. Sometimes they even ride bikes and smoke at the same time. To be honest, Angelo might not be judgemental about my smoking now, but I can tell it's only a matter of time before it's a deal breaker – and guess what? The stress of that impending moment makes me want to smoke even more.

Obviously, now Angelo's on the scene, it means I've been able to finally cut ties with Robby. And by cut ties, I mean go back to ignoring him for the most part. Which I think is for the best. For me, Joy. And that's what matters most in every situation, right?

Angelo says 'hi' by the way. He stayed over last night, and made me a lovely – and extremely protein-rich – breakfast, and now we're spooning on the couch. No, not spooning. Scissoring? That doesn't sound right either. He's up one end, I'm up the other, and I have my feet on his chest. It's an optimal position, so he can't see what I'm writing about him. I haven't told him about you yet, Lil – he thinks you're a perfectly normal sister, so just play along.

What? He's inviting you to stay with his family in Sicily. Oh, he's not finished. Angelo invites you to come next spring when the orange blossoms are in bloom, they are very beautiful. Okay, wrap it up now, Angelo. He says you can bring a boyfriend if you like, so that'll be a first – I've set him straight about that – and he apologises and says please bring your girlfriend, or any friend you like. He really is sweet, Lil.

Oh, speaking of, your social worker friend ex-colleague Alexandra messaged me the other day, which was super nice. She'd heard I'd left London, and just wanted to see how I was going, and to send her love, which was very thoughtful. You have good friends, Lil, kudos to you.

Right, I better stop writing, kick Angelo out and get ready – Sara's taking me to my first Lopermarket (flea market). I still haven't done anything to my room – Harville is really the only decoration so far, if you can call a raggedy teddy bear, with one missing eye 'decoration' (sorry, Harville), so Sara decided we needed to remedy the situation immediately. She's going to show me how to barter like a local. I'm good cop to her bad cop. I'm also learning the art of the walkaway (and guess how we're getting to the market? On a bike. Will miracles never cease?).

Bye for now.

Your sis on wheels,

Jo-oy

LETTER EIGHT

Wednesday, 13 June

Okay, I need to tell you about two embarrassing episodes in my life recently: cake day, and my… um, smear test.

(Also, hi, Lil. Forgot to start with the conventional letter formalities.)

Let's begin with the more humiliating and exposing of the two, shall we? Yep, you guessed it – cake day.

Cakes are good, right? Mmmm… delicious cakes?

Wrong. So wrong. Cakes are social anxiety made manifest.

Backstory: at our office, we have a lot of informal meetings. I get it, we're slaving away, isolated on our own computers most of the day, and sometimes we barely speak to each other, so the breaks are engineered social times. We have a team meeting on a Monday morning, and every Friday there's a breakfast meeting, with bread and cheese (for some reason, but I'm not complaining). Remember, this is on top of the – pretty much mandatory – communal lunches. As if that's not enough already, Wednesday is cake day. Sometimes the occasion is a birthday, or someone leaving, but often there seems to be no reason for the cake, there's just cake. Cake. I love cake, right? What's your problem, Joy?

Well, cake is not cake at all. It's a trap.

On my first cake day, I was finishing off something at my desk and so I arrived a little late. That was the first black mark against my name, and I received a few funny looks (which from an eye-contact avoiding Dane is the equivalent of being shanked in the kidney with a knitting needle). The cake itself was horrible and tasted like chocolate dirt. It was the worst cake I've ever had the misfortune to pass through my lips, and it's safe to say I've eaten my fair share. It congealed instantly in your mouth in a greasy, oily clump and stuck to the back of your throat. If this constitutes cake in Denmark, I thought, you can leave me out.

The following Wednesday, when cake time was announced, I told my team to go ahead without me. They resisted, Jakob even screwing up his stubbly face in protest, but I batted them away light-heartedly, and told them I'd join them soon. My plan was to avoid going at all, but you know me, I start to feel guilty immediately, so after twenty minutes of excruciating insecurity, I finally caved and joined everyone around the cake. I was pleased to see it wasn't a chocolate abomination this week, this cake was more a tart with glazed fruit on top – well, that's what I'm assuming it was, because there was only one piece left, and it was pretty mushed up. As I helped myself to it, I could sense something happen, a silent ripple of disapproval, although I had no idea why. It was cake day. I was eating cake. What more did these people want? Touching base with Sara later (who has become my go-to person for everything Danish etiquette related), I learned it's bad manners to take the last piece of cake – no, more than that, IT'S THE RUDEST THING YOU CAN POSSIBLY DO. As a way of avoiding this ultimate taboo, Danes do this weird thing where they cut the last slice in half and take that, and the next person does the same, and so on – and that's obviously what'd happened before I arrived late and helped myself to the final sorry slice. Basically, I embarrassed the whole office in one fell swoop, because they would never have molested the last piece if they'd known I was coming to claim it. The shame! The cake-related shame of it all!

Armed with this new information, I tried my best to conform, although by now cake was triggering a strong sense of PTSD. If I even looked at a picture of cake, my hands started to sweat and my mouth became dry, but each week, I made sure to get to the cake on time, claim my slice, make lots of appreciative sounds eating it, and ignore every impulse to have a second slice (and never the last piece – better to throw yourself out the window). Things were slowly getting better, and I was no longer turning pale at the sight of cake, when Nansi whispered to me that the following Wednesday, as it was my birthday week, I should bring the cake (Note: I officially ignored my birthday in protest of getting yet another year older. It. Does. Not. Stop.).

That night, I rushed to the supermarket to assess baking ingredients. Now, I'm not the world's most devoted master baker, but I can whip up some muffins if I have to. The bar was set very high, however, as all the office cakes, even if they didn't taste great (e.g. the chocolate soil abomination), at least looked very professional, with proper icing, and glazed fruit and shit. It would also have to be quite a big cake to feed everyone, and to stop the embarrassing showdown of people avoiding the final slice. Fortunately, the one (and only) perk of living with Greta the Inexorable is that she keeps an extremely well-stocked kitchen, with every appliance and all the baking gear you might think of. My quandary was this – should I make an English classic, like a Victoria sponge (or even Mum's Persian speciality, the ubiquitous cardamom and pistachio cake) – or a Danish one, to show I was assimilating well, and generally being a team-player? After agonising for days, I decided I would go with a traditional Danish cake for extra marks. How hard could it be?

Smash cut to me the following Tuesday night, sobbing into my third attempt at making a – little too ironically named – Danish Dream Cake. It was close to midnight – I'd already raised Greta's ire by sending the baking trays crashing to the ground, and kicking them around the floor in my hurry to pick them up. I also had to send Angelo home after he'd popped round for moral support, but kept getting in the way, trying to instigate a sexy make out session while I was frantically measuring ingredients. The problem was that I wasn't used to the oven – Greta's ran much hotter than I expected – and so I'd burnt the first attempt to a literal crisp. The second attempt didn't rise properly (I think I might have over-beaten the batter in my panic). My third attempt was neither a carcinogenic risk, nor particularly squat, but I was running low on sugar, so I was unsure exactly how sweet it would be (Greta doesn't eat anything with sugar in it, even fruit. I thought she was diabetic for the first couple of weeks until I realised she was just being difficult). I decided to make up for the lack of sugar with extra icing on top. And extra icing, I did. The resulting cake was about two parts icing to one part cake, but I bunged it in the fridge, exhausted, and went to bed, hoping for the best.

In the morning, I paused before opening the fridge (what would you like for your birthday? How about crippling anxiety over baked goods?). There was a lot riding on this creation, but my colleagues would appreciate the effort, I told myself, even if it didn't look perfect…

I needn't have worried, Lil. It was not perfect, it was not really a cake even. In the night, the tray had fallen to one side and the icing had slid down one side before congealing. It was a baking-related landslide. For some time I squatted in front of the open fridge in shock, until my face started to get freezer burn and I was afraid Greta would walk in and accuse me of wasting electricity. I took the lopsided cake out (it seemed to have gained ten pounds overnight) and tried to smooth the icing back somehow, but it was not budging. Maybe it tasted better than it looked? I cut a small square from the corner of the cake and tried it. It was not sweet, it really had no taste. The icing was much better than it appeared (although that wouldn't be hard), but overall, it was like rich butter icing on a crispbread cracker. I couldn't take this to work – it would undermine what little goodwill I had already built. I binned that cake. I binned it, dressed hurriedly and ran out of the house to buy a common store-bought layer cake with white marzipan icing, which I transported to work in a taxi, and handed it in shamefully, knowing I'd be judged for failing the homework assignment. But I didn't care: I had been requested to bring cake and there it was. Let them eat cake, oh God, let them eat it!

All morning, I sat in a numb bubble of failure and when cake time came, I tried my hardest to look happy. As the cake was revealed, I searched people's faces for judgemental reactions, but the Danes are generally inscrutable and the reckoning didn't happen. Several of my colleagues even congratulated me on my cake's deliciousness. Were they being sarcastic, knowing I didn't bake it? Did they all talk behind my back? Or was I given a pass because I was a stupid foreigner?

I was telling the story to Sara when she burst into laughter.

'Everyone buys the cake,' she explained merrily.

Everyone buys the bloody cake, Lil. Of course, they do. Who wants to be slaving away on your third cake at midnight ON THE WEEK OF YOUR BIRTHDAY? Makes perfect sense. Guess I'll know for next time. Thanks, everyone!

Ugh.

I've been racking my brain trying to think of a suitable segue to talk about my pap smear, but I've come up with nought (also, never Google 'vagina' and 'cake', unless you want to be heavily traumatised).

So, my pap smear.

Double ugh.

You know what a ~~hypochondriac~~ ~~neurotic~~ sensitive person I am. I do not like needles, or blood, or the germs on the door handles at doctors' surgeries. You would think, however, that a person with as many concerns as I have would constantly be getting check-ups. Not true. I put off everything – STI tests, boob lump tests, that hereditary heart thing Dad has – and then I really luxuriate in the feeling of panic and impending doom. Once I've worked myself up into a frenzy, I'll arrive at the clinic in tears, only to be told it's a pimple and not skin cancer or whatever. So, full disclosure, I haven't been so great at remembering my pap smears. But new country, new me. And I was due a test in England before I left. Well due. Overdue, some might say. I signed up to a doctor, and when he looked at my notes, he commented on the fact I hadn't had a smear test in a while, and I should have one then and there with the nurse. Just like that. Your normal, casual pap smear. In the UK, it would take four months to get a referral. And then the referral would be lost in the post. Everything was moving much too fast.

I started to make excuses – 'I have to get back to work…', 'It's almost the Equinox', 'I'd forgotten to bring my vagina with me' – but somehow, moments later, I found myself in a room with a female nurse, who instructed me to take off everything below my waist. Now fortunately, FORTUNATELY, I'm in a relationship, and so my legs were shaved and my lady garden was relatively well-kept (kempt?), but I worried somehow the nurse would know I'd been having quite a lot of sex with an energetic and lovely young Italian – and judge me for being a harlot. Look, I'm not saying my fears are rational. Also, it was quite cold in the room – and so would it be okay to leave my socks on? The nurse had said everything below the waist, but… socks? Also, my socks had a (small) hole in the heel of the left foot. Should I take off the socks and risk cold feet? Or keep them on and risk disobeying the nurse, and being earmarked a troublemaker, or being judged for being a messy slut, who was probably having so much sex that she didn't have the time to buy new socks? I finally decided to strip off everything and go full commando – better cold feet than ill judgement.

Once on the bed, the nurse came back in, only to be met by the image of me posing with both legs daintily crossed, as if I was about to be painted in oils.

'I'm a bit nervous,' I said.

'We'll get this done quickly,' the nurse replied. She was about Mum's age, and reminded me a bit of Mum actually, which was both off-putting and calming in equal measures.

'Can I make a request?' I asked, before she started. 'Could you use the smallest speculum?'

The nurse looked at me impassively.

'We only have one size,' she said.

'How big is it?'

She showed me – and it was plastic, not metal, which made it slightly less scary looking, but only very slightly.

'I've done this many times,' the nurse said.

I'm sure she has, but my heart was pounding. Usually, I just go along with everything, but I imagined what you'd say in the situation. Advocate for yourself, it's your body! Don't be forced into compliance!

'I'd feel better if we could use a smaller speculum.'

Really, speculum is the most horrible word in the world. You can't say it without spitting.

The nurse shrugged. 'I will see,' she said and left the room again.

Oh no, I thought, I've angered her. You don't want to get someone who's just about to jam a thingummy up your wotsit offside. But it's a reality – the normal-sized speculums are uncomfortable. I have a petite wotsit! Petite!

When she came back, I had curled my legs up behind me in a sort of mermaid pin-up pose. I don't know who I was trying to impress.

'I found a smaller one,' she said, without any level of excitement, and it looked the same size really, and I wondered if she was lying to me, but really, what could I do? So, I lay back (I didn't need to put my feet in the stirrups), and the nurse said, 'You are very tense. Take a deep breath and relax. It will help.'

And I always hate it when people say that. Nothing makes me feel less like relaxing than having to relax. But I dutifully took a few deep breaths and prepared myself for the inevitable painful/uncomfortable feeling, when the nurse said, 'You are English?'

I nodded in agreement, still breathing as if I was going into labour.

And then she said, 'Have you read "Harry Potter"?'

Have I read 'Harry Potter'?

I kid you not. It seems anyone who is about to enter my vagina needs to bring up this children's book series and challenge me on why I haven't read it. How can I possibly be British and not have loved 'Harry Whatsisface and the Goblets of Whatever'???

This made me even more tense, because the nurse noted, 'You're not breathing,' but then suddenly it was all over, and she was taking off her gloves and saying, 'I was so sad when… died' and I thought, SPOILERS, LADY! I mean, what if I did decide to read it?

After all that, the test came back inconclusive because they didn't get enough cells, so I have to go back and do it all over. Sigh.

In fact, I should book the appointment now.

Or I could make a peanut butter sandwich?

Mmmm… sandwich. I think I'll do that instead. No time like the present, right?

xxxxJ

P.S. I've booked my flight to come back to see you (and Mum and Dad, of course). I'll be there in three weeks! Argh – soon!

P.P.S. Speaking of the mother, this was her text yesterday: 'Enough is enough, darling, you've proved your point. Also, I saw on your Facebook, you still haven't thrown out those shoes I told you about last summer. I only say this because I care.'

Save me from her, Lil!

P.P.P.S. With all this talk of cake, I just want to assure you I'm completely fine, and haven't had another bad turn re: eating xxxx

LETTER TO MARGARET

Hi Margaret,

The connection got really terrible there, I don't think you could hear me. I'd been speaking for about five minutes (really important, breakthrough stuff too), when I realised the line was dead.

It still won't connect, so I thought I'd give old technology a whirl.

Where was I? Oh yes, I'm cross with Lil. I know I shouldn't expect responses to my letters, you and I even talked about this – but I still do. There's something about writing a letter, and knowing the person isn't even going to try to respond. I take it personally, I know that's ridiculous. Even at the best of times, Lil hasn't exactly been a 'get right back to you' type of person. So why should she start now, what with everything that's happened?

But there's this part of me that looks for her envelope, with a British stamp, every time I check the mail. Each time I start a letter I think, 'Lil'll love this'. But that's just projection, as you've taught me. Everything's a blinking projection. The whole bloody world – projection upon projection upon, well, you know this stuff better than me, Margaret. I'm probably not even writing these letters to the 'real' Lil, but only a projected version of her – one who wants to hear my witterings, and thinks my jokes are hilarious, and is fascinated by her big sister's exploits in a strange new country.

In reality, Lil doesn't have a lot of time for my shenanigans. She watches documentaries and has an important job helping vulnerable children. She's not 'serious' serious – she can be fun and silly too, that's part of our comedy routine. I'm the mad emotional one, Lil's the one to bring me down to earth again – but she can get very quiet, which always unnerves me. She doesn't like being hugged. She hates loud sounds – like a firework suddenly going off, or if a car honks – it makes her wince. She can be very secretive with who she's dating, even with me. Sometimes she can go silent with her communication for a few days, and then I get paranoid and think I've done something to make her mad with me, and then she pops back, and everything's completely fine. I shouldn't take the lack of letters personally, I know that. Okay, I've convinced myself. You're very good at this, Margaret.

And look, not one joke.

Oh, I think you're calling me again…

Thanks,

Joy

LETTER NINE

Thursday, 14 June

Lil – oh my God, Robby is here!

Robby. Is. Here. In. Copenhagen.

This is not a drill. THIS IS NOT A DRILL. He just called from the airport. FROM THE AIRPORT, LIL.

What do I do?

I'm going to tell him to get straight back on the plane.

WHAT WAS HE THINKING????? (I know technically, I invited him, but it was obvious I didn't mean it. Not obvious enough, obviously…)

And what will Angelo think?

Dad is arriving tomorrow too.

WHY DOES EVERYTHING HAPPEN AT ONCE? WHY?

LETTER TEN

Saturday, 16 June

Dear Miss Lily (no middle name) Taranaki,

(Haha, I know you hate being called 'Miss' almost as much as being called Lily.)

I've been awake for half an hour, but I daren't step outside my bedroom, even though I'm both dehydrated and really need a wee, because I'm not ready to wake everyone up and start the gears of the day whirring.

Currently, my idiot ex-boyfriend is snoring on my couch, while our hallowed father is sleeping in my flatmate's bed, fully clothed (not with Greta, thank mercy – she's away). My actual boyfriend is M.I.A., probably – deservedly – sulking at his place.

I miss you, Lil. I wish you weren't so far away. You were always so great in situations like this. Remember as kids how you always wanted to be a hostage negotiator? You'd make a loud speaker using a toilet roll and I'd sit on the stairs with my doll, Pollyanna, who was planning to blow up the toy box if her demands weren't met. I was never very good as the antagonist, I always giggled when you'd say things like, 'Pollyanna, we'll get you a helicopter to Santorini, just let Harville and the teddies go free'. When we'd have friends over from school, you'd try to instigate a multi-person scenario, but the guest would inevitably say, 'This is weird and boring' and you'd look at them like, 'You're weird and boring' and I'd have to smooth things over. Actually, in hindsight, maybe I was the better negotiator?

I even miss Mum. She'd say, 'Lazy boys and girls don't go to heaven' and make everyone get up, and give us all jobs, and I'd hate it, but at least I wouldn't have to think what to do and we'd all be distracted. She'd send Robby and Dad off on some quest to buy sour cream for the scrambled eggs, and you and I would be forced to change all the bedsheets, or peel potatoes, or source chairs, grumbling the whole time – Mum is the master of assigning busywork – but when we all came back, the windows would be wide open, and there'd be bread baking, and everything would be organised and lemony-fresh.

I could do with some additional feminine energy too. All this testosterone is stifling. I feel like I'm in some weird men's group, where they play the drums, cover themselves in mud, and make wolf sounds around a campfire. Not for the first time in my life, I'm considering giving up men altogether. I mean, really, what's the point? All the posturing, and the fragile egos, they're like monkeys – constantly touching their junk and flinging faeces at each other (metaphorically).

But I'm jumping ahead. Let's go back two days, shall we?

THURSDAY

When Robby's taxi pulled up outside my flat, I was in a very strange headspace. Mostly, I was annoyed at him – because, what a jerk move, coming over unannounced (yes, I realise I did invite him. What are you, his lawyer?) – but I was conflicted too, because part of me was happy to see a familiar face, and there's one more thing, Lil. I wasn't completely honest when I said I'd cut all ties with Robby. Whenever I was really homesick, or tipsy (or both), I would occasionally message him. Occasionally. Before Angelo, of course… To be fair, Robby was always up late working, and it was only text messages, and sometimes you want to chat with a person who knows everything about you, and tells you everything's going to be okay…

When Robby stepped out of the cab, he was wearing some ridiculous new trainers and a coat with a chain brocade on the front pocket, and a black baseball hat with 'solid' written on it – and when he kissed me on the cheek, I shook my head in resignation. Part of me had wondered how I'd feel seeing him – would there be a wobble of regret? Would I want to throw myself at his lanky goodish-looks, or ruffle his jet-black hair (I've always felt personally aggrieved he doesn't have a single grey on his head) – but I am happy to report I was not overcome with love or lust, I only felt residual affection, and slightly annoyed, like he'd crashed the neighbour's car or something. And that was good, I suppose. It's good to feel there are no longer any major emotional stakes. That's progress.

Maybe not good for Robby though. Probably definitely not.

He was even more sheepish in person. In fact, if there had been a rock nearby, he would have definitely crawled underneath it. Once he'd paid the taxi, we went into the burger place downstairs, not talking for a long time after we'd bought our food.

'Robby,' I said, at last. 'You know I'm seeing someone over here?'

He nodded.

'Your dad told me.'

'Wait, why have you been speaking to Dad?'

Robby looked even more sheepish. I really thought his head would retract into his shoulders like a tortoise.

'We're Facebook friends,' he said finally. This alliance was news to me – I didn't think Dad even liked Robby much. 'He said I should come over, speak my piece.'

'Did he now?' I said between gritted teeth. 'You know Dad's arriving tomorrow?'

Robby seemed genuinely surprised at this.

'Great minds,' he said with a shrug.

No, not great minds, Robby. Not great minds at all.

'Look, I'll say my bit and go,' he said.

And I could feel it then, this build-up of tension, and I thought, don't ask me to marry you, Robby. Not in a burger joint. Have some class!

'I know I was never good enough for you…'

'That's not it…'

'And it was always tough with me working nights…'

'Robby…'

'And I wasn't as faithful as I should have been…'

My eyebrows shot up in surprise.

'Wait… What do you mean by "not as faithful"?'

'You know. The thing I had with Debbie…?'

'What thing? Who's Debbie?'

I've never seen Robby look so pale.

'I thought you knew…'

'About what, Robby? WHO'S DEBBIE?'

'She's a barman. A barwoman, I mean – a barperson.'

'And you slept with her while we were going out?'

The group of Danish people waiting in the queue for their burgers were pretending not to listen.

'We were on one of our breaks, I think…'

'You THINK?'

'I lose track. Yeah, we were definitely broken up.'

'But you kept seeing her after we got back together?'

'It was hard not to – she's at work all the time.'

'Because you're her boss?'

'Technically. But – hang on – are you seriously telling me you didn't know?'

'Obviously not, Robby, if my reaction is anything to go by.'

'But… but… You had an attitude. Like a knowing, disapproving attitude. You've always been able to read me like a book.'

'Not well enough, it seems.' I cleared my throat, realising some of my weaker moments of paranoia were entirely justified. 'So, to recap, you made a surprise trip to Copenhagen in order to tell me you were unfaithful in our relationship?'

'Ah, yeah. But also, to win you back.'

'How is that working out for you?'

Robby pressed his palms into his eyes.

'Not good, mate. Not good.'

I laughed. A lot. Robby started laughing too. We laughed for what felt like twenty minutes – people outside the burger place stopped to look at us – and it felt good.

Robby was there during a lot of my bad eating days – sitting with me when I was having an out-in-out binge, buying me canned chicken soup in the days after, when I didn't want to keep anything down. Holding my hair if I did puke. He toed that difficult line between being supportive while someone you love does something horribly destructive. You might not be able to make them stop, but you can hold their hand and help them when they're ready. And Robby held my hand, countless times. I don't give him enough credit, Lil.

It makes me think I should open up to Angelo more about stuff, but even though he's great, I'm not quite there yet.

By this time it was close to midnight and I felt mean sending Robby to a hostel or whatever, so I begrudgingly told him he could stay the night on the couch. I guess that's what you might call a tactical error, because in the flat we opened one of Greta's fancy bottles of red wine (Oh, man, I must remember to replace it before she gets back or there will be hell to pay! Writing myself a note now…), and when we'd almost finished it, Robby gave this little heartfelt speech about how we'd been together through some really tough times – his mother's scare with breast cancer, all my stuff, the recent political climate – and it's true, Robby has always been there for me, and maybe that's why I needed to leave him too, because he represented a part of my life I was running away from, the darkest part. But it wasn't fair to just cut him out completely, I can see that now, and he deserved better, and I was thinking all this when he put his hand on my knee, and I knew if I'd made the slightest move we'd start kissing.

Cut a long story short, Robby slept in my bed, but we didn't, you know, do anything. And it was sort of nice to have him there one last time. It was like really saying goodbye.

Until I woke up, of course. Then I felt terrible.

FRIDAY

I'd already taken the day off because of Dad arriving (not that anyone does much work on a Friday, it's practically a half day in Denmark) so all I had to do when I woke up was feel extraordinarily guilty for nearly kissing Robby. There were two texts and a missed call from Angelo, and ten messages from Dad, documenting his journey to the airport, the flight and his arrival (obviously, reportage runs in our genes), so I threw Robby into the shower and was frantically cleaning up the flat – the smell of near-miss betrayal permeating the air – when Angelo messaged ('Please welcome your father to this country for me') and Dad simultaneously buzzed downstairs.

'You're here already!' I said to Dad, as he trudged up the stairs.

'Great to see you too, sweetheart.'

We hugged, and entered the flat just as Robby was trying to sneak through the living room wearing nothing but a towel. Honestly, my life is like one of those Hangover films: 'Hangover 5: Nordic Nonsense'.

'Robby, this is a surprise,' Dad said, his eyes full of mischief, and as they shook hands, Robby almost lost his towel. THANK BLOODY HELL HE DIDN'T. I attempted to make Dad leave and get some breakfast with me, but I could tell he was enjoying the scenario, and he kept saying, 'Let's wait for Robby to put on some pants and we'll all go.' And so we all head off for breakfast at this place around the corner and Dad orders a beer, right off the bat ('I'm on holiday!'), and fortunately, the Danish all drink like fish so the waiter didn't bat an eyelid, and Robby ordered one too, and I got a Bloody Mary to be social, and breakfast turned into lunch. It was pretty fun, to be honest, and Dad was on top form, telling all his old stories of playing second-degree rugby for Wellington ('I could have been a contender!'), and meeting Mum in that pub in Bristol, being the only two brown people in the place, and both drunkenly and incorrectly thinking the other was the same nationality as them – and his glory days as a stockbroker on the trade floor in New York – and when I next looked at my phone it was nearly 3 p.m. and I still hadn't messaged Angelo back.

Excusing myself, I stood up and went outside to call him, realising as soon as I did that the three Bloody Marys had taken an effect.

'I'm so sorry,' I slurred slightly, when Angelo picked up.

'I was worried,' he replied, sounding rightfully pissed off. 'Did your dad arrive okay?'

'Yes, he's here now.' Currently having an arm wrestle with my ex-boyfriend. No biggie.

'Good. I'll let you get back then.'

'I was ringing to say you should join us? Tonight, we're going to see JP's band play. I know I said before it might be too soon to meet my parents, and I didn't want to put that pressure on you, but I've changed my mind.' (Well, the Bloody Marys and the guilt had changed my mind.)

'It would be an honour to meet your father,' Angelo said. 'But I have an event tonight for school.'

'Ah, okay. Dad's here until Monday, so maybe we can have dinner together before then?'

'Great, let's talk tomorrow. Joy?'

'Yes, Angelo?'

And he spoke Italian to me then, and the hairs stood up on the back of my neck, it was so beautiful.

'Oh, wow! What does it mean?'

'I'll tell you later,' he replied.

As I walked back to the table, I was already formulating a plan. Stop drinking, put Robby on a plane, have a nap, and get up feeling refreshed for the evening's frivolities. A victimless crime.

Dad had other plans.

'Robby's not going anywhere,' he said, grabbing him around the shoulder and squeezing him to his chest. 'We're best mates now. Aren't we, Robert?'

When Robby went to the loo, I pinched Dad hard.

'Stop encouraging Robby,' I said. 'And he says you two have been chatting on Facebook. What the hell, Dad?'

'Sorry, doll – he seemed so downhearted, I just suggested he grew a spine. I didn't actually think he'd actually come over. But looks like it's worked out anyway,' he said, trying to poke me in the ribs.

'No, it did not work out. Robby and I are not back together. I'm seeing someone called Angelo, which you well know.'

'What's so good about this Angelo fellah, eh?'

'He's very sweet. And intelligent.' I didn't say he reminded me of Prince Eric from 'The Little Mermaid', but he does. I didn't mention his pointy abs either. 'He also likes me a lot (in an ocean of blonde beauties, nonetheless), so he obviously has very good judgement. I feel like I'm a better version of myself when I'm with him.'

'You're already a better version of yourself, sweetheart. You put too much pressure on yourself. Garçon? Another beer, if you please.'

'No more beers!'

I got the bill (Dad paid it, of course – he wouldn't take no for an answer) and managed to get us all back to the flat in one piece, but by then it was almost 4 p.m. and we had to go out again in a couple of hours. Robby and Dad were practically singing sea shanties together, so I ordered some burgers from downstairs (they are doing a roaring trade from me) and suggested Robby look at flights, and Dad unpack his suitcase, but it was like trying to herd cats (Minnie! Wonder what that hairball is up to?), and in the end, I gave up. We were meeting Sara and Geoff at 7 p.m., so I had just enough time to close my eyes for five minutes, drag a comb through my hair, put on a splodge of make-up, and hustle everyone out the door.

When we arrived at the bar, only Sara was there.

'Geoff is having some intestinal issues,' she said, and we all voiced our condolences, before Dad and Robby started bickering about who was going to buy the first round. Dad won eventually, but Robby bought the second one hot on his heels, so we were basically holding two drinks each. Classy, guys.

Sara was on good form, joking with Dad and laughing with Robby, and seemed unperturbed that we were all pretty pickled from day drinking.

'I'll have to catch up,' she said, before buying herself a shot of tequila.

At some point (my concept of time last night is hazy) we went for dinner together, and then moved on to the place where JP's band was playing. What we must have looked like – the four of us – hollering and whooping when they came on the stage. Poor JP. The band were amazing though, and Robby kept buying everyone pretentious and obscure cocktails, and I was drinking something called an Old Irish Mame and sort of dance-jumping on the spot when who do I see walking into the bar, but Angelo. My first thought was, 'oh, shit – I drunk.' And my second was, 'Oh shit, Robby here.'

Angelo comes up all smiles, and dressed really smartly: a blue blazer and an immaculately ironed white shirt, the collar so stiff, it looked starched, Angelo's thick wavy Italian hair all perfectly groomed. I introduce him to Dad, who gives him an inappropriate hug, of course, practically picking him up off the floor, and to Sara, and lastly, to Robby. And the world doesn't explode (not yet). Robby is normal and nice, and shakes Angelo's hand, and the music is loud, and Robby says something, and Angelo can't hear, so Robby repeats it in his ear, and my heart pounds. But when Angelo pulls away, he looks unruffled, and I take a sigh of relief and a big sip of my pretentious drink. Gulp. Then a song comes on we all know, and Dad and Robby are practically moshing with a group of Danes who have been roused by alcohol, and Sara's top has slipped and her boobs are in danger of being on full display, and Angelo squeezes my hand and watches this assemblage with a frozen grin on his face.

'Your father is very fun,' he says, a slight look of panic in his eyes.

'That's one word for it,' I reply, squeezing his hand and hoping he can't smell all the cigarettes on my breath.

When Angelo next tries to buy drinks, Robby saunters over and tries to suggest better, more ostentatious cocktails. The band takes a break, JP comes up to me and I'm telling him how wonderful they are, when he nods towards Angelo and Robby at the bar and says, 'Now, you have two men fighting over you. You English girls!' And in slow motion, I turn my head and I see Robby leaning in, and Angelo sort of scowling, and then he pushes Robby back a bit, and Robby says, audibly, 'Only in the same bed!' ROBBY. I'm sure they're about to fight, and I worry because Angelo might look slight, but he has lots of pointy muscles under those smart clothes. But Angelo just shakes his head in what seems like disgust, and makes eye-contact with me. I know I've fucked up then, Lil. I can see it in his eyes, he can see it in mine. He storms out of the bar, and I start to cry, and Sara takes me to the bathroom, but she's almost more drunk than I am, and when we come out again, Dad is asleep in a booth, and Robby is nowhere to be seen, so I put Sara in a taxi and load Dad and I in the next one, and when we arrive back at the flat, Robby has somehow managed to make his way to the burger place and is drunkenly stuffing onion rings into his face.

So that was my night, thanks for asking.

Angelo hasn't texted yet, and I haven't texted him. I want to, but I'm scared. I'm ashamed, and being a coward, I guess. It's almost midday. What should I do, Lil?

I can hear them stirring in the other room.

I wish I felt more hungover today – I don't actually feel that awful. My punishment is to be relatively clear-headed and experience the consequences of my actions, I suppose. Or maybe I'm still drunk.

Why did we share the same bed? I didn't kiss Robby though, Lil, I didn't. Even though I was tempted, I didn't. That counts for something, right?

Do you know what will make everything better? A good English fry-up – sausages, fried eggs, bacon, the lot. It's worked before, countless times. And I know you don't approve of meat-eating, but I need it today…

Ugh.

I think I'll make Robby cook breakfast as punishment.

God, he's an idiot. A lovable idiot.

God, I'm an idiot. A slightly less lovable idiot.

What if this is it between Angelo and me? I never found out what he said to me in Italian either…

Joy 😵

LETTER ELEVEN

Sunday, 17 June

Lily-Palooza,

Remember when I said I didn't have a hangover yesterday? Guess what? I <u>was</u> still drunk! Classic Joy.

Robby took the first flight to London this morning, and back into the warm embrace of Debbie – good luck to her! Actually, we had a nice send-off, and I didn't blame Robby too much for what happened with Angelo. I blamed him a little, of course. And I was passive-aggressive about it. And I enjoyed seeing him squirm. But ultimately, it was a nice goodbye. And I wish him well. As long as he hasn't ruined my relationship with the youngest, sweetest, fittest man I've ever dated. If Robby has, then I retract everything I just said, and wish a plague of locusts on all his houses.

Once Robby had gone, Dad and I mooched around the flat. I suggested putting on a film, but we ended up watching old episodes of Dad's favourite 'The Young Ones' instead, but all the characters were jarring or grating, so we zonked out in front of music videos on YouTube instead. You know you're properly hungover when you only have the attention span for a three-minute music video.

Lil, I have to tell you something about Dad. I wouldn't mention it to anyone but you, because it makes me feel disloyal even bringing this up – I noticed it when he arrived, but everything was going on with Robby, so I didn't have time to process – but Dad isn't looking his usual self. He's put on some weight. No judgement there, you're talking to the yo-yo queen herself, but he's also, I don't know – he seems <u>older</u> suddenly. I know that's cruel to say, and he's hungover, and he's on holiday, but I found myself sneaking looks at him as we were sat on the couch together, trying to figure out what was so different. He's jowly for the first time, and the bags under his eyes are bigger, and his hair's gone greyer, and it feels horrible saying this, but I was shocked when I first saw him come up the stairs. He's always been so active, but he was puffing when he made it to the top. He seemed smaller somehow too. I don't know, maybe I'm overreacting, and I can imagine you getting cross, reading this – you're such a daddy's girl in denial – but I felt you should know. That we should, I don't know, keep an eye on him (just read that back and realised how ridiculous that sounds – what, we should stop him from ageing?).

'Are you looking after yourself?' he asked me at one point.

'Of course,' I said, cigarette hanging off my lip (Greta will kill me because the place stinks of cigarettes, but I can't go down in the freezing cold right now), and then I started to feel paranoid that maybe Dad thought I was getting fat and older too.

'And you're enjoying it here?'

'Enjoying might be too strong a word,' I said, sucking in my belly.

'But it was worth it?'

That was such an impossible question to ask. <u>Was it worth leaving us all?</u>

'Angelo's great,' I replied, and then wished I hadn't, because I didn't want to build him up before Dad could have a proper (sober) conversation with him. I wanted Dad to see Angelo's greatness on his own terms. I then started blathering about all the things Angelo was into, the parkour, the exercise, the nutrition, but spoken out loud they didn't seem like positive attributes.

'Does he want kids?'

Boom, there it was. I didn't think Dad had it in him to drop such a loaded question like that – that's usually Mum's terrain.

We're playing like that, are we? I thought.

'I don't know. We've only been dating a few weeks.'

Dad sniffed.

'How old is he again?'

Double boom. I'd already told Mum Angelo's age, so Dad would definitely know. Gloves off.

'He's twenty-five.' I almost added, 'but he's very wise for his age,' but stopped myself because that's what every skeezy older person dating a younger person says.

'Dad, are you happy in Brighton?' I countered.

He stared at the laptop. On screen, the Cranberries were singing in an Irish drawl about having to let it lingeeerrrrrrrr.

'Your mother has been working a long time to get a position like this. Yes, we had to up sticks from London, but they really like her at the university, and it's easy to forget all the years she was bringing up you and your sister, while I was off travelling. She's coming into her own, doll, and if that means I have to take a back seat for a while, then so be it. It's the least I can do. She's a wonderful woman, your mother. She loves you a lot.'

This speech was so unexpected, it sort of knocked me, and made me scared all of a sudden.

'Is she okay?' I asked.

'What?' Dad looked at me blankly.

'There's nothing wrong with Mum, is there?'

'I told you, she's fine.'

'And you would tell me if it wasn't? With you as well?'

Dad grunted.

'Dad?'

'Yes, hun, of course. It's just taking me longer to settle – retirement isn't really my bag.'

'What about your consulting? I thought you were going to do it part-time?'

He shrugged.

'That didn't really pan out. It's the technology, it's moving so fast. Everything becomes obsolete the moment it's implemented.'

'So, what are you going to do?'

'I have my furniture restoration, I have you.' He squeezed my hand, and I felt that horrible wave of pressure then, to have grandchildren, and I felt cross at myself for being snappy with him earlier. Dad would make the best grandfather ever. That's what he was designed for. He was a good Dad sure, but he was ambitious, and unavailable, and needed to be the life of the party, but now he's mellowed, and he has the time. And there's this void in Mum and Dad's world where grandchildren should be – neither you nor I are coming up with the goods anytime soon. Ugh, it hurt my soul, Lil. I can't have the pressure of him waiting for me to have a baby, I just can't. It's another one of the reasons I had to leave home. I think Dad knows that. Oh, man, the complex, complex emotions.

'I'm thinking of telling Mum about Lil,' I said. Since we're being recklessly honest, why not?

Dad said nothing, but raised his eyebrows.

'Did you hear me?'

'I heard, doll.'

'What do you think about that?'

'I think your mother's been through a lot over the past few years.'

'That's always the excuse though,' I replied.

Dad nodded. It was true, he couldn't argue with that.

'When did you know?'

'About Lil?' Looking to the ceiling, Dad took a big breath in through his nose and then out his mouth. 'When she was fifteen? I picked her up with a friend after a movie, and they both sat in the back seat. She usually only wanted to sit in the front.'

'And you didn't tell Mum?'

'I didn't feel it was my place.'

Dad grunted – out of guilt or resignation, I couldn't tell.

I still hadn't messaged Angelo, so taking the plunge I left Dad watching Beyoncé in the living room, and nervously called him.

Angelo picked up on the second ring as if he was expecting me.

'Hello,' he said, flatly.

'I'm sorry,' I blurted out.

'Okay,' he replied, but his voice sounded steely.

'I didn't know Robby was coming over. And nothing happened, really.'

'Did you kiss him?'

'No.'

'Okay,' he said again after a pause.

'You can be mad if you want.'

'Mad?'

'I mean angry.'

'I'm not angry. I wanted to meet your dad, I left without saying goodbye. It was disrespectful – I shouldn't have reacted like that.'

Dad didn't mind, I wanted to say. What about ME, my stupid feelings?

'Can you forgive me?' I asked. 'I shouldn't have let Robby stay in the same bed. It crossed a line.'

There's another pause.

'Of course.'

'Good, I will make it up to you, I promise.'

'Joy, can I ask you something?'

'Yes…'

'Do you like me?'

'Of course I do.'

'Am I the rebound guy?'

I thought about this for a moment.

'No, you're not.'

'If you're just going to leave and go back to your ex-boy-friend…?'

'Believe me, that will never happen. Seeing Robby ended things, categorically.'

'That is good to hear. Because I like you.'

And Lil, even though I wanted to hear him say it, there was a twinge in my heart at the responsibility of Angelo's like. What if I hurt his feelings? What if I broke his heart? Was I being flippant with him because he was young and fit and hot? Where was this going? Did I see a future with him? Would I have a baby with him? Argh – questions! But I've had enough hangovers in my life to know when to put these sort of questions on ice. Angelo and I were on the mend, that's all that mattered. We said our goodbyes, and I told him to come and have dinner with Dad tonight, to which he agreed.

When I came back into the living room, Dad was watching Christina Aguilera singing 'Dirrty'.

'This is quite good,' he said, 'she really gets into the spirit of the thing.'

I really love him sometimes.

I miss you. And Mum. Stupid families, making you have emotions. Maybe I can convince Dad to stay and open up a Danish furniture making shop?

Better go – I need to get ready for dinner with Angelo. Best not ruin this great thing I have, right?

Loads of love,

xxxx Joy

LETTER TWELVE

Saturday, 30 June

To my favourite sister in the ENTIRE UNIVERSE,
    (Yes, I'm totally buttering you up, it'll make sense later – stay tuned.)
    I can't believe it's been a whole two weeks since Dad's visit. Nay, I won't believe it. I must have blacked out at some point, or I've read the calendar wrong, or I bought a Mayan calendar by mistake. Where. Does. The. Time. Go? I've been so super busy – trying to be an exemplar upstanding girlfriend to Angelo, of course – but mostly, I'm swamped at work. My first big project, the (hopefully) revolutionary new medical software we're designing is at the make or break stage. Three weeks on Monday, we're delivering the software to the higher-ups (which is called 'Ariel' after the little mermaid – which was my idea – because she lost her voice, get it?), and there are still so many kinks to iron out and we're ~~slightly~~ vastly behind schedule, and I'm away in the UK for a couple of days visiting you lot soon, so that's extra pressure too. BUT YOU KNOW ME, I'M GOOD WITH PRESSURE HAHAHA.
    The stress on my teammates is clearly showing, however – literally, with some of them. Hagen has a bad rash on the side of his face – hives, he says, which he gets if he eats too many tomatoes, but I'm convinced it's work related. Jakob has completely lost his

sense of humour and can't be roused even when we have sausages for lunch (he used to do a little play for us with the sausages as people, it was only borderline entertaining, but honestly, there are so many lunches here, you start to look forward to any deviation from the norm). We're trying not to let Nansi get too stressed, because, guess what? Yep, <u>she's preggers</u>. Nansi was so nonchalent (spelling) about delivering the news too. She swivelled around on her chair, and said, 'Joy, I will be leaving soon because I will be taking my maternity leave,' and swivelled back. Just like that. After all the weeks of mystery, I wanted more of a pay-off. To be led, blindfolded into a room full of balloons that read 'bun in the oven' perhaps, or for her to have announced the news with a glitter cannon, or offered to name the baby after me. Something.

'Oh gosh, congratulations,' is all I managed to mumble in response.

The intense pressure has undeniably brought the four of us together, and I'm beginning to learn more about everyone's personal lives, although only in dribs and drabs, as they're still annoyingly private. Nansi has been with her partner for two years, a man she dated briefly at high school, and then years later, he messaged her on Facebook out of the blue, and boom, they fell in love. Maybe not 'boom', Nansi is not really a 'boom in love' type of person. In fact, she didn't even say they were in love, what she actually said was, 'He was fatter, but he still had a nice backside, so I thought, why not?' Hagan was married for fifteen years, but divorced last year, and is now hot on the dating apps. The more I get to know Hagen, the more I realise he's a big sweetie – like six foot four big – but part of me would love to be a fly on the wall when he arrived for one of his dates wearing his typical uniform of camo jacket, military boots, and wild sideburns. Or maybe the women love it, and he's cleaning up?

Oh, and big news: Jakob broke up with his girlfriend. I think she called it off with him, considering how crestfallen he's been.

Literally. His hair is sitting flatter on his head, as if it's been overcome by emotion. I've obviously wanted to find out all the details, but I'm hampered by being his boss and trying to be even a tiny bit professional, so I keep willing Nansi or Hagen to ask some probing questions – but nothing. Danes can be so boringly tactful. I wonder if it had something to do with the addiction thing though?

To help with the software project, our team took a day trip to the local hospital last week to interview patients using older versions of the device we're working on, and to test our prototype. The first person we met was a fourteen-year-old girl called Lærke (pronounced 'lager'), who had been in a car accident when she was ten, and suffered injuries to her throat and chest so severe the doctors thought she'd never be able to speak again. She sat very still, answering all our questions (in English too, so I could understand), and let us take photos, and generally prod and poke her, smiling charitably whenever we made terrible jokes to try and lighten the mood. She had these beautiful translucent eyelashes, and pale, almost invisible, eyebrows, and you could see the aggressive scars too, and I thought, how amazing to have been through this horribly tragic thing, and yet to be so calm and assured. At fourteen, were we ever as self-possessed? You were, perhaps, struggling with your sexuality, but I was a nightmare, what with all my anxiety, imagining what would happen if you, or Mum and Dad were murdered (for some unknown and fantastically unlikely reason) and sobbing hysterically on my bed.

After we'd finished our interview with Lærke (you've already forgotten, haven't you? Hint: lager), we started talking to her surgeon and a few of the specialist nurses, when I noticed Jakob was missing. I was furious – we'd come all this way and he was AWOL (recently heartbroken or not, we still had a job to do) – so I stomped out of the room to go find him. I didn't have to look far – Jakob was sitting in the hallway, hunched over on a seat – and

I was about to start lecturing him and wagging my finger when I noticed his shoulders were trembling. Now, my tears I'm used to. My tears are fine. But someone else's tears? Nope, do not like. My impulse was to run, but against my better judgement I found myself perching next to him instead, and it's the most awkward thing in the world, silently observing another human being crying when you're not even sure if they know you're there. Should I have politely coughed, or said, 'There, there'? Eventually, I placed a hand on his shoulder, and the moment I touched him, Jakob sort of jolted and laughed/cried, looking up with tears and mucus all over his face. I hunted around in my pockets for a tissue, but he'd wiped most of it on his sleeve by the time I found one, which would usually gross me out, but somehow in the circumstances, I could nearly tolerate it.

'Are you alright?' I asked redundantly.

'I will be,' he said sniffing, but he didn't apologise for crying, and I respected that. 'I don't know… Lærke's story really moved me.'

'We're under a lot of stress too, what with the deadline…' (and your girlfriend dumping you, I thought, but tactfully didn't say).

'Fuck the deadline,' Jakob said. 'It's not important.'

This time it was my turn to jolt, first in anger at Jakob's lack of professionalism and his loyalty to the project, and then at myself, because I realised he was right. Sure, we were trying to help a niche group of people improve their quality of life with this new software, but I'd treated Lærke like a specimen. I'd let the questioning run on too long, because I was worried we didn't have enough info, even when it was clear from her body language she was getting tired. I'd become that woman with the clipboard you'd always warned me against being, Lil. And I felt awful about it.

This was sinking in, when Jakob turned to me.

'Are you scared of dying?' he asked.

'Of course,' I replied hesitantly. 'Isn't everyone?'

'I mean, do you get scared every day? Do you think of death?'

And I could feel this protective wall of ice starting to creep over my chest. I think of death all the time. In my mind, I don't even call it death, I call it the 'd' word instead, to try and sap it of some power.

'I think we have to focus on living,' I said, carefully, 'because otherwise it gets too difficult.'

Jakob nodded.

'When my sister was very young,' he said, 'she fell off a fire escape and hit her head. She was concussed – my mother thought she was dead when they found her. I was at a friend's house when it happened, and I remember this strange woman coming to collect me and take me to the hospital, and when I saw my sister, her eyes were rolling in her head, round and round.'

'That must have been terrible,' I said. 'Was she alright?'

'After a while. But when I saw my sister, I thought, what if her eyes never go back to normal? What if they're always like this and people stare?' Jakob covered his face with his hands.

'You must have been very worried for her,' I said as calmly as I could muster, thinking about you, and trying not to cry myself.

'I was only concerned for myself,' Jakob said, starting to weep again. 'What people would think of me with a sister like that. I should have felt guilty for not being with her, for not stopping her from falling. I was her big brother. But instead, I was embarrassed.'

Jakob really started to sob then, loudly and gasping for air. Lil, you know how I get in the face of someone else's overwhelming grief and emotions – it brings out the ~~annoyingly know-it-all~~ logical side in me. It's a defensive mechanism, I can't help it. It's much easier to hide behind logic.

'Hey, hey there,' I said, trying to be soothing, 'what you did was only natural. There's even an evolutionary imperative for those feelings.'

'A what?' Jakob asked, between sobs.

'To be grossed out by weird bodily things. It's a normal human response. That's why we don't like blood or snot or pus or anything, it's why we're squeamish – to keep us away from potential danger and disease. When you saw your sister, it was only your survival mode kicking in. You were freaked out – it was scary to see her like that – and you were worried it could upset other people too. You shouldn't feel guilty. If anything, it shows what a kind, empathetic person you are.' There were other things I thought to say, but the ice wall stopped me. I'm his boss anyway. Better to keep it general. He doesn't need to know my life story, right?

Jakob smiled through his tears. 'You always know what to say.'

'Do I?' I replied. 'I don't feel like I do. I feel like I'm always rabbiting on.'

'Rabbiting?'

'Talking too much.'

'No, Joy – you talk just enough.'

And his eyes were so wet and large and red from crying, and his eyelashes were all stuck together, and he was absolutely covered in snot, but I really wanted to dry Jakob's face with my hands and bring his head into my arms and hold him.

'I feel better now,' he said, fortunately before I actually did cradle him to my bosom. 'We can go back inside if you like.'

After such an intense afternoon, I was relieved to get into the office again, but no sooner had I arrived at my desk than Ingerlise sauntered over. Remember her? The nice chatty older woman who kept coming along to see how I was doing? I wasn't sure if she was my boss or not? (Twist: she is!) Ingerlise asked how the trip went – and I felt a twinge of guilt about Jakob, had I overstepped the mark? Surely not, I was completely professional… Those big wet eyes though… – and then she ~~invited~~ instructed me to present a project update at an important meeting next week. I heard myself saying, 'Of course, Ingerlise (I even think I pronounced her name right), you can count on me.' <u>You can</u>

count on me? I've never uttered those words before. Maybe Copenhagen is changing me?

That evening, I had a proper get dressed up and go-out-of-the-house date with Angelo – we were heading to a nearby restaurant called BOB (Biomio Organic Bistro) in the Meatpacking District, which I've always liked for its incongruous but romantic red neon 'Bosch' sign (a hangover from its days as a factory perhaps? I forgot to ask). Angelo arrived at the apartment with a bunch of daffy tulips, looking very dashing. Even Greta – busy lighting her nightly 4,000 candles – seemed impressed, his suit jacket so fitted he could barely bend his arms. But bend his arm he did, and wearing my nice green dress, I held onto Angelo's elbow, and we walked the ten minutes down the road to the restaurant, feeling slightly self-conscious that we looked like munchkins out on the town.

It's finally starting to get warmer here, and maybe everyone was sensing the impending summer, or perhaps I was just feeling the glass (or two) of Pinot Grigio I'd ~~sipped~~ chugged, getting ready, but everything felt – what's that horrible sounding word, which means something lush? Fecund. The world seemed abundant and content (except I wanted a cigarette, of course – when don't I?).

At the restaurant, there'd been a mix-up with our reservation, so we could only sit along the window on stools, but I actually preferred it, because this way we could look out onto the road, which made a sweeping bend in front of us, and watch the cars and bicycles go by. It was very filmic and cosy (sorry, hygge).

Angelo always asks a lot of questions when he gets a menu – the provenance of the food… How 'organic' was their organic? Were the growing vegetables serenaded to? – and usually I get anxious we're taking so long, but tonight I was relaxed, feeling like everything was back on track after my hiccup with Robby.

'You know what I like about you, Angelo?' I said, feeling generous, once the waitress had taken our menus. 'You're so wonderfully Italian, but you're also not Italian. Does that make sense?'

Angelo squinted at me.

'I'm not Italian enough?' he replied.

'No – you're the absolute right amount of Italian. But you're not defined by your Italian-ness.'

'Are you expecting me to be flipping pizzas and riding Vespas?' He spoke in a loud hokey Italian accent then, 'Mamma Mia!', 'Luigi', 'Maka da pasta', doing that thing where you pinch the air with your hand, and I laughed. (See, it was light! We started off light!)

'I mean, it's what happens when you go overseas,' I said, still giggling. 'There's a level of assimilation, isn't there? I'm doing it too. I guess it softens some of our cultural edges.'

'But you said I'm not Italian. How am I not Italian?'

'Well, you're cosmopolitan. And sensitive. And sweet.'

'I cannot be Italian and sweet?'

'Of course you can – that's not what I meant at all. You're getting defensive.'

Angelo shook his head.

'I thought I was sensitive, not defensive. Is this also not Italian?'

'You're not letting me explain,' I said. 'It's good to be a chameleon, it's good to evolve. I think we get too hung up on being from a certain place, a certain culture. It stops us from growing.'

'That is – how do you say? – 'rich' coming from you. Joy, you're always talking about how things are better in England – the soap is better, the water tastes better, they have better clouds in the sky…'

'Am I? I'm sorry then.'

'I don't mind. But maybe you will realise things are different when you've been away longer. You will understand that your connection with your past is a wonderful thing – it anchors you, it shows who you were, so you know what you have become.'

'Sorry, I didn't mean to offend you.'

'I'm not offended. Remember, my English is sometimes not as fast as you, and then I get… defensive, as you say…'

'Okay, well, my point is… you're a wonderfully diverse person who has a wide range of interests. You've travelled. You speak Danish. You've taken the best bits of being Italian and added to them with the being the best parts of being international.'

'So, I am not a stereotype?' Angelo said, 'Newsflash, Joy, no one is a stereotype.' (He says 'newsflash something' a lot, I don't know where he picked it up…)

'Well, you are being slightly stereotypical now.'

'Why, because I'm a hothead? Because I get angry? Now I'm a bad Italian?' Angelo shook his head. 'This is about your ex-boyfriend – Robby – isn't it? Because I didn't yell at you and make the drama, I'm being punished now for not being Italian enough? You want the yelling? Because I can give you yelling!'

'Angelo, keep your voice down.'

'Oh sorry, I'm so Italian. I can't!'

(Full disclosure – he looked kind of adorable as he did this.)

'Stop it, Angelo,' I said, half laughing, half serious. People at other tables <u>were</u> looking.

He lowered his voice again.

'It causes me a lot of pain to be away from my family, my mother. You know I'm the only one to leave Sicily. It is not typical. And over here' (he lowered his voice even more), 'we are treated differently. I always feel like an outsider in Denmark, so different. You of all people should know what that's like.'

'Me of all people?'

'With your family's… heritage.'

I wrinkled my nose.

'I consider myself English,' I said. 'It's simpler that way. I've never been hugely attached to where my parents are from. I've never lived in New Zealand or Iran, it's not my experience.'

'You don't look English though.'

'What does that mean?' I said, annoyed. 'What does an English person look like?'

'See, it's not so easy when someone else says it. Joy, you're English, but not so English. But in the best possible way!'

'That's not what I meant at all.'

'Joy, you are a <u>contrarian</u>.' (He said this in a thick Italian accent.)

'A what?'

He repeated the word more slowly, but with no less attitude.

'You like the opposite of things,' he continued. 'You don't like cute animals or reading popular books. You always talk about living a healthier life, but you never do anything about it. You dislike Greta and your flat, but you don't look for a new place. And I don't mind, I think you're fine the way you are, but it's exhausting.'

'Exhausting?' I repeated quietly to myself.

'You are always two steps away from being happy,' Angelo continued. 'You never arrive. Happiness is always over there. If Greta is a better flatmate… If your Danish is better. Over there, over there always.'

Oh, Lil, is Angelo right – am I a contrarian? Was I being a douchebag? You'd tell me, wouldn't you? That's why I've transcribed this conversation for you, warts and all, to get your honest opinion. Although, thinking on it now, you'll probably side with him. You've always loved our complicated heritage, relishing our bi-cultural roots – the girl wearing the Maori pounamu fishing hook necklace reading 'Persepolis' and eating Vegemite flatbread sandwiches. In my defence, you managed to carve out your own identity, but also, you were younger, and a hipster to boot (yes, I'm calling you a hipster) – while I was the eldest, and had everything thrust on me, whether I wanted it or not, Mum and Dad competing to see who could indoctrinate me the most. No wonder I turned out the way I did. And it's not like you and I didn't have our fights and disagreements. We could be horrible to each other, like only two sisters can, but does that make me a contrarian?

I'm not really selling my case to you.

Ugh, I am a douchebag.

This whole conversation between Angelo and I was good-humoured though – maybe I've made it more intense in the retelling. As proof, I felt comfortable enough excusing myself for a cigarette before our food arrived.

'Go, smoke,' Angelo said, rolling his eyes, 'I will wait here being Italian, but not too much.'

I kissed him on the cheek as I left, and waved at him from the other side of the window when I was outside, but he was already on his phone.

I nipped around the corner of the restaurant, so I'd be out of sight, and huddled against the wall, taking out a fag. They have the most horrible pictures on the cigarette packs over here too. It's a full-on gore-fest – gaping larynxes and cancerfied lungs – although no one seems to pay any attention, plus cigs are also half the price in Denmark compared to the UK. As I smoked the filthy thing, I remembered Lærke (lager), and how brave she was, and the clever metal box we were making for her throat, and Jakob, and his tears, and my being a contrarian. The wind whipped up, and it was so cold, it took my breath away, and I realised something, Lil: this was going to be my last ever cigarette. I smoked it all the way down to the filter and stubbed it out under my shoe, in that French way JP has, and then I ran back inside to my boyfriend, and the warm candles, and expensive but delicious organic food, and the most successful version of my life I've carved out ever, I think. I didn't quite tell Angelo about giving up smoking though, not yet. I wanted to tell you first. And I still haven't had a cigarette either, and it's (looks at watch) 10.31 a.m. the day after the day after. So that's (uses fingers. Stops and uses calculator app) – more than thirty-six hours. Which is almost two days. How do I feel? A bit like I want a cigarette, but I'm going to be strong this time – I have to be, I do.

I can't believe I'm going to the UK in a week. I'm looking forward to seeing you, but I'm also a little scared about coming back. That's normal, right?

Love you,

Joy xxxx

LETTER THIRTEEN

Sunday, 1 July/Monday, 2 July
(AKA middle of the blinkin' night)

My sweet, sweet Lilith,

I slipped up, I did – literally, figuratively <u>and</u> metaphorically (alright, grammar police, maybe not metaphorically).

My biggest mistake was forgoing a thorough sweep of the house when my resolve was at its height yesterday – I can see that now. You have to remove temptation. Lesson learnt. I'd forgotten about my black leather 'going-out-to-trendy-bars' jacket, and the mangled pack of fags stowed in one of the pockets from the now infamous Robby weekend-of-regret. It's amazing how memory and the subconscious works. An hour ago – when I woke in the middle of the night, desperate for a cigarette – my stupid, crafty brain was giddy with the information. 'Here, look at this,' it went, rubbing its metaphorical hands together, delivering the image of delicious cigarettes so realistic I could almost taste the tar. Now, it's scientifically proven that convictions are weaker in the dead of the night, with no witnesses around – everything feels much more covert and forgivable in the darkness (e.g. stuffing your face from the fridge. Or peeing with the door open. Or stuffing your face while peeing with the door open) – and minutes later, I was flinging handfuls of clothing out of my wardrobe until I found said jacket (which smelled gorgeously of stale smoke). Inside, there were three battered cigarettes in a mangled packet – one fag ripped in half, but two were salvageable, and after I'd found my lighter (keeping that was another tactical error), I opened my bedroom window, because if you're going to fall off the wagon completely, you might as well break all the rules and smoke inside too. My hands were shaking, and my heart was beating, and with those astronomically high levels of anticipation and withdrawal, I was still terrified Greta would get a whiff of the smoke and yell at me, so I leant (leaned?) out the window as far as I possibly could. I was lying on my stomach over the ledge, standing on my tippiest of tippy toes, ready to waft smoke away with my free hand – and as I tried to light the fag, I felt myself starting to tilt forward, my legs flailing – and Lil, my life actually flashed before my eyes: Minnie purring on my lap, those spirited routines we created as kids to Annie's 'It's a Hard Knock Life' which were so convincing, guests weren't sure if they were genuine cries for help (haha, remember the broom choreography?), Jakob and his stupidly lovely lip freckle, Angelo doing a backflip off a water tower, Robby trying to get two Cadbury creme eggs into his mouth at once. And of course, the image of Mum, shaking her head because she was right all along… I would leave this world a cold, barren vessel. But do you know my biggest fear, greater even than the judgemental mother unit? That Greta would have to clean me off the pavement in the morning, and she'd be so annoyed! So luckily, for both our sakes, I managed to grab onto the side of the window just in time, banging my hip in the process, and losing the cigarette, but at least avoiding a headfirst descent onto solid concrete.

Hoisting myself back inside, and trembling on the floor, I realised once and for all, smoking REALLY WAS GOING TO KILL ME if I didn't take affirmative action. But I'm weak, soooo weak – and who has always had the most conviction in the family? Who went vegan for a whole year and didn't falter once (not even during Persian New Year?) That's right – you, Ms Takarangi. You're full of the stuff (conviction, that is), with tonnes to spare. So, help me! I read somewhere that if you entrust a person whose opinion matters to you, it makes you more beholden to the goal. And I know what you're thinking – I didn't sign up for this, you can't make me – but this will be very low commitment your side, I promise. All you have to do is what you know best – silently judge me (haha, I kid. Sort of…). I'll chronicle the next few days – historically, the relapse danger zone, as tonight proves – in real time, and maybe, just maybe, this will work? I hope so, I NEED IT TO – I can't go on like this, repeating the same old patterns, over and over. Imagine how wonderful it will be if I'm a non-smoker when I see you next week, the good feels I'll have?

   Recording starting NOW.

MONDAY: 3.48 a.m.

The adrenaline has worn off, and I think I can sleep again. But first, I have to destroy that last cigarette.

MONDAY: 3.52 a.m.

Mission accomplished – cigarette ripped up in the dark like a madwoman and tobacco doused under water. Goodbye, lung cancer!

MONDAY: 7.36 a.m.

Off to work. I normally smoke about ten cigarettes a day – one on the way to the office, one at elevenses, two at lunchtime, one in the afternoon, one or two after work, and then a few in the evening. I try to ration them out, and have one less than I actually <u>want</u>, but usually this plan backfires, and I smoke two extra before bed, like some dirty junkie. Today, I'm going to listen to

Oprah's Super Soul Podcast interview of Maya Angelou and chew sixteen pieces of sugar-free gum instead. I know all the aspartame isn't good for me, and can cause diarrhoea, but honestly, I need something to balance the unavoidable weight gain.

MONDAY: 9.30 a.m.

Was thinking about my first ever cigarette. It was when I was four-teen, so you were eleven. I went down to the park (the one with the slide that was always greasy for some reason – unaware kids would always get marooned halfway down) with Joanne Parker without telling you. We shared a cigarette, and then swung on the swings until we felt dizzy and sick. But the thing I remember most is coming back home, and having you asking me all these questions – you said I smelt funny, and I was sure you were going to tell Mum. Lil, you were so cross with me, and I don't think you've ever smoked one cigarette, and I know it's because of that day, the betrayal of me going to the park without you. It was also the beginning of the end of our childhood together, because after that, I pretty much became a horrible teenager, and then you became an even worse one, and we weren't friends again for years.

MONDAY: 10.32 a.m.

Zero cigarettes consumed.

Danish words committed to memory = 0

Hours apart from Minnie = several thousand.

I'm worried about overeating at lunchtime. Maybe I could hide under my desk? Speaking of hiding, I'm writing this on the toilet, as it felt too strange and conspicuous writing in longhand at my desk – like I was getting out a loom and starting weaving or something. So yes, this piece of paper has been in a public bathroom. You're welcome.

How do I feel? Shaky. Jakob commented that I looked 'pale' and I explained to him I'd stopped smoking. He looked at me like I was insane – I could almost see the subtext in his eyes: 'Smoke, damnit, woman! This is no time to better yourself, we're under constant fire!' (I don't know why he speaks like a RAF pilot from WW2), but what he actually said was, 'Hope it goes well.' You and me both, buddy. Although, I have to say we've become much – I don't want to say closer, because that sounds unprofessional, but yes, closer is the only word for it – since the thing in the hospital. We're subscribed to each other's Spotify playlists now, and Jakob teases me much less, which I appreciate (I can give it, but I've never been able to take it).

MONDAY: 7 p.m.

Got to the end of the day. Lunch wasn't as bad as I thought, because today was tacos, and I'm not a huge fan of tacos, so the anti-cigarette gods were smiling. That being said, I really felt like smoking after lunch, and I wondered if I should go and buy some nicotine gum (although I've tried them before with no success – them, patches, hypnotherapy, you name it). Especially as Ingerlise (my boss-lady) keeps walking by my desk on the hour 'checking in'. She's like the secret police, passing by for a friendly chat, but it's really because of the approaching deadline.

In the afternoon, I found out Nansi will be going on maternity leave in September so I'll need to hire a new person and get them trained up, and ah, I really, really, really wanted a cigarette! But then I thought of your wonderfully disapproving face, wagging your finger at me and tutting, and it helped. I don't want to be a woman in her mid to late thirties that smokes. It's gone on way longer than I ever intended. Remember when I was only a social smoker? Those simpler, halcyon days… I'm trying to think, what was my turning point from social to ~~chain~~ regular smoker? When did I start having a fag in the morning? That's so gross when you really think about it. The whole thing is so gross when you think about it. I have a cough now too, all the phlegm coming up, but that's a good thing, I suppose – except the phlegm is luridly coloured.

MONDAY: 11.13 p.m.

After work, I decided to go over to Angelo's (now we've smoothed over everything from dinner the other night, and Dad and Robby's trip), because I reasoned it would be good to have someone keep an eye on me. We settled on his couch to watch stuff on his laptop, but everything annoyed me – the way his flatmate kept coming into the room to start a conversation, how Angelo never maximised the screen on YouTube, and the fact all his viewing suggestions were sports related (there are only so many compilations of exhausted marathon runners crossing a finish line I can stomach – it creeps me out how emaciated and veiny they get at the end of the race when they're so super dehydrated), so eventually, I made my excuses and left.

Out in the cold, with all the fresh air filling my lungs, I fought the impulse to swerve into every corner shop on the way home and buy some filthy cancer sticks. I made it home successfully, finding Greta on the sofa painting her toenails – white, of course (wouldn't it be deliciously terrible if she accidentally spilled some nail polish on the sofa? Just a little bit… even if you could barely see it, because it's white, of course), and talking to someone on her iPhone headphones in a low murmur, almost solemnly, in Danish, never smiling or laughing, or making any emotion of any sort (who is she talking to? A lover? Her mother? A friend? Does Greta even have friends she calls?). The fumes from the nail polish made me want to run over and snatch the bottle out of Greta's hand and start sniffing it right on the spot. Instead,

I quietly made myself a cup of peppermint tea and went to my bedroom, where I lay down to see if I was tired enough to sleep (I wasn't). I needed something to take my mind off things, and I remembered I hadn't listened to an audiobook for years, not since we were teenagers. There was a point in my life when I couldn't fall asleep without an audiobook on CD (remember those!). I went into my phone, and scrolled through the audiobooks, and I almost did it, Lil, I almost bought 'Harry Potter'. This was my lowest ebb, surely? I was all, 'Oh, it's narrated by Stephen Fry' – but I came to my senses finally. I bought 'Wind in the Willows' instead because it was on offer, but actually, that's a lot scarier than I remember, with the rats trying to take over everything, and then the toad character would appear again and his voice was so big and booming, it would wake me up, so eventually, I turned it off completely, and wrote this. So that's a whole day done without smoking, even if my life feels a bit empty, and I have no reason to get up in the morning. Hooray?

TUESDAY: 11.30 a.m.

Still no cigarettes.

Earlier, I was innocently at my desk, doing my actual work and minding my own business, when Ingerlise sauntered over and asked if I was ready for the presentation.

I said I definitely would be, eventually.

She stared at me blankly for a few seconds.

'That is good,' Ingerlise said after a while. 'But you know the presentation is now?'

No, I bloody did not know it was NOW. I thought she'd said next week!

Ingerlise gave me a hopeful smile, and I thought she might say we could reschedule – obviously – because I hadn't prepared anything, but what she actually said was, 'Well, do your best,' and beckoned me to follow her. DO YOUR BEST? Jakob's crinkly forehead creased even more than usual, Nansi averted her eyes, and Hagen gave me a mock salute as I was marched away to my demise.

The meeting room was on the floor above us, and we made polite (and on my part, frantic) small talk as we went up in the elevator, but I could smell the subtext wafting off Ingerlise: don't fuck this up. But how could I not? There were no slides, nothing prepared – I hadn't even wrapped my head around all the recent milestones. Waiting in the meeting room, there were four people: two men and two women I hadn't met before. All pretty corporate-looking for Danes. Ingerlise introduced me and I shook everyone's hand. Please don't fire me, I thought, as I slipped my limp, moist fingers into theirs, each in turn.

'As we know,' Ingerlise began, 'Joy has come over from the London office, and this is her first project here. She's going to tell us how she's progressing.'

Oh, Lil, I would have liked a cigarette, that's how I was getting on. They give people a final cigarette before they face the firing squad, don't they? I could feel the nicotine seeping out of my pores as I started to sweat, and I thought, 'Don't go, nicotine, not right now – I need you! Stay with me, beautiful tar!'

The five people stared at me expectantly, and I experimented with opening my mouth to see if anything would come out. Nothing did initially, but then, finally, words:

'Thank you for having me here today. It's a real honour (what am I hosting, the Oscars?). As you know, I'm British so I hope you don't mind if I speak English?'

They all shook their heads, smiling.

'The project is going well. We are slightly ahead of schedule, even though we've had quite a few issues with the initial testing.'

'Such as?' one of the women asked.

'Just the sheer number of tests. The team is working extremely hard, but I've had to think of some inventive ways to keep us on track.'

'What sort of ways?'

'Blackmail and bribery…' I laughed manically, but everyone else was stone-cold silent. I also have to remember that while the Danes' English is pretty exceptional, it's not perfect. If I speak too fast (which I often do) or use colloqualisms (spelling), or I'm too detailed in a story, they can get lost. 'I mean, I'm looking for inconsistencies in the testing cycles, auditing the data so we bring up anything sooner, so I catch errors that slip between the cracks. The quicker we can get the feedback loop going, the better.'

'How do you find it, working in Denmark?'

'Everyone is so nice,' I said, feeling like a Miss America contestant. 'Very supportive…'

'What do you mean by blackmail and bribery?' asked one of the men, the most serious-looking of the group.

'Oh, it was a joke. Sorry, it's my English sense of humour. I mean, sure – have I promised one of my teammates I'll drink his home brewed beer if he hits his deadlines? Yes. Am I bribing another one with liquorice? Possibly. But it's all in good fun,' I garbled like a lunatic.

The stony silence turned even stonier.

'You know, we take blackmail and bribery very seriously here,' unsmiling serious man said. My career flashed before my eyes. Well, that time animal activists shot me with a paint gun at least (just to confirm for the zillionth time, we never tested on animals. Med students, yes. Animals, no). And I've never liked working enough to be one of those 'all in' career women, but I do like my job. What else would I do with my time? But then I saw something in the man's eyes, a spark of light, some might even call it a 'twinkle' – and everyone started laughing, the tension evaporating instantly.

'It was a joke,' he explained. 'Our Danish sense of humour.'

Hilarious – I'm sure I'll find it funny once my pulmonary heart attack is over.

Since the meeting wasn't a complete shambles I felt quite high on success, and usually, I would go and have a celebratory smoke, but instead I went for a walk along the waterfront, and the wind was bracing, and I felt so alive – and part of me wanted to run, run anywhere, run in excitement and happiness. Why don't we ever do that – just run and see where it takes us, without worrying what people will think of us, or where we're going, or if our bits will get wobbly as we run, and perhaps we should have worn a better bra – just run for the sake of it? I didn't run though, because I still had an afternoon of work ahead of me, but there was a definite spring in my step.

TUESDAY: 9.30 p.m.
Something happened tonight. No, I didn't smoke a cigarette. Worse, much worse.

When things go really badly, my impulse is to hide away, or eat a whole tub of chocolate ice cream or a jar of peanut butter until my stomach's so sore, I have something else to worry about. I've eaten so much ice cream/peanut butter these past few years, watched so much crappy TV. I'm bored of my coping mechanisms, there's no imagination to them. At least with these letters I'm using my brain. That's something, right?

I'm not sure if I can write this down yet. Oh, why aren't you here?

I was so happy still from the day, and it was a nice sunny evening, so I walked home, taking the more scenic route back. It's one of those moments when you realise summer is actually here, it's not a figment of your imagination, and your body yearns for the vitamin D of it all. When I arrived onto Istedgade, it was its usual bustling self, with all its characters: the little old man in the walker who drinks a can of dented beer outside the corner shop, the sweeping blonde beauties with their long, lustrous hair, the hipsters, and hipster children, all dressed so cool. When I approached the flat, I was surprised to find Angelo waiting outside the coffee shop, with his bike, and my heart skipped a little, and I took him in before he spotted me, and how lucky I was to have met someone who was so kind and also had such great hair.

When Angelo turned and saw me, there was something different in his eyes. Oh no, I thought, I hope nothing's happened. I hurried over.

'Are you waiting for me?' I asked, as brightly as I could manage.

'Yes,' he replied, and there was that steeliness to his voice, and the dullness to his eyes, as if he was looking slightly to my left instead of directly at me. Remember when we used to do that to babysitters to freak them out?

'I hope you haven't been waiting long. Do you want to come up?'

After locking up his bike, we both went up to the flat. It was stuffy as the heating had been on all day by accident, and I opened the window (terrible waste of energy, I know), and put the kettle on, but Angelo said, 'I won't stay long.'

I won't stay long. Bon voyage, I suppose. Ugh.

'What's up?' I said finally, sensing some impending dread.

'Joy,' he said, perching on the arm of the sofa. 'I wanted to tell you this in person. I've really enjoyed meeting you.'

'Meeting me?' I interrupted. 'Meeting me was weeks ago.' I already knew what was coming, Lil. I knew how this panned out, but I wasn't going down without a fight.

'I just think we want different things,' he said. 'I need to focus on my studies. I'm really sorry.'

'Okay,' I said, 'I understand' – although I did not understand and I was definitely not okay.

'You're an amazing person…'

'Just not amazing enough to be with,' I replied quickly.

Angelo rubbed his eye as if he was exhausted. As if I was exhausting him. He dropped his hand to his side, as if even rubbing his eye had been too much effort.

'You've only really arrived in Copenhagen. You're just out of a relationship. You should be taking time for yourself.'

'Isn't that what I should be telling you? You're too young, you should be out sowing your wild oats?' I was feeling a new emotion now that was cutting through the sadness: anger. 'Don't turn that excuse round on me. I'm thirty-six years old. I shouldn't be TAKING TIME FOR MYSELF.' (I might have been almost shouting this.) 'I need to <u>hurry up</u>. I know that's not very sexy to say out loud, but as you seem to be breaking up with me, it's making me a little reckless. And I liked you, Angelo. No, I like you, present tense.'

'I'm sorry.'

'Not as sorry as I am,' I said contritely.

'Do you want me to go?' he asked.

'No, I want you to stay with me. Stay the night.' I realised how desperate I sounded, but I didn't care.

'I don't think that would be a very good idea.'

'Is this about Robby?' (Stupid bloody Robby.)

'It's about a lot of things.'

'Such as?'

'I don't think it helps to bring everything up.'

'<u>Everything</u> up? Everything? I thought you liked me, Angelo? Five minutes ago, yesterday morning, last week, at some point you liked me?'

'I do like you. But we're very different people.'

And I wanted to challenge this statement, but in a (brief) moment of reflection, I realised he was right. Cultural differences. The age barrier. The smoking, the drinking.

'Joy,' he said carefully, slowly, deliberately, 'there's a part of you I can't access, a part which is closed off...'

He trailed off, unable to explain what he meant in English. I didn't try to help him find the words, because I already knew he was right: there <u>are</u> things I don't want to open up to him about, things I simply can't say.

But wasn't this proof I shouldn't have?

'Are you going to be alright?' Angelo asked, his stupid handsome face frowning with concern.

I nodded.

'I haven't had a cigarette,' I added sulkily.

'That's great.' But it was the 'that's great' of the postman when you tell him you did well at your exams. No real enthusiasm, polite encouragement. (THAT'S GREAT.)

'Remember Nietzche (spelling?)?' Angelo said. 'That which does not kill us makes us stronger.'

'Yeah, he was a laugh a minute, that Nietzche,' I replied despondently.

Angelo shrugged, as if my reaction proved everything.

Standing up to leave, he was so different, like someone wearing a bad Angelo costume or unconvincing Angelo CGI. He left without saying anything else, without a hug or a goodbye kiss – he simply nodded his head, signifying the end.

I'm not sure how long I was sitting there, but eventually, the cold air coming in from the window was making me shiver.

'I didn't tell Angelo about my presentation,' I thought. I'd been excited too, I'd rehearsed all these bits in my mind to try and make him laugh – and my first impulse was to text him, but then I realised I couldn't, my communication rights had been revoked, and it hit me then. Angelo had broken up with me in the best way possible, face-to-face, giving me the respect I deserved, and Lil, it pained me even more that I'd blown it with a great guy, one who was the consummate gentleman, even when he was breaking hearts.

Sorry to end on such a bum note, but I still didn't smoke any cigarettes. That counts for something, right?

J

LETTER FOURTEEN

Wednesday, 11 July

Dear Lil,

I'm back in Copenhagen. It feels like I was never away – back to work, back to Greta's candles, back to my Danish life. England was a welcome break, but to be honest, it was tough as well. Not only because I was dealing with the fallout of my breakup with Angelo, but because of the usual parental issues, and – I'll be super honest – I had mixed emotions about visiting you. So, while I really wanted to turn up in the UK, and be the best version of myself, and show everyone I was a better, changed, new and improved Joy, it didn't exactly happen like that. Instead, there was some pretty impressive backsliding.

After I visited you in Brixton, I headed straight to Brighton on the train. Dad picked me up at the station – he was in a good 'up' mood, and that helped evaporate some of the awkward feelings left over from his trip to Copenhagen – the weirdness of him being so supportive of Mum, my reaction to his weight gain, your stuff. Their new place is closer to Hove than Brighton, in the nice part of town, but the house they're renting is the worst one on the best street, and apparently the neighbours are sick of Dad's power tools, and all the sawdust he makes sanding down his furniture. It's hilarious how much of a workaholic he is – even in his early retirement, he can't keep still.

'Do you like this?' he'd say, proudly displaying some old side table that he'd just denuded of varnish.

'Are you going to paint it now?' I asked.

'No, that's the style. The grain's beautiful.'

'Okay,' I'd say, shrugging.

Each day, Dad and I had a long walk along the lovely pebbly beach together. I didn't tell him too much about Angelo – I was in a weird place emotionally – and fortunately, Dad didn't press me too hard. I couldn't fight the feeling I was a failure though, and I had to keep running through my many (minor) accomplishments in my mind, to stop from spiralling. And I love Dad, love him to bits, but it's always been better when you're there too. Dad and I are too similar emotionally, we can make each other a bit flat – we've always needed some Lilyness to bring a backbone to the proceedings, and balance out all the squishy feelings and moody silences. I think he would also appreciate you helping with the furniture sanding – I get too scared and drop things. Dad keeps saying the sanding machine won't hurt me, but what if it catches my skin and rips off a layer? I'm sure that's happened to someone before. I could Google it, but I'm afraid it would be too gross (I already do about 25% of my Googling while squinting so I don't see any horrible images by accident. Such is the life of a hypochondriac, I suppose.)

'I was thinking,' he said on one of our walks along the beach, 'about Lil. I wonder if she wanted me to see her holding hands in the back seat that night?'

'Probably,' I replied. 'She was always very out and proud in real life.'

'Maybe I should have a chat about it with your mother?'

'Really? You'd do that?'

He shrugged, looking out towards the horizon, 'Possibly, yeah.'

Possibly? Great, just great.

To be fair, Dad looks better in Brighton than he did in Denmark – although he's still drinking a lot – but I feel mean saying he seemed fatter and older, he's just acclimatised to life in Brighton, everyone is a bit windswept and laid-back there. Dad worked his whole career in a fast-paced corporate environment, supporting us all, so it's good he can relax a bit now.

Mum, on the other hand, is go, go, go! She's at university every day, even the weekends. I sat in on a couple of classes (Mum teaching health sciences to baby pharmacists), and she's really good, Lil, she knows her stuff, and you can tell the students like her. I don't know, it sort of made me feel jealous, like Mum had replaced us with these young, invested students – getting careers in medicine that we never quite achieved (wow, what would Mum have done if we'd actually had the grades and ambition to become doctors and not just a hand holder and a child wrangler?). There was this one girl, she stayed after the class to talk to Mum, and the way they joked and smiled, I wanted to take a big fistful of the girl's hair and yank it. I know, it's taken Mum a long time to get to this point – all the years she put her career aside to raise both of us big lumps of clay – and it's great she's finally doing everything she dreamed of, it really is. But why has she become so hip, and young and fresh <u>now</u>, when it's of no use to either of us? Dad and she seem to live on completely different schedules, and although they don't fight, they don't really interact much either.

I did get a few enjoyable snippets of time with Mum – she was very interested in how the Ariel project at work was going, she took me out to brunch at a lovely local place where all the bread was baked on the premises, and it all had bits of fruit in it, yum – and she asked me questions, and seemed genuinely interested about my life in Copenhagen (I must remember that Mum is way harsher and more abrupt over texts).

At brunch, I told her about the breakup with Angelo, and afterwards Mum said, 'How do you feel about him now?'

'I miss him,' I replied, chomping through my third slice of bread filled with sticky, jam-like apricots.

'What do you miss exactly?' she asked.

The sex, I thought immediately, but actually no, I don't miss that. Yet.

'The not being alone.'

'But you didn't see him all the time, did you? You were at work, you were busy, you were sleeping. How often during the week would you be with Angelo?'

'A weekday evening, maybe two – a Friday or Saturday night.' (And morning, but I didn't tell Mum that, of course.)

'So actually, not that often. The majority of the week you were alone.'

God, she's so pedantic. I got her point, but sheesh. Not exactly come here, darling, everything's fine.

'But we were texting and messaging,' I countered. 'We would send each other hundreds of messages in a week.'

'So perhaps you're missing the person in your phone that tells you nice things, and listens to your day?'

'I guess so.'

'Going over there, making a fresh start, you've done well, darling. We know it hasn't been easy for you, what with everything.'

And that's when Mum got me – it's a long time since she's told me anything positive like that: she made me cry.

Afterwards, I told her about visiting you in South London, and really, it was the first time in I don't-know-how-long that it felt like Mum and I were having a proper conversation. She told me gossip about the university (basically, who was sleeping with whom), and gossip about Aunt Yasmeen (who isn't sleeping with anyone after poor Uncle Shamil died, and doesn't plan to – 'She's hanging up her vagina' is how Mum described it, gross). Mum is also planning a trip back to Iran, which instantly made me feel nervous – mention of travel to Iran should always come with a trigger warning...

Overall, I had the strangest sensation of 'Have I made a mistake? Should I come back to Brighton and live nearer everyone, and go out with a hippy, and sit on the pebbles every day, and just enjoy my life? Am I enjoying my life now? Could I enjoy it EVEN MORE?'

But then the next moment, Mum would harass me about having babies or be passive-aggressive because someone forgot to replace the bin liner, and I couldn't get away from Brighton fast enough. Haha, family!

There was one bombshell though.

I mentioned to Mum I wanted to pick up a few things from the house in London, and she froze, eyes to the heavens, in the way that always means I'm not going to like what comes next out of her mouth.

'Darling, there have been changes at the house.'

'Are you redecorating?' Maybe they were getting some work done while they were staying in Brighton, I thought.

'We're selling, sweetheart.'

Our family home. The house we grew up in. The one with all our childhood stuff in (well, mostly mine, the hoarder I am). I know it was a problematic place for both of us, and we couldn't wait to move out when we were teenagers – me because I was reading 'The Pursuit of Love' and wanted to be part of the aristocracy, but instead found myself in the suburbs of West London, and you because you wanted to be ripping off your head scarf in Iran, or reclaiming land in New Zealand, but instead, you were doing your O-Levels and babysitting for the Nielsons next door – but it was still ours, with memories good and bad.

'When were you going to tell us?'

'"Us" darling? Your sister will be fine. It's time to move on, for everyone.'

But I'm not convinced – could you please tell her you're as furious as me? Some solidarity here? K thanks.

And I didn't feel like I could argue, what with having officially left the country, and I'm sure you're fine with it, now I come to think about it, your lack of nostalgia and sentimentality is frustrating (Harville excluded), but I don't want some strangers to own OUR house. There are memories there. Important memories.

Ugh.

The return trip to Copenhagen was not great. I was chosen for a random bag search, and you know how alarming that is for a Persian-looking person. Airports are never easy – we can't help but feel guilty, and I felt like I radiated guilt. The woman at security was very nice and mumsy though, which I appreciated.

'That bag looks roomy,' she said charitably, as she swabbed it down thoroughly, looking for, what? Explosive materials? Residues of drugs? Terrorist dust? 'And good straps. You can't be too careful with your back, you only get one.'

When I arrived at the flat in Istedgade on Sunday evening, Greta was sitting watching 'American Idol' on her laptop (you wouldn't think from looking at her, but she is a sucker for a singing reality show).

'How was your trip?' she asked without removing her eyes from the screen.

'You know how it is with family – can't live with them, can't fake your own death, claim your inheritance and move to South America.'

Greta processed this.

'How would you claim your inheritance if you'd faked your own death?' she asked. Good question, I really should have thought that one through, Greta.

'Anything interesting happen while I was away?' I asked, trying to make conversation, really.

'The building is getting new – how do you call them? – balconies on all the outer windows.'

'Really, that will be cool. Will they finish them before the end of summer?'

'One hopes,' replied Greta.

'We can have balcony parties, invite people for barbecues on our porch. Party on the veranda and everyone's invited.'

Greta didn't respond to my enthusiasm.

'I saw Angelo the other day in the supermarket,' she said. 'He told me you had broken up. I'm sorry to hear that.'

Oooof.

'Thank you,' I said, slightly winded at the mention of him. 'How did he look?'

'Angelo? Fine. Normal.'

'Did he look like he missed me?' is what I wanted to ask, but of course, how would Greta know?

'Was he with anyone?'

'No, he was by himself. Actually, there might have been a girl with him.'

'A girl girl or a woman girl?'

'I do not understand. Do you mean age?'

'What did she look like?'

'She was blonde, Danish, normal.'

My heart screeched in my chest.

But Angelo wouldn't have gotten a girlfriend so quickly, would he? It was probably a fellow student from university, but the image created a massive cloud over my head for the rest of the evening. It still hadn't cleared in the morning, and I just couldn't face the start of the working week, so I took the day off sick. I know… With the big deadline looming too… But my reasoning is, I wouldn't be much help to the team, feeling like I was. They'd already managed three days without me, what was one more?

When I heard Greta leave in the morning, I stalked around the flat in my pyjamas, feeling guilty for missing work, relieved, sad and something else – that little flicker of mischief you always called 'the beast'. 'The beast' wants to mess things up, to drink wine, and smoke illicit cigarettes, and eat until I hurt, so I knew

I'd have to find an outlet for this energy or things would go south quickly. I considered Skyping FaceTime Margaret (FaceTime has been a little patchy recently), but she was busy anyway, and I wasn't ready to be reflective yet, I was ready to <u>do</u> something. Taking my bowl of fancy Danish granola back to bed, I brought up Angelo's social media (thunder clashes) and started to poke around for any sign of this supermarket blonde, but there wasn't anything incriminating. Angelo is not great at updating his social media – except when it comes to videos of people jumping off things. Once I'd online stalked enough (but really, can you ever <u>really</u> online stalk enough?), I was practically vibrating with pent-up potential mischief. I wanted a cigarette badly, so I whisked myself out of bed, had a ~~cold~~ lukewarm shower, and told myself in no uncertain terms that I was <u>not to have one</u>. Then I dressed in my freshest daytime pyjamas, which felt like progress, and went straight back to Angelo's social media because I'm something of a masochist and I thought, hey, I still want Angelo in my life, he's a good guy, and I should communicate that in a roundabout way. We could still be grown-up online friends, right – even if we're DEFINITELY NOT DATING? This is the modern world. I'm a modern woman. IT COOL. So I – quite brazenly – liked his most recent Instagram picture, which was of him hanging out, watching sport with his flatmate. Then I felt a surge of emotion – as I would never be in that flat again – regret, sadness, arriving at anger, and I felt like blocking him, and I considered my options, and yes, he did deserve to be blocked, he had broken my heart, and I shouldn't be liking his bloody photos. I should be taking a stand. I unfriended him on Facebook, and stopped following him on Instagram – which felt good for, oh, all of about three minutes, before a wave of horror spread over me. What had I done? I might as well have tampered with his bike brakes! After another bowl of fortifying cereal, I considered the fallout. Should I message Angelo and explain my reasoning? Could I say I was hurt and needed some time without his lovely face constantly coming up in my timeline, and that's why I defriended him? But then I'd actively liked one of his photos. The combination made me seem loopy. I could lay it all out for him, beg for forgiveness. Nothing seemed like a good solution. In the end, chomping on my third bowl of granola, I sent him a new friend request, which read:

Hi Angelo, had a moment of weakness and defriended you, but feeling remorse. I'd still like to be online friends, if you would? xJ

And then I waited. And waited. And waited. Refreshing the page over and over until I started to develop a weird clicking twitch in my hand. As I was reloading Facebook, I received a text message from Jakob: 'Hey boss lady, hope you're not feeling too bad. You're probably pulling a sick day anyway, so I shouldn't get too sad for you! Haha Jakob'.

Oh great, so Jakob's figured me out.

Update: It's 4 p.m. and still no word from Angelo. I'm looking at pictures of botched celebrity plastic surgery before and afters, interspersed with manic refreshing. Would it be too much if I went and stood outside his flat until he comes home? And to think, I once imagined Angelo and I would be a story we could tell people – two immigrants in a foreign country, just like Dad and Mum. I'm trying to remind myself of Angelo's bad points. He once called Greta 'fat-thin' and mocked her shakes, saying they were full of sugar. All discreetly behind her back, and much less worse than the horrible things I've said about her, but still… Angelo wasn't perfect.

*

Update: 8 p.m. Angelo blocked me on Instagram.

I feel horrible. It seems nasty on his part. I made a mistake, and now I'm being punished. I'm not some mad, obsessive girl: we had a relationship for several weeks.

Should I text him? Or email him? Or write him a letter?

No, you're right – I shouldn't.

Oh, why, Lil? Why do I have to ruin everything? Tell me?

Your chronically-single spinster sister,

Joy

LETTER FIFTEEN

Thursday, 12 July

Oh, Lil,

Being blocked by Angelo really affected me, and I woke up the following morning, utterly defeated. I even rang work and pulled another sickie without the slightest pang of guilt – although I feel plenty now, like whiplash.

I don't want to be defined by the men I'm dating (or not, as the case may be), I really don't. What if I'm just not cut out for relationships? I'm not even being dramatic when I write that. Wouldn't it be better if I accepted my lot, and start planning for a future by myself?

Thought experiment: how would my life look if I wasn't constantly worried about finding love? Where would I be – physically, emotionally, mentally – if I wasn't afraid of how my family saw me? (disclaimer: not you so much). If I wasn't so scared of being alone?

I think I could do without the physical stuff. Of course, I'm saying that after several weeks of high-intensity sex – come back to me in a few months when I'm grinding up against the balustrades (haha, gross). But I don't think it's the sex I'd miss. It's the having to cook all my own meals and washing my own laundry FOREVER. I know it sounds banal, but life seems so much better if there's someone there with you, on your team to 'wash your gruts' as Dad would say poetically. I want someone to ask me, casually, 'What do you feel like eating tonight, J-Bird?' (in this fantasy, J-Bird is my nickname). 'A pizza? Chinese? Shall I have a rummage in the fridge and see what I can come up with?' I just fell instantly in love with this fantasy boyfriend, rummaging in the fridge for me. That's all it takes for me to get squishy.

What happens when I get older? When I get really old? It's not as if you're going to look after me (oh, you'd <u>love</u> that…).

Practically, though – I'm thirty-six years old. Say I meet someone, even in the next two years, who might be conceivably worth marrying, I'll be thirty-eight by then, thirty-nine at a push. If we start trying to have a baby, maybe I'm forty, forty-one, forty-two and pregnant? That makes me fifty when they're in their teens. What if I want two kids? Do I need to pop them out one after the other? Or will I have to go on hormone replacement therapy and have sextuplets all in one go? The papers will love that – 'Great Joy! Copenhagen Woman's Sextuplet Happiness…' I'm tired of all these mental calculations, I've been doing them for twenty years.

I could have a child by myself, but I'm overcome with dread at the thought of it. All that hard work, completely on my own. And Mum – I wouldn't be able to take her out of the equation (of course, I'd probably want her around, what with the sextuplets…).

Okay, here's the worst-case scenario. I never meet anyone, I never fall in love, I don't get married, I don't have kids. I progress with my career, untroubled by parenthood. Mum and Dad never forgive me, but what can they do? Cut me out? Hardly. They're stuck with me as much as I am with them. In my spinsterhood, I live in a one-bedroom flat, which I buy at the ripe old age of fifty-two (the first time I can finally afford one). I take solo holidays to the remoter Greek Islands (no, not Lesbos) or go on biking tours with Austrian couples. Maybe I'll have lovers, maybe I won't. Perhaps I can hire a male gigolo every so often and feel all empowered. Or I could just become celibate. Would it be a relief to cast off all this expectation? I don't know, I can't even imagine it. When I try to still my mind, I just hear this roaring sound, like the waves of a tsunami approaching – it's still some way off, but it's travelling fast…

Worst-case scenario? Worst-case scenario is I give up caring. I get even more fixated on food. Worst-case scenario is I look older than my age. I keep smoking. And drinking. I see the disappointment in Dad's eyes. Mum voices her concerns, constantly. These are all outward things.

Maybe I could go to New Zealand? Stay with Dad's family? Perhaps I could move to the Coromandel, and live in a bach, and eat chips (crisps). All Dad's side of the family are bigger, there'd be no judgement. I could wake up each morning and walk along the white sand beaches, and I don't know, start writing again, fiction this time (not just these letters – the melodrama of my life).

Who knows, I could take a lover, an older man who lives up the road. Not very attractive, not many of his own teeth, but honest, and good, and lonely like me. We could make each other happy, with no expectations. That could be real happiness, living on the other side of the world, far away from the parental gaze. But then I think of you, and I falter. That would be running away. But I've gone this far, to Copenhagen, I suppose. Was that running away?

I wish you'd reply to my bloody letters! Call yourself a loyal sister – when I need you most. Damn you, Lily, being so far away. Damn, damn, damn!

I know you felt you lost me with the eating stuff as a teenager, because I became so secretive, but I lost a piece of you too with the sexuality stuff – you were in a club I couldn't be part of, selfish as that sounds.

Maybe giving up all this wanting is the answer. Maybe it's the problem in the first place: I want too much. But what else are you supposed to do with your life, tell me that? I'm not sure if I believe in God – not after everything. Ugh, this is what you get when you grow up with a mother who is culturally Shia Muslim, but very pick-and-choose in practice (who nonetheless used religion as a way of scaring us into submission), a father who is a lapsed-Christian atheist, and a younger sister who identifies as a 'spiritual questioner of things' (whatever that means).

What about when Mum and Dad get too old, or sick? I can't be off gallivanting in New Zealand then.

You see, there is no easy out. Not even in my worst-case scenario. That's really a worst-case scenario – when your worst-case scenario is unobtainable.

By the way, the Danes are no prize winners when it comes to happiness, it's all a ruse. They just have lower expectations, which they easily meet. It's about perception. The Danish are just much happier with their mediocre lives than us Brits.

I spent the whole day in bed, not eating much, not even Greta's stash of chocolate she thinks she's hidden from me in the back of her cupboard (I am, and always will be, a horrible snoop). I turned off my phone and left my computer alone. I was, as Mum would put it, having a 'proper sulk'. My mood only worsened when I remembered our family home had been sold off without being consulted. What if I'd wanted to say goodbye to the place? To reflect on some of those precious memories? I buried myself in YouTube videos and mindless memes. When I heard Greta get in, I was slightly bewildered – why had she come back early? – until I realised it was the evening, and she was returning from work at the normal time. Later, only once she'd gone to bed, I snuck out to pee and brush my teeth (teeth brushing is my only consistent hygiene standard), but I was wide awake when I returned to my room – the mintiness of the toothpaste having perked me up – so I turned on my laptop and marathoned a reality TV show called, horribly, 'More to Love', which is 'The Bachelor', except with overweight people (hey, I'm no size zero, but fun fact, most of it is peanut butter weight). The programme is from 2009, and only ran for one season, and I could see why – it's diabolical, and offensive, and I. Couldn't. Stop. Watching. You'd think with my eating issues I'd find it tough to watch, but it was strangely cathartic. I cried three times during the nine-episode run, and spent an hour Googling all the contestants to see where they are now, cheering when I discovered if one of them seemed happily married.

I was woken the next morning by Greta banging on my bedroom door.

'I was just checking you are alive,' she said, after I'd acknowledged my existence by groaning loudly.

'I'm not feeling very well,' I called, giving an impromptu cough.

'I will tell them at the office,' she responded. 'Get better soon. Drink hot tea, and I have some sick sweets in the bathroom if you need them.'

Those sounded revolting, but it was a nice thought, which Greta quickly undercut with, 'And if you vomit in the toilet, please clean it up afterwards with the bleach.'

'I won't,' I called back.

There was a pause.

'You won't clean it?' Greta asked. 'Why?'

'No, I mean I won't vomit,' I said, coughing again to illustrate my fake illness was all throat-based.

'You can never be certain of these things,' came the response, and I had to admit, Greta did have a point. You can never be certain.

Her bluntness does remind me of you sometimes. And since you're so far away, I guess it's good I've found someone to fill the void. Bossy. Check. Demanding. Check. End of List. Haha.

Possibly it was psychosomatic, but I did start to feel slightly under the weather once she'd left, with a slight headache (which I'm always convinced is an undiagnosed brain tumour) and a scratchy throat, so I decided it would be good for me to leave the flat to get some air – and some food, as I was starving. On the way to the supermarket, I called into a pharmacist, because my stash of painkillers and cold remedies I'd brought over from England was running perilously low. I looked and looked on the shelves, but I couldn't find anything – not a Lemsip or a Night Nurse to be found – so I asked the pharmacist where their cough syrup was kept.

'We don't have,' she said unhelpfully.

'Do you mean you've run out?' I asked. Maybe there was a shortage, I thought. The great Lemsip drought of…

She shook her head, and I waited for her to elaborate but she didn't.

'Do you have ibuprofen then?' I asked finally.

'We only have paracetamol.'

At least they had something. I followed her to the counter, where the pharmacist removed a comically tiny packet, which could only hold two pills – max.

I actually laughed out loud.

'I'll buy three then, please,' I said, once I'd composed myself. Three felt like a good number. Not drug addict or suicide worthy.

'Nej. To buy more, you have to visit the doctor.'

FOR PARACETAMOL? Mum used to give us paracetamol like it was vitamin C, and she has a Masters in pharmacology. As kids, paracetamol was a universal panacea. Stub your toe? Paracetamol. Pale complexion? Take two. Actual headache? Crush three and snort them. Between that and the hydrocortisone we slathered over every inch of our young bodies, we were children of the ~~revolution~~ medication. And now I'd have to go to the <u>doctor</u> for PARACETAMOL on a PRESCRIPTION??

But the pharmacist was not finished blowing my mind.

'Even if you go to the doctor, they might not give you any-thing,' she insisted.

I wanted to ask for the manager – no, I wanted to talk to the manager of DENMARK. I could feel my headache getting worse (upgrading it mentally to a lesser migraine).

I stomped home, feeling sad AND angry now, and homesick because I'd just gone back to visit, and I'd have to wait a respect-able time for another trip to stock up on medication, otherwise Mum would smell blood in the water and start taking bites out of me in the hope I'd return (or maybe she wouldn't bother now she has her new surrogate student daughters). I was in quite the mood when I arrived back at the flat, one where I was capable of really effing something up – like binge eating Greta's stash of chocolate, or secretly smoking a cigarette – and I didn't want to do either, so I phoned a friend instead. Obviously not you, like you ever pick up.

'What are you doing?' I asked when Sara answered.

'I'm at university, but I'm leaving soon. What's going on?'

I told Sara about Angelo, and she instantly said, 'I'll be right over,' and I felt so relieved, because isn't that what we want to hear from someone, 'I'll be right over'?

I had just enough time to clean myself up before Sara arrived, brandishing a bottle of champagne.

I looked at the bottle as if it was ticking.

'Come on,' she said, 'it will cheer you up.'

'I have a sore throat,' I said, unconvincingly.

Sara snorted. 'Then this is the best medicine.'

'I'm trying not to smoke.'

'Then don't smoke! Drinking isn't smoking! Anyway, why don't you want to smoke?'

'Because it's killing me. And making me look old.'

Sara shrugged. 'Life is killing you and making you look old.'

That's Danes to a tee, shrugging and saying something defeatist in a way that sounds mildly optimistic. Do you know how many times Copenhagen (the city) has burnt down? About six times. Why? Because of all the bloody candles. They can't stop lighting them. And what's the remedy for all life's ailments (including, probably, your house burning down?): lighting some lovely candles.

But, oh man, the sound of the cork popping DID make me feel better, and the taste, and the bubbles, and the instant giddiness – and Sara sat down on the sofa, and we went over everything. Every. Thing. And she knows Angelo, of course, and said he wasn't the sort of person to rush into another relationship, so the girl in the supermarket WAS probably another student working on a project with him. Sara also said Angelo was a bit of a know-it-all in class, and was slightly arrogant, always bringing up nihalism (spelling?) and Nietsche (sp?) and he was obviously too immature for me, and she knew lots of hot single straight men to set me up with, and I knew it was probably lies, but it was good lies only a true friend can give (sorry, you've always been <u>too</u> honest. Sometimes I want sugar coating).

When I went to refill Sara's glass, she hesitated.

'I shouldn't really,' she said. 'I'm being bad. We're trying for a baby, but I'm not ovulating for another week and a half…'

'Oh my gosh, congratulations,' I said – but I felt the words stick in my throat.

'Geoff has been tested, and his sperms are irregular. They are the wrong shape, and don't swim very fast. The tails are deformed. I'm not getting any younger either. We aren't sure if it will work, but we are trying. Otherwise, I will just have an affair with his brother the next time we are in Toronto.'

Sara said this with such a poker face, I didn't know how to react until she started laughing. Sara is great – you would really get on with her, Lil.

'What made you wait?' I said, feeling emboldened by the booze to ask personal questions.

'Until I was old?' she laughed. 'Before Geoff, I was with a married man for a long time, and he already had kids. Before that, I was having too much fun. Men are allowed fun, so why not us?'

I wondered what Mum would make of Sara. I know Mum has a career now, but for a long time, her main achievement was bringing up us two denigrates. I wonder what she would have been like as a mother if she'd waited until my age?

We were close to finishing the bubbly when Sara suggested,

'It's such a beautifully sunny day, we should go out and do something fun, somewhere in Copenhagen you haven't been before. Oh yes!' she said, 'we should hire a boat and go on the canals!' And you know how I am about boats (chronically unsure), but it did seem like a fun idea, so before the booze left our system, we'd ordered a taxi, and on the way, I had the sudden brainwave to invite JP on a whim, because Sara liked him, and I remembered he told me he'd once worked on a luxury yacht, and so it was reassuring to have someone vaguely nautical with us. JP had only just woken up – at nearly 3.30 p.m. – but was on board for our impromptu excursion, so he cycled to meet us on the waterfront. Sara and I must have looked quite the sight when we arrived, because JP shook his head, muttering French to himself with a wry smile – and we all crowded into a boat, clinking with the many bubbly bottles we'd bought on the way, and I thought the boat people might be against two tipsy women and a groggy-looking Frenchman taking control of an actual vessel, but they seemed nonplussed, and anyway, they sold booze in their shop, and there was an actual picnic table on the boat, so they were pretty much encouraging drinking, what with the inclusion of a flat surface for glasses and bottles, etcetera.

It was COLD on the water (even with the sun), and scary, not only because I was afraid of falling in, but also because I was terrified of getting hit by another boat. To begin with, JP drove us (there was a route we were supposed to follow along the canals), and there were quite a few other smaller boats like ours, but mostly larger tour-type ones, and I felt self-conscious with people peering down on us, which made me drink harder. JP smoked a cigarette (making me crave one) as he steered, looking the epitome of French cool, like a rakish gondolier driver, but then he made Sara and I take turns driving, because of 'liberty, equality,' and – what's the third one? I want to say 'paternity'? Anyway, that. Sara went first, but had to be relieved of her duties when it was evident she was too drunk to drive straight (re: baby making – whoops!) and I was petrified I was going to crash us into the canal wall, but fared considerably better. The wake of water from other boats was worrying, and seagulls swooping around our heads was problematic, but it was exhilarating too, and we laughed, and the sun even came out momentarily, and JP was sitting at the ~~stern~~? ~~Hull~~? Front of the boat, looking like Lord Nelson. Oh, hang on – maybe that's not appropriate/culturally sensitive. Like Napoleon then?

'How's your girlfriend?' Sara asked JP at some point (time is not very linear in my memories), making wiggly eyes at me for some reason.

'She is good,' but he looked sheepish, so Sara pressed him, and JP revealed they had opened up their relationship, and his girlfriend was now shagging an Icelandic club promoter on the side.

'Have you been with anyone else?' Sara asked point-blank (she is good like that).

'Not yet,' JP replied, and we all whooped so much that the boat pitched dangerously, and I begged them both to calm down and not stand up on the boat, but really, it was fun, and we were all in hysterics.

I told JP about Angelo breaking up with me, and he said, 'Why, is he an idiot?' and I think I blushed, and felt a little better.

Really, when you're going through a breakup, you ultimately want to be drunk on a boat with your friends (Friends! I have actual friends here!).

When we were almost back at the start, JP decided he wanted to take a dip, which I didn't think was a good idea for multiple reasons – I had visions of police boats dredging the water, and helicopters beaming spotlights into murky waters – but he ignored my concerns, and stripped down to his (slightly baggy, but spot-lessly white) Calvin Klein's. His body was very lean, almost bony, in that heroin-chic kind of way, and he was perhaps the palest man I've ever seen – he almost glowed – and yes, there was a moment when I wondered how bony he might feel, pressing up against me, and whether he was more or less bony than Angelo (what is it with me and bony boys?). And then I got sad about Angelo's bony bits, but then JP dived into the water with a big splash, and Sara and I nervously watched to see he was okay, but then he popped to the surface, trying to look cool, but he was obviously FREEZING, and we had to haul out his soggy butt (and his baggier, and now almost see-through, pants – I averted my gaze politely from his groinal region) into the boat again. JP was shivering a lot, so we made a beeline for the shore, and who was there to greet us, but Geoff – taking pictures on his phone as we approached, and smiling lovingly at Sara (aw, those two – I want a husband who accepts my random bouts of boat day drinking). Geoff's car was nearby, and he'd brought towels, so we got JP dried off, and allowed ourselves to be whisked away to a restaurant, and then JP took us out to a bar, and the rest of the evening is a blur, and if you've made it this far, you deserve a friggin' prize because this is another long letter, but I didn't think about Angelo's stupid Instagram once (well, maybe once), and you know the very best thing, Lil? I DIDN'T SMOKE ONE CIGARETTE.

BYE, SIS

K bye xxxxxxxxx

LETTER SIXTEEN

Sunday, 15 July

Hey Lil,

I wanted to write a follow-up to my last letter because, well, sometimes I think I write these things to convince myself of events, because I gloss over so much – ugh, okay, let's just get into it. (Also, please destroy this letter on reading.)

You know after the boat trip, I said everything was 'a blur'? That's not an exaggeration. There are whole stretches of the evening I can't remember at all – starting from when we were at the first bar.

All I know for certain is I woke up in my bed the next morning with the most splitting headache of my entire life. It was so intense, weird sparks flashed before my eyes if I moved too quickly, as though my brain was short circuiting. More worryingly, I couldn't find my bag – the one I'd taken on the boat – anywhere in our flat. Then it dawned on me: how did I get home at all? I frantically searched my bedroom – luckily, finding my phone on the dresser – but there was no sign of the bag (with my wallet inside), so I texted Sara and asked what happened, trying not to sound too panicked.

Here's what she told me: We actually visited two other bars. I was great fun (and not embarrassing, which I'm not sure I believe, but she was adamant I was well behaved). I took a taxi home with JP, and I definitely had my bag with me when I left with him.

Lil, I got really scared then, because I didn't remember <u>any-thing</u>, and what if something had happened? I could have walked out in front of a car, or (more likely) fallen off something. What if I'd tried to have another cigarette out my window?

Another thought emerged, through the mental haze: did anything happen with JP? This caused me to do something I'm not proud of, Lil – I found my underwear, and I inspected them, in case, you know… But I couldn't tell. I tried hard to remember getting home, and I could almost picture the taxi… and me in the back with JP… But it was very foggy, and maybe I was making it up? I texted JP then, trying to sound breezy, and he responded straight away – yes, he had my bag. I'd left it in the taxi, much to my great relief.

'Hope I was well behaved,' I texted back, fishing for details.

JP replied, simply, 'You English girls.'

I didn't know what that meant – did we kiss, or something more? Should I take the morning after pill or an STI test? I followed up this line of thinking with a panicky text saying, 'Haha – but did anything happen? In the taxi? Or afterwards?'

JP replied, 'Of course not. You were very drunk, and I made sure you arrived at home safe, after we had some food.'

'Some food?' I replied.

JP: 'Yes, a kebab.'

And Lil, I felt it in my stomach then – I'd wondered why my belly was so heavy-feeling. When I looked at the clothes I'd worn the night before, there were tomato ketchupy stains all down the front, and I felt horrible, knowing there was something inside me – even if it was only a kebab – that I had no recollection putting there.

I believe JP, I do – but what if I'd been with someone less trustworthy? Or I'd been by myself and the taxi driver had tried something? (I can hear you screaming into the page as you read this, 'Be more bloody careful, Joy!' I know, I know, I'm sorry.) Or what if I'd tripped, walking up the stairs? Or I'd called Angelo? Or even Robby? Oh God, I didn't even think about that – what if I actually did message Angelo? (Just checked, and I didn't – small mercies.) Even though I don't think I smoked a <u>full</u> cigarette, I almost certainly had a puff. In my drunken state, I would have considered it a loophole. Puffs! Just puffs! And honestly, when I invited Sara over, I secretly hoped she'd bring booze. Subconsciously, I wanted to get drunk and have an excuse to sneak puffs of cigarettes. Not blackout drunk, though. That is scary, that's a new development.

I'm too old for this, Lil. I'm not twenty-one anymore. I came here to fix my life, to find happiness, but it's not working. Now I realise something: I was never going to quit smoking without stopping drinking too. They are inextricably linked.

I try to think about a life without alcohol. Imagine going out on dates and not drinking – would it be weird if I couldn't have a glass of wine with a lovely meal? I could never go on a tour of vineyards in France (or Tuscany). Or toast someone's wedding with champagne (speaking of, I've been invited to two weddings back in the UK since I've been here, which I've been able to squirm out of. I couldn't face them, especially when I'm feeling so lonely). Maybe I could just cut down on my drinking? But I've tried before, Lil – I have, multiple times, you'll testify to that – and here I am again.

I kept going round and round like this all day, with this dreadful hangover, and the dead weight of a kebab in my stomach, as I tried to scrub the stains out of my top in the cold, communal laundry, hiding the garment whenever anyone came in because I didn't want them to think I was the sort of person who tipped food all down herself ON A THURSDAY NIGHT WHEN SHE WAS BLACKOUT DRUNK AFTER SKIIVING OFF WORK ALL DAY, but Lil, I am that person, I am. I'm good at finding the funny anecdote, and laughing at myself, and I have some legendary nights out – many of them with you – but <u>I have to give up drinking</u>. It's now or never. If I give up drinking, I can give up smoking. If I can give up smoking, I break the cycle. Break the wheel. Break the door down. Break something finally. Break it good.

But honestly, I don't know how to do it. Read a book? Watch a TED Talk? My blinking FaceTime therapist had chosen next week to be away on holiday (it's FaceTime, Margaret – I should be able to contact you anywhere, anytime, when I have a crisis. That's the whole point, isn't it?).

I was actively trying to avoid Greta all day, because, well, she's Greta and I didn't need the added judgement – and I thought she was in her bedroom, but instead, I found her on the couch EATING A YOGURT, like some freakishly normal sane person does on the weekend, instead of wallowing in self-pity. God, her skin looked lovely and dewy, her eyes bright, and I'm never sure if she's wearing make-up, but she always looks <u>enhanced</u> somehow (false eyelashes, maybe?) and she glanced up from the magazine she was reading, and said, 'Hello, Joy.'

I don't know if it was simply because it was the first face-to-face human contact I'd had all day, but I started crying.

Greta watched me, holding the yogurt pot in front of her still in the air, frozen in place.

'I'm sorry,' I said in a wail. And in that moment, I suddenly realised how she must see me, this crazy, over-emotional drunken British girl, bonking young men on her spare bed and smoking cigarettes out the window (even when she asked me very nicely not to), and never getting anything right.

'Are you still sick?' Greta asked.

'Sort of,' I said. 'I couldn't buy any ibuprofen at the shop either,' I sobbed.

'Would you like to have some of mine?'

The kindness of her gesture set me off again, and I just stood weeping in the doorway nodding, as Greta fetched some ibuprofen pills from her bedroom. I know big displays of emotion are the biggest no no when you're living with someone. You don't air your dirty laundry so publicly (well, in England we don't, we just bottle it up until it causes us cancer) – we all have our own neurosis (spelling?) – but maybe this was my rock bottom? Eventually, I sat down on the edge of the sofa, snivelling and holding the packet of painkillers, while Greta fished out a tissue from her pocket.

'Are you feeling homesick?' she asked, handing it to me.

I shrugged.

'It must be hard, being away from your family and your home.'

I wiped my face and nodded. And then I told her everything about the night before, or everything I could remember at least. It all just came tumbling out. To Greta. Who I work with. She could tell people at work! Greta listened patiently, occasionally feeding a dainty spoon of yogurt into her mouth and gently masticating as I blurted out all the vile thoughts that were marinating in my brain.

When I was done, she put the yogurt pot down on the coffee table.

'Do you think I should go to Alcoholics Anonymous?' I sniffled.

'No, I don't think so,' she replied. This made me feel better. 'Not yet at least.' Slightly less better. 'Have you asked for help?'

I shook my head. I mean, these letters help, but I didn't really ask if I could write them to you, Lil – I just did.

Greta sat back on the sofa. She has such good posture. I was slumped over like a pile of wet rugs.

'I used to drink a lot when I was younger,' she said. 'I was very unhappy.'

Really? That's not the picture I have of Greta.

'How did you change?' I asked. 'It's the changing part I'm not so good at.'

'I will show you.'

Greta went into the kitchen, and poured something into a short glass, returning with it. The liquid looked like water, and I was about to take a grateful gulp when she raised a finger.

'This is vodka,' she explained.

WTF? Great abstinence counselling, Greta, I thought. Remind me not to come to you with my alcohol problems again. But she wasn't finished.

'I want you to drink it.'

I started to protest, but she held up her finger again, 'Bah, bah, bah. Drink the vodka and <u>really</u> taste it.'

'I can't bear to,' I wailed. 'I'll be sick, I'm so hungover.'

'It does not matter,' Greta replied, and I knew she was not messing about if she didn't mind potential vomit.

In recess of my mind (the only part not hideously hungover), I sort of knew what she was doing. It was like a father who makes his son smoke a pack of cigarettes to put him off smoking ever again, but I wasn't a child, I was a grown-ass woman who had years of drinking under her belt (literally, there's a whole roll of fat made solely out of Chardonnay). And I was still in shock that Greta was being nice to me in any way, which made me strangely compliant.

'Your body is hurting because of a poison, but you have forgotten what it is (if I'm making Greta sound very yoda-esque, that's because she is). Slowly drink.'

I picked up the glass, and my hand was shaking, and I almost retched before I'd put the glass to my lips, and every fibre of my body was saying no, no, no, but doing <u>something</u> was at least better than doing nothing. I took a small sip, and it was revolting, and Greta said, 'Feel the sting of it, the sharpness on your tongue. What does it taste like?'

'Horribleness.'

'Good! You are really experiencing it. Drink some more.'

'I don't think I can.'

'Yes, you can. More.'

I did, and I gagged, and it was traumatic, but I drank it all.

After I'd finished the vodka – my eyes streaming tears – Greta instructed me to do the following:

1. Clean my ashtray and give it to her.
2. Hand over any booze I had in the cupboards (bottle of dessert wine, cooking wine, a bottle of champagne).
3. Take my favourite glass I like to drink wine from outside and break it (I kid you not – wrapped in newspaper, like the breaking of a glass at a Jewish wedding).

When this was all done to her satisfaction, Greta got up and went into the kitchen again to start chopping things up, and I didn't like the noise of the chopping, but she was very good with the knife, very professional, and in the smoothie blender the things would go – plop – beetroot, an apple, green stuff (herbs?), powders, seeds – plop, plop, plop, and then it was all whisked up (I hid, like Minnie, from the noise) before she presented the concoction to me in a tall glass.

'It will help,' Greta said, as I sniffed the glass gingerly. I wanted to say I wasn't hungry because of the blackout binge eating and now the vodka, but that didn't feel like a ceremonious way to start the process, so I took a tentative sip and it actually tasted good – like liquid health, Lil – and the moment I swallowed it, my stomach relaxed slightly and I realised I was hungry after all, and I drank the whole thing down (full disclosure: not the last quarter, because it was very fibrous). I might have had another little cry while I was drinking it, just because Greta had been so kind, and I was always stealing her food (although mostly replacing it again) and I didn't deserve this treatment, but it was just what I needed, and I thought everyone should have a Greta in their life.

Afterwards, Greta sent me off to have a nap, but not before she promised to cook us both a light supper. I protested – she'd done so much already – but she would hear none of it.

So now I'm in my bedroom, and I can't help wondering, HAVE I MADE A PACT WITH THE (SHE) DEVIL?

Only time will tell, I suppose. (But really, Greta's been wonderful – I'm an unappreciative jerk face sometimes.)

Love you loads,

Joy xxxx

LETTER SEVENTEEN

Tuesday, 17 July

Hi Lil,

Now Greta is running my entire life and everything I consume, it's been an odd few days. What's weird, is 'it' – whatever this is – is actually working. The trick seems to be having someone to be accountable to – like a personal trainer, I suppose, or a personal chef. I have a personal Greta, and in the morning there's a note from her, which might say, 'Eat an apple on your way to work,' with a cheesy inspirational quote underneath ('Mistakes are the proof you are trying', 'All things are possible if only you believe'), and so I do, and the apple eating takes my mind off not having a cigarette, and the quote makes me groan and roll my eyes, but then I think about it on the way into the office, and it sort of stays with me the whole day. It's hard to explain. Greta likes having me as a project, I think. Project Joy. Gives her a purpose. Or maybe she's sick of me, and just wants me to be a better flatmate finally, so is aggressively taking matters into her own hands? Or, maybe she just actually <u>likes</u> me, we are becoming friends, and I should be more appreciate of her generosity?

Greta's also there, at lunchtime, peering at me, omnipresent, so I'm less inclined to overeat. In the evenings, she's teaching me about food and cooking and nutrition and stuff. I mean, I know how to cook a little, but it's the same old five meals Mum would always make (Monday: stew with rice, Tuesday: chicken with rice, Wednesday: lamb with rice, Thursday: vegetarian with rice (at your insistence), Friday: anything but rice – mostly always chips – for Dad, Saturday: takeaway, Sunday: family potluck), so I know a lot about RICE, but I don't really know about nutrition per se.

I'm taking supplements now, Lil (remember, I used to make fun of you for taking magnesium tablets, because of your twitchy eye?). I'm drinking many, many smoothies. And I'm choosing to consume things because I know they are nutritious, not because I'm avoiding something (fat, carbs, sugar) or because I desperately want something (fat, carbs, sugar). Angelo used to say smoothies were full of sugar, and were actually terrible for you – the way he described them, they were worse than heroin, but I don't know – they taste healthy (especially the greener they are), and I feel healthy. I'm actually adding something to my diet instead of subtracting something for once, and I feel less bloated, and my skin looks clearer, it does. I don't feel as full all the time, but I'm also not hungry. Sometimes, when I've finished a big meal, I actually feel like my skin is puffy, and I have grown an instant double chin. Greta says that's inflammation, and a sign I was not giving my body what it wants.

Alright, alright – I can sense you being sceptical of my sudden turnaround with Greta as my totally unqualified sobriety counsellor (and maybe jealous we're… bonding?) But it's more than the sum of its parts somehow. I feel GOOD, Lil. And this is the culmination of a long line of changes – moving here, stopping smoking, my alcohol epiphany, even writing these letters, little things that have all added up. Greta was just the final link in the chain. Anyway, we'll see.

I haven't told Mum or Dad anything yet, because Greta and I have created a fragile reality, and I don't want its membrane pierced yet (or slashed to bits by Mum. She always has this way of saying 'I suggest…' which isn't a suggestion at all, but a way of anglicising her inherent Persian directness). Because, isn't everything all hugs and smoothies until you're really tested? And boy, have I been tested this week…

Okay, I wasn't sure if I was going to tell you about this, but here we go… Being blackout drunk wasn't the worst thing to happen to me this week after all.

It kicked off when I went back to work, after my debauchery on the canals. Max from HR arrived at my desk, promptly, and asked if we could have 'a chat'. Jakob looked as if to say, 'What's his deal?' and I shook my head, but I felt nervous. It turned out I had reason to be.

Max led me to a meeting room, and after getting the pleasantries out of the way ('Do you want water?', 'No, good'), he began.

Lil, someone had seen me. On the boat. Drunk. When I should have been at work. When I'd told them I was sick. Too sick to come into the office. While we were struggling with a big, important time-sensitive project.

'This is quite serious,' Max announced, the understatement of the year.

I froze; I stared at him. Max stared back. For what felt a million years. I'm being fired – I thought, I'm being fired. Just as Greta was fixing me. Just as I'd started enjoying the flat, and learning the rare moments when the washing machine was free. Just as I had started making friends.

Max peered over his designer glasses.

'In England, it might be okay to take an unannounced leave, but here you can get in serious trouble.' (No, actually, Max, in the UK, it would be a justifiably fireable offence too, but I didn't tell him that, I just nodded mutely.) 'I know we seem relaxed in terms of hours,' he continued, 'and you might want to take a stress day – how do you call it, a duvet day? – but it's not a good look to be found out joyriding on a boat.'

Uh, a pun. Usually I like a good Joy-related pun, but not this time.

Why did I go on a bloody boat in the middle of a bloody work day, in a (relatively) tiny city, in the centre, where I stand out like a sore thumb because I'm tiny and not blonde? Am I some sort of idiot?

'It won't happen again,' I told Max – and I meant it with every fibre of my being. THIS WOULD NOT HAPPEN AGAIN.

'I understand what it's like, moving to Denmark – the culture is very different here. It was strange for me too.' I blinked, because I thought Max was Danish. Obviously not. 'We all like to party hard sometimes. I like to party pretty crazy too, Joy. Of course, people get drunk and call in sick the next day, but you have to be more discrete.'

Keep it classy, got it. And maybe don't GET VISIBLY PISSED ON A BLOODY BOAT.

Also, I wonder who spotted me.

After the grilling, I mercifully did not lose my job, and I would usually have craved a cigarette, but instead I had a glass of cold water. A GLASS OF MOFO TAPWATER. And it felt good. Refreshing.

So, just to recap: I'm teetotal, and a non-smoker, and I'm living my best life, although it's at the cost of being in a (probably unhealthy) interdependent relationship with Greta. Plus, one more strike and I lose my job and have to move back to England in disgrace.

So, yeah, that's me. How are you?

X J

LETTER EIGHTEEN

Saturday, 21 July (morning)

Dear Lil,

The thing about not drinking is that it severely limits one's going-outness. Or your staying in-ness. And I 'love' Greta, but she's KILLING ME with this healthy lifestyle stuff, she's constantly watching me – I'm under 24-hour surveillance – and I'm getting a lot of single white female vibes about my current situation. I know I asked for it, and I realise Greta is being totally amazing to me, but still.

I love Sara too, but she's clearly a boozy friend, and I think I should keep my distance for the time being, just in case I relapse. What do you do with all this <u>time </u>though, Lil? What do other people do? Go to the gym, I suppose, but I haven't sunk that low yet (ha). You always played computer games in your spare time, when you weren't trying to save the world's deprived children single-handedly. I have been taking longer bike rides and cooking more elaborate meals (even if all the vegetables are kind of horrible-looking over here, because they don't import everything from Chile, like we do in the UK – they're eco-conscious, of course. Alright, Danes, we get it, you're amazing – stop showing off, sheesh).

Friday nights are the worst, because it's been a stressful week and I want to unwind, and really, that glass of red wine after work is what makes life worth living. What do you replace it with? Cake is my immediate answer. But then Greta zaps me with a taser and I come to my senses.

I could download the dating apps, I suppose, rip the sticking plaster off and go on a couple of soul-destroying first dates, but I'm scared I don't know the first thing about dating in Denmark, and what if I don't get any messages? It will bum me out. So, no apps for the time being.

No apps. No drinking. There must be something else to do in our society, right? Something to give our life shape and meaning? No? Fine.

I've tried. I've gone to the cinema twice by myself, and I was anxiety-ridden the first trip, but otherwise it was okay. Except, Danes are frequent and chronic talkers during the movie. I had to shush people. Yes, me – Joy, the chronic talker. A shusher. Fortunately, when they turn to see who has told them to be quiet, they can barely see me, I'm so small in the cinema seat.

I even thought about joining a choir, but although I'm practically Maria Callas compared to you, I'm not a singer per se, so I began to look at other things I could do. There's no shortage of extra curriculum activities in Copenhagen, but the one that caught my eye was something called 5 rythms (spelling?), which sounded mysterious. What sort of rythums (sp?) are we talking about, and why five of them? From what I could understand (using Google translate), it seemed to be some kind of dance class. Now, you know I'm a bit of a mover and a shaker (I did choreograph all those 'Annie' routines as a kid, after all) and it sounded intriguing, despite my nerves – and really, anything was better than staying in with Greta. I kid, I kid… I love her, really. She's my rock (SEND HELP). The 5 rhythyms (spelling? infinity, I never know how to spell this) class was every two weeks on a Friday, and the venue was only about fifteen minutes' walk away, so the next time it was on, I packed my exercise gear and struck out after work, feeling uneasy.

Fine, go home, I told myself. Or have a cigarette. Blow everything. Start over. You'll only be here again in a few months. I kept walking.

When I arrived, there was jingly-jangly music playing, and I paid my entrance fee to an older woman who kept the money in a biscuit tin. People were getting changed out in the open (there weren't any changing rooms, and the toilets had a long line), and so I nervously stripped off my top and jeans – I already had my exercise gear on, thank goodness. Everyone was sort of milling round on the dancefloor, stretching and warming up, so I wandered over with my drink bottle, and claimed a spot, and waited for the class to start. A new song came on with more of a beat, and I wondered where the instructor was – and we were all sort of jiggling together when it hit me – <u>this was it</u>. This was 5 rythtms. It was free-form dance. With strangers. Sober.

My blood ran cold. I picked up my drink bottle, about to make a break for it, when a cute guy came and stood by me, and I thought, well, I'm here now, haha, and it's better than walking home in defeat, and I guess I can shake my bootie freestyle when the need arises. A woman with blonde hair came on the microphone, and spoke in English (woot!) over the music, and told us to relax into the space, and I started wiggling my arms from side to side, thinking, what am I doing here with all these hippy weirdos? Do they think I'm a weirdo? Probably. Eventually, the music began to get even crazier, and people were spinning around and kicking, and I think I laughed a few times, but then you sort of get carried away with everything, and it's easier to join in than stand there looking like a numpty, so I started with a few pirouettes and some jazz hands (did not break out the 'Annie' moves just yet. I mean, I didn't have a broom. Or a dog. Or a bald millionaire), but then we were back to panpipes and swaying, and I was slightly disappointed, because it felt like only twenty minutes had passed.

But it wasn't over – oh no, it was only beginning.

The DJ woman told us to form a big circle – there must have been fifty of us at least, two-thirds women, and the men were a real assortment, from straggly beanpoles to a few pimply teenagers who were obviously with their girlfriends, and a couple of older guys in their sixties. There was one woman who must have been knocking on ninety at least (she looked incredible for her age). The DJ lady welcomed us officially – we should follow what our bodies needed, she explained, and pay attention to the dynamics in the room. Then she instructed us all to go around the group and say our names. Lil, you know I have nightmares about this sort of thing. It had already started, there was no escape – and what was worse, after you said your name, everyone repeated it. All the names sounded exactly the same, too – so, it would go:

Woman with dark leggings: 'Mette.'

Everyone repeating: 'Mette.'

Woman with blonde braid: 'Melke.'

Everyone: 'Melke.'

I was standing exactly halfway around the circle, and I could feel this wave of public humiliation approaching. Would they understand my name? Would my voice sound squeaky? Would they laugh at my incongruous English accent?

It was my turn.

'Joy!' I said – a little too loudly.

'Joy!' everyone repeated (some of them giving it a bit of the old Eeyore Danish inflection).

And then we were back to the dancing, but it was easier this time because we were all warmed up. I still felt silly, but now there was a unity to our silliness because we'd all spoken our names out loud. It was odd dancing with no booze in my system. The handsome man danced near me too, which helped – he looked like he probably went hiking a lot, he had a beard, and closed his eyes as he danced in one spot – and I noticed I was always trying to keep my distance, while staying just close enough so I could feel the heat radiating off him. I gave some shoulder isolations, and a few more ballet moves (a plié or two), and I might even have shimmied – and before long, the music kicked up a notch, and I started to glisten, and then up another notch, and now it was proper banging hard house clubbing. People were throwing themselves around, going crazy. I flung myself around too, and at one point I thought I might be sick, and at another point I bit my tongue, so I had to have a sit down at the side by myself, and the ninety-year-old woman came over and asked if I was okay.

Eventually, I swallowed my mouthful of blood and got up again and continued to bop, and the music became all flouncy, and I know it SOUNDS cringeworthy, Lil – but in the moment, it really wasn't. As I danced, I started to think about Angelo, and I realised it had never really been right between us. We were too different, and sure, there was a sexual connection, but after a while that fizzles out if there's no compatibility too. I had a bit of a cry (maximum three tears), but nobody could probably tell because my face was so sweaty anyway. Just to be sure, I went to hide in the loos for ten minutes (if I ever write an autobiography, it will be called 'My Life in Toilets') and then I thought about JP, and remembered I had to get my bag from him (I've been using a wad of Danish kroner Dad gave me in a small plastic bag as my backup purse), and I wondered if JP came over, would anything happen between us? I also thought about Dad, and how distant he was when we were kids because of his high-powered job, and I wonder if that's why I put men in boxes a lot of the time, because it's easier if they're removed slightly – it's the way I handle the emotions. Then the music stopped, and I realised I'd been swaying with my eyes half-closed for the last twenty minutes.

We all came together in a circle again, and I kid you not, this time when I looked round, it wasn't full of weirdos and hippies, they were people just like me, and I loved them all. I felt like I was radiating love, and I sensed everyone was feeling this too, and I suddenly missed you a lot, <u>like a lot</u>, and I wanted to bring you here, so we could dance together, and I know you'd never do anything like that, but I enjoyed imagining you would.

When I got back to the flat, Greta was in her bedroom, but she'd left out a kale salad, with a note that read: 'Lots of magnesium. Good for thin hair'.

I really don't deserve Greta. (I WONDER IF I SHOULD RUN AWAY AND JOIN THE CIRCUS?)

That was the Friday before last – this Friday was work's summer party. There was dancing there too, but a very different variety.

I was nervous on several counts: it was my first official work do, I was still stinging from the telling-off (and I still didn't know who had seen me on the boat, which made me paranoid), and it was my first going-out experience as a non-drinker and non-smoker. Greta was going to be there, so I'd have my sobriety counsellor on hand, at least.

It all started off pretty inocuously (spelling?), with some standing round with drinks and nibbles. The event was held in a lovely conference place near the Danish Queen's Palace, and there were waiters in crisp uniforms, and lots and lots of booze. Jakob, Nansi and I stayed tightly together – we've pretty much imprinted on each other now (Hagen was off fraternising with the other blokiest of blokes). I could tell Nansi is not a crowd person, or a party person, really – she kept patting her belly nervously, and her sleeves were pulled down over her hands. I know she was itching to play her jewel game on her phone. Her belly is huge now – she looks like a concrete mixer.

'How's the pregnancy going, Nans?' I asked, feeling I could risk a personal question, considering it was a social occasion.

'It's fine,' she said. 'My breasts are very tender.'

Okay, great. Good to know.

Jakob looked nervous too (and youthful – he'd shaved his designer stubble off completely and looked very fresh-faced and striking), but I wasn't sure why – he was usually the energy source of our team, but I noticed he became much more introverted in a bigger group. He kept getting Nansi and I drinks (lemonade, obviously), and didn't seem particularly interested in the beer he was drinking.

'I don't like the taste,' he said guiltily, when I quizzed him about it.

'Don't let Hagen hear you,' I said. 'He'll force-feed you one of his horrible ales.'

People kept coming over and chatting, and it was nice to connect with new colleagues in the office. I was surprised how much I didn't miss a drink – I felt light and confident, and I didn't have to worry if I'd drunk too much, too quickly, or if I'd eaten enough, or if I'd wake up the next morning, cringing. If I was going to make a fool of myself, it would be on account of me, my actions – and not the alcohol – and that was marginally reassuring?

At some point, one of the scarily high-up bosses clinked a glass, and the room fell silent, and there were speeches, long ones made in Danish first, with lots of laughs, and then considerably shorter ones in English, where the jokes didn't seem to land (or maybe it was because for most people, they were a repeat). I felt a pressure to laugh especially loudly during the English version, because it was mostly for my benefit, but this did mean me guffawing a couple of times when it was maybe supposed to be more serious.

'One of the things we are very excited about,' announced the boss, 'is the new larynx software and device pioneered by Team Seven,' (that's us). Everyone clapped. Nansi looked at her feet, or she would have if her belly wasn't in the way, Jakob went a bright beetroot colour, and Hagen stood up on a chair briefly and whooped, much to everyone's amusement. Jakob caught my eye as people were clapping and gave me a shy smile, and I winked at him, but caught myself mid-wink and thought better of it – maybe it wasn't a good idea to wink at your subordinate while everyone in your company was watching – so to style it out, I simply kept my winked eye shut for ten seconds.

After the speeches, everyone started to really drink. Hagen was absolutely hammered, his big booming voice omnipresent throughout the room. Even when he went to the loo, you could hear him booming away each time someone opened the connecting door to the hallway. At one point, I saw Greta talking to him by the bar. Oh no, I thought instinctively, but I didn't know which one I felt more of an impulse to save from the other, so I watched helplessly instead. Greta looked as if she was enjoying their interaction, I even saw her smiling. I had a sudden panic that they were gossiping about me, but as you've tried to teach me over the years (unsuccessfully, obviously), the world does not revolve around Joy. Maybe they were swapping inspirational quotes? I'm sure there's some overlap between Hagen's burly-man practicableness, and Greta's cheesy meme-based inspirationalism: 'Prepare today, because there might not be a tomorrow. But if there is, make it the best one ever!'

At about nine, I had to stop Nansi getting a shot of champagne for her lemonade ('Just a little won't hurt,' she said defensively), the dancefloor filled up, and the waiters quickly pushed the tables back to stop them being toppled over by lurching bodies. There was some pretty awkward, erratic dancing, bless them all. Jakob, Nansi and I boogied in one place, with Jakob trying to stop anyone jostling Nansi like some protective sheepdog, and apologising each time he brushed my hand with his (ugh, swoon!). But you'll never guess who broke out the moves? And I mean THE MOVES. Max from human resources (he's Norwegian, I've since discovered). He. Broke. It. Down. I saw him do the worm, at least one death drop (losing his shoe in the process), and there was definitely some duck-walk vogueing. I. Was. Here. For. It.

I felt slightly more confident with my dancing after my 5 rythms the week before, even experimenting with a few dips and slightly more complicated turns. Jakob and I danced together for a bit. He's not bad, actually – he nods his head and pumps the air with his hands, and does these hip gyrations, like he's humping the air. Okay, I just read that back, and it doesn't sound particularly good, but Jakob makes it work. I mean, he's no Norwegian Max, but then, who is?

At about 10 p.m., Nansi finally went home, and Jakob was talking to someone else, when things started to get freaky. A very drunk man (definitely wearing a wedding ring) sauntered over, and started saying very inappropriate things to me: how nice I seemed (we'd never met, to my knowledge), how his wife was cold and distant, that they didn't have any intimacy anymore – all great stuff you want to tell a female colleague. When Jakob returned, he gave me an 'Is everything alright?' look, and I gave him the 'Not really' one back, and he manoeuvred the man away. For the record, the guy wasn't really creepy, he was just a bit sad and desperate. I think he genuinely just needed someone to talk to.

Unhappily married chap wasn't the last one either – I would suddenly find a strange man hovering beside me, ready to give me compliments and tell me how much his wife/girlfriend didn't love him. And I thought Danish men didn't even notice me?

'Do you want to get out of here?' Jakob asked after attempt number three, and I giggled, because it sounded like a line from a film.

'I thought you'd never ask,' I said, cliché for a cliché.

We stood outside in the warm summer-evening air – it was strange to go outside at a party and not light up a cigarette. There was a mob of people smoking, however, so Jakob and I moved out onto the street and over to the lakes. The lakes are right in the centre of Copenhagen, but I think of them more as rivers, because they're rectangle, and not circles like any self-respecting lake should be. Tonight though, I was lenient.

'The lakes are beautiful,' I said, because, well, you have to, don't you? The lights from the buildings glittering in the water, the swans gliding silently (one swam up to us, staring expectantly until we failed to give it food), the gentle mid-summer murmur of people enjoying themselves.

'It must be beautiful in London too? With St Paul's Cathedral.'

'Have you ever been to London?'

Jakob shook his head.

'I'm worried they would all look at me like I was stupid.'

'Why would they do that?'

'Everyone speaks very proper English, like the Queen, like you. And I don't know anything about football. I also don't like tea.'

'You don't like beer OR tea? How do I not know this?'

'There's a lot you don't know about me.'

'Such as?'

'How much I like your voice. The way it sounds. Your accent.'

I felt very tongue-tied and couldn't speak.

'I like you, Joy.'

I thought I'd misheard him for a second.

'What?'

'I like you.'

Oh, wow!

How was this different from all those other men in the party? I hear you ask, Lil. Because I wanted it, I wanted Jakob to like me. So badly. It was like finally hearing a song on the radio going round in your head all week.

I felt a pang of uncertainty – I was his boss, after all and I'm already on thin ice – but I don't know, it felt right. And I was sober – the alcohol wasn't an excuse. It was all me. Me instigating the kiss. Me brushing my lips against his. Me slipping my tongue into his mouth (okay, okay, gross, I know. I'll stop. I got carried away. Phew – is it getting hot?).

'My sister would love it here,' I said, when we'd taken a break from all our heavenly smooching (yes, I hope you enjoy being brought up at totally inappropriate moments. YOU'RE WELCOME).

'Has she come to visit yet?'

'No,' I replied. And then I told Jakob about you, and why you were one of the reasons I left the UK, and all about these letters. Afterwards, we held each other, and looked at the water. Then we kissed again. It was like being in a delicious trance. Before long, we were both being eaten alive by mosquitoes, so we tiptoed back into the party, as innocently as we could – but everyone was so trashed by then, we could have rocked up wearing each other's clothes and no one would have cared.

I left shortly after, and Jakob sent me one text on my way home: 'Finally.'

It made me smile, a lot.

I know, I know, I should feel bad about kissing Jakob, my colleague, my subordinate, and I sort of do, but mostly, I feel kind of… proud.

But it won't happen again. I'm not losing my job over a kiss. One and done. And you know I'm a woman of my word (ha!).

Miss you.

xxx Joy-Ride

LETTER NINETEEN

Ohmygodohmygodohmygodohmygodohmygodohmygo-dohmygodohmygodohmygodohmygodohmygodohmy-godohmygodohmygodohmygodohmygod… I kissed Jakob. Ohmygodohmygodohmygodohmygodohmygodohmygodohmy-godohmygodohmygodohmygod… I can't stop thinking about the softness of his lips. His bottom lip especially. It's like a fat grub, like those Huhu grubs you tried in Hokitika over in New Zealand (the memory of it wiggling between your teeth is forever scorched into my mind).

I'm his boss. I'll be fired. Humiliated. Deported.

Was it worth it?

Actually, Lil, the answer comes immediately: yes. Yes, it was.

LETTER TWENTY

Monday, 23 July

Dearest Lilliput,

The weekend took forever to be over. It was excruciating. I didn't message Jakob, and he didn't message me again, but there was a palpable tension in the air. PALPABLE. We were both actively NOT texting each other, I could just feel it. I knew I'd see him on Monday, and I also knew Nansi and Hagen were both on holiday, because... I'm their boss, remember? Oh God, I'm his boss! To be fair, I spent the weekend punishing myself – I cleaned my bedroom twice, got up early, did all my laundry, colour-co-ordinated my underwear drawer and made healthy low-carb muffins. Even Greta was impressed – although the muffins were still too high-carb for her, she did have a bite of mine. Her verdict was they were 'chewy'.

Oh, and I nearly destroyed my computer. I was in a café ~~working~~ watching back-to-back episodes of 'Love Island', and there was the smell of burning metal, and I realised it was a candle behind my laptop. I've burned a blinking great black splotch into it (fortunately, the laptop still works).

Come Monday morning, I was practically trembling with anticipation and excitement while also berating myself. I had more than just butterflies on the walk to work, it was like a squirming snake pit in my belly. I kept telling myself, 'Be cool, Joy. Be cool,' but the stakes were so high. Would I rather lose my job, or date Jakob for a few weeks until it inevitably petered out? Perhaps I was only attracted to him because I was his boss? The transgression of it all. I tried not to overthink it (lol, who am I kidding? I overthought it A LOT), but I was practically twitching by the time I arrived at the office. There was Jakob, at his desk. I took my time observing him before he noticed me. The curve of his back as he hunched over his computer. The fine weave of his grey cotton top. He was really good with those browser windows, flipping between them with such dexterity. But then I shook myself. What was I doing? I was mooning! I had to BE PROFESSIONAL FOR ONCE IN MY LIFE, for the sake of my career.

I marched professionally up to my desk.

'Morning,' I said, as professionally as I could muster, but it came out loud and aggressively, as if I was annoyed.

'Good morning,' Jakob replied, and then the silence sunk in as I tried to think of something to follow up with.

'Good weekend?' I asked, finally. There was no one around us, about two-thirds of the office were on holiday, but it felt like every movement, every word, every expression was being monitored.

'Pretty good,' he replied.

Pretty good, I thought. What does that mean? <u>Pretty good without me?</u> i.e. I'm fine without you. Ergo, it was a mistake never to be repeated again? OR <u>pretty good</u> BECAUSE we kissed and I will do everything in my power to make you mine, if it's the last thing I do. WHICH ONE IS IT, JAKOB?

'Great,' I replied, booting up my computer, and making a nonsensical note on a notepad so it looked like I had a lot on my plate. Important things.

Just then, someone arrived with three kids in tow (this happens all the time here, people's kids in the office – it's like a bloody day-care centre, especially over school holidays), making a raccous (spelling?), so Jakob and I both popped on our headphones.

I WONDER WHAT SONG HE'S LISTENING TO? I thought desperately. He was so close, yet so far. I wanted to reach out and touch him, but I didn't.

I didn't, Lil, I promise.

We had a catch-up scheduled at 11 a.m., but the kids were still being noisy, so Jakob suggested we go to one of the breakout rooms. YES, went my heart, as I grabbed my laptop. NO, went my professionalism. Suggest somewhere highly visible, said my future lawyer – make sure there are witnesses.

'The padded meeting room?' Jakob suggested.

'Sounds good,' I replied professionally.

Walking there, I felt in slow motion – like I was on runners and my path was already mapped out. We went inside, and shut the door, and sat down next to each other, and we didn't even open the laptop, Lil. I looked at Jakob, and he smiled, and something just dropped away in his face, like he was holding himself together, and the façade came down, and they'll probably use this letter as evidence against me in court when I inevitably get arrested, but there was no way we couldn't have kissed. After we'd made out for a while, it all came tumbling out: Jakob said he'd had a lousy time of it over the weekend, and wanted to text or call, and nearly did twice, and I told him the same, that I couldn't stop thinking about him, and every song reminded me of him, and every funny thing that happened I wanted to tell him instantly. Then suddenly, we both realised we were talking when we could be kissing, and – wow! – kissing was available to us, and we were literally grinning and laughing AS we were kissing, like two freaking idiots who aren't afraid they're about to lose their jobs, and possibly get arrested by the Danish police, for – I don't know – being too damn cute.

This I'm certain of: in the padded meeting room, no one can hear you kiss. But can they see you? CAN THEY?

We'd been a very long time in the room, with zero work done, and I was worried my face would be red and raw from

Jakob's stubble – I was amazed his freckle was still attached to his beautiful lower lip – so I told him to go on ahead to his desk, I'd wait for the rash to subside, and meet him in the canteen for lunch. I sat, trying to fill in an Excel spreadsheet, but in reality, I was alternately basking in the warm fallout glow of our kisses, and the overpowering heat of guilt. Happiness, guilt, happiness, guilt. Tide in, tide out. After what felt like an appropriate length of time, I exited the love cave and pretended to be a normal professional-type person again.

When I arrived in the canteen, it didn't take me long to spot Jakob, because it was only a quarter full – and just as well – because he had very sweetly, but not very subtly, created a romantic picnic area for the two of us. I don't think he'd meant to – Jakob just knows I always drink fizzy water, and liked the yellow pears, and extra black pepper, and of course I was always going to have a dessert with jam in it, and so he'd assembled napkins and cutlery, and really anything else I might want or need, and it was such a lovely gesture, but he might as well have scattered rose petals around the table, lit a candle, and invited a violinist to start playing. Fortunately, I don't think anyone really took notice. Max wasn't at lunch, and I couldn't see Greta, and Jakob managed to hold himself back from feeding me peeled grapes at least, but I was enjoying it too much to care. Lock me up and throw away the key, I thought, as I tried to pay attention to the words coming out of his luscious mouth.

We somehow managed to spend the rest of the afternoon seated separately at our desks, focusing on our monitors (although, I had the distinct sensation that we were holding invisible hands the whole time – like phantom limb syndrome, but with like, romance). When the work day was finally done, Jakob and I said our usual goodbyes, although they were much more formal and performative than normal, and the moment we left the office, we were texting each other furiously, and again, it all spilled out, it was like messaging you, Lil – there was no filter, no judgement – I'd just tell him exactly what was on my mind, and what I was feeling. It felt wonderful, but reckless – wonderfully reckless – and I smiled at everyone on the way home, resulting in some funny looks from passers-by, and the seagulls seemed to be cartwheeling in the sky, and when it started to rain a little, it felt like tiny drops of joy, actual joy. That word has lost any real meaning for me, for obvious reasons, but now I realise why people would name their goddamn daughter it. It <u>was</u> nominative determinism, my parents hoped I would feel this happy, one day. Before I was even born, they hoped I'd meet someone who made me feel understood and special, and I had, I had claimed my birth right. Not putting huge expectations on an office fling or anything…

And there was another feeling too, Lil – worry that something would go wrong. Something big, like before. Like, with you. That I wasn't worthy of this joy, that I would jinx it, that by feeling this happy, I would bring darkness into my life again to counterbalance it. How could I possibly feel true joy again, after everything? How dare I even consider it.

There was also still the question over Jakob's therapy. I really wish I didn't know about it. Maybe I'm blowing it out of proportion? But what if it's something big? What if he killed someone? Only accidentally, in a canoeing trip perhaps, but still… Would I still kiss him? Depends on the circumstances. I mean, he's a really good kisser…

Lil – guess who literally just texted?

Mum: 'Darling, I'm coming over to visit. How does this weekend sound?'

This weekend? Has she sensed I've started something with Jakob? I wouldn't put it past her – some kind of witchcraft? Or does she have my room bugged?

I'm so happy, I don't even care. Let her come! Let them all come – the whole extended Persian family. Bring the cousins and second cousins, and even the third cousins, twice removed. I'M READY.

xxxx J

P.S. I went through old texts from Robby on my English phone and what surprised me was how sweet and tender, and well, LOVING we were to each other. You forget, don't you? And I was so ready to make a change, I demonised Robby and made him my whipping boy. Sorry, Robby.

LETTER TWENTY-ONE

Sunday, 29 July

Hi Lil,

Oh, I really wish you were here. I don't quite know how to process this all by myself.

Hurricane Mother rolled into town on Saturday. It was batten down the hatches, hide Jakob under the floorboards, and hope for the best. Ugh, the best! Mum had announced (after I'd finished scrubbing the flat down for the third time) that she'd be staying in a boutique hotel up the road, which made me wonder where she had the money all of a sudden – not from the uni, surely? And then I remembered our parents had gone and sold off our family home – the one you and I grew up in, with all our childhood memories – and they were probably happily squandering our inheritance.

The hotel she was staying at was nice at least, super slick and modern, everything minimalist and bang on trend – although there was a big centrepiece of fresh lilies in the reception area, and they absolutely reeked, so you'd have hated that. Mum even had pot plants in the granite-tiled bathroom, which I liked, but she asked the porter to move.

'I don't like soil where I clean myself,' is what she told him (the porter was nonplussed).

Mum also wanted a spare hotel key (you remember her weird childhood hang up about always having exit strategies planned out in advance before she can sleep – and needing multiple keys for everything?).

'Have you lost weight?' she asked after we hugged, looking me up and down. I have, but after the years of battling her opinion and/or eating disorders, I wasn't exactly jumping at the chance to earn her tacit approval.

'I might have lost a little,' I mumbled.

'You're skin and bones,' she said, grabbing my wrist, and I had to stop myself rolling my eyes – I'd missed the magical perfect weight again, the pendulum had swung the other direction. 'We can feed you up tonight,' she added, squeezing my hand, 'I'm taking us out for dinner. We can try this place, it won all of the awards. I want to see what all the fuss is about.'

'You have to have a reservation at least a year in advance for one of those trendy restaurants.'

'Nonsense! There are always cancellations. I'll see what my friend Simon can do.' (Simon was the concierge Mum had befriended, God help him.)

'Let's go to a more relaxed place to eat,' I suggested. I was thinking of my clothes – I didn't have anything fancy enough to wear to a super-cool place. 'You'll only get disappointed and start sending the food back.'

'Darling, I've come to visit my daughter who has abandoned me, running away overseas. I can at least take her out for a belated birthday meal.' (Love how Mum does that – make out as if it's a present for you, when it's really what she wants.)

And so it was decided. I went home to rake through my wardrobe, and try and find something suitable – knowing nothing would be quite right for Mum. Little did I know what I was actually preparing for…

At 7 p.m., I met Mum back at the hotel. I was shocked when I saw her: she looked great. I mean, Mum always looks great, but she was wearing this incredible slinky dress, and she was showing quite a bit of leg, and (slightly crinklier than I remember) cleavage, and I should have realised what this dress meant, I should have seen the signs. Maybe you've guessed already, but sometimes I can't see my own hand waving in front of my face.

The restaurant was disappointingly normal – I was expecting avant-garde shapes sticking out of walls, and the tables on the ceiling or something. There was no menu, however, which was slightly quirky. We had to tell the chefs ahead of time if we had any food allergies – Mum said she was allergic to coriander, which is an out-and-out lie, she's just not very fond of it – and then the meal would be delivered in a cloud of secrecy (and, as we discovered later, weird flavoured bubbles).

'Not here,' Mum said to the waiter, when he showed us to a table which was in the very centre of the low-lit restaurant. 'Can we have somewhere more private?'

Again, I should have seen it coming, Lil – but I've historically never realised things – your gayness, Robby's unsuitability as a boyfriend, the fact that yellow is not a flattering colour on me – until someone hits me over the head with it (literally, on that last point – you once bonked me with your umbrella, and said, 'That raincoat is awful, it makes you look <u>exhausted</u>.').

We finally ended up at a table that was closer to the loos, but much more tucked away, and so Mum was pleased.

'Wine,' she said, brandishing the menu (they did have one for drinks, which I thought was conceptually lazy – why not give them your preference a decade or two in advance, so they could grow the right type of grapes and produce a personalised vintage for you? Opportunity missed).

'Oh…' I said.

'What?' snapped Mum.

'I've given up.'

Mum surveyed me, you know how she does, with her eyes – assessing.

'Where did that come from?' A good decision for once, is what she clearly meant. 'Well, I can't drink a bottle to myself,' she said, handing the waiter the menu sadly. 'I'll have a cocktail then, whatever you suggest, Simon, is it? (It wasn't.) And do you have any bread and olives?'

They didn't, and that was the first official Mum strike against the restaurant.

When the waiter left, she grabbed my hand.

'Now tell me,' she said, all concern. 'How are you? Do you get all my texts? I'm never sure if your phone is broken or you're just not replying to me.'

'My phone's fine.'

'You didn't drop it again?'

'That happened years ago, Mum.'

'Look at these cheekbones suddenly. You need to get your eyebrows threaded again though, darling. I've found a nice girl in Brighton, a trusted source, we'll go when you're back next – have you booked your flights?' and on, and on, and on like this until the amuse-bouches arrived.

Mum was not amused.

'What's this?' she asked the waiter before he could begin an explanation.

'It's a jelly made out of a cactus called…'

'A. Jelly.'

'Mum,' I whispered across the table, 'why did we come here if you're not going to give it a chance?'

'Tell me, Simon (still not his name) – is there a cracker or a stick of bread in the kitchen? Can you ask them. For this… paste.' She practically spat out the word.

'Jelly,' Not Simon said tartly and marched off to the kitchen.

'They're not very polite here,' Mum sniffed.

'How's Dad?' I asked, trying to move the conversation forward.

'Your father's your father.'

It was now or never: strike while the cactus jelly was warm.

'I've been talking with Dad, and there's something we want you to know about Lil.' (I know it must be weird reading about us talking about you in the third person. I'd hate it, but I can't see any way around it. Sorry!)

'What could he possibly tell me about my own daughter?' she replied defensively. Dad obviously hadn't said a thing. God damn it, he can be so useless! 'I don't want to talk about your sister right now, anyway. I want to talk about you.'

Here it comes, I thought.

'There's something different about you, and it's not just the weight loss. Your skin's different too. You're not eating dangerously again, are you? I thought we sorted all that?'

'No, Mum!' I basically yelled at her, but luckily, we were so tucked away in the corner of the restaurant, no one else batted an eyelid. 'And anyway, you don't "sort" it – I'm not a pack of cards.' Lame comeback, I know, but it's all I could think of.

The waiter returned with – I kid you not – what looked like two massive croutons on a wooden board.

'What's this?' Mum asked, poking one of them (it did not yield to her finger), but the waiter was already departing, so she and I wiped the jelly paste onto our over-sized croutons, and bit into them – the crouton exploding into bits as soon as pressure was applied (maybe it was supposed to happen as part of the experience? Bomb bread?).

'There's something you're not telling me,' Mum said, wiping the crumbs off the table into her hand with a napkin.

'I'd really like to talk about Lil for a moment...'

'I know – you're pregnant!'

'I'm not pregnant!' I basically screamed back, as the waiter arrived with a plate full of weirdly coloured leaves. 'I'm not,' I hissed again, as he presented the plates to us.

'Are you dating anyone?'

I paused, and Mum's eyes opened wider.

'Not that Sicilian child student again?'

'No, Mum – and he was a full twenty-five years old.'

'Who then?'

I should have lied. But you can't lie with Mum – even you couldn't, Lil. That's why you avoided her so much. She traps you in her lie-detector gaze and it's all over, Rover.

'His name is Jakob.'

'Jakob? Jakob?' she said, turning one of the leaves over to see what was underneath (Spoilers: nothing). 'Why does that name ring a bell…?' I stuffed a fork full of very bitter leaves into my mouth. 'Not the Jakob who works under you?'

I had a lot of (very weird vinegary) plant matter in my mouth, and so I chewed furiously.

'Darling, no,' Mum continued, unhindered by any response. 'That will not end well. What if you break up with him and he reports you? Or if it compromises your career?' I could almost hear the cogs whirling. 'No, no, no, darling – you need to end this now, and delicately, so it does not become a problem.' (I was still chewing. It was chewier than one of Greta's super green smoothies.) 'Have you slept with him?'

I took a big gulp of water.

'Mum, no…' (But full disclosure, Lil, yes, we have now – last night, in fact. I think Jakob was nervous, but it was really lovely, and definitely TBC.)

'You're lucky, darling – you have a career, you don't want to throw it all away over some man.'

'You're always the one trying to marry me off.'

'I am not, darling.'

I blinked at this bare-faced lie.

'You're constantly pushing your agenda,' I said.

'What agenda?'

'You want me married, with kids, and a mortgage. It's all you've ever talked about, Mum – my entire life.'

'Darling, I want you to be happy, that's all. I wanted you to get married, and have babies, because it was important to you. As a child, you were always talking about your wedding dress and the man you would marry…'

'But that's when I was a child…'

'I don't know, you've never told me what you want now. You just humour me, so I'm quiet – so yes, I push and push, but what can you expect? I'm your mother, I want you to have everything you can possibly want – that's my job.'

'But it's so much pressure,' I wailed.

'Love is not pressure. When you have your own family, you'll understand what pressure really is…' Oh, here we go, I thought. 'But if you really like this Jakob – good. I'm in support.'

That took the wind out of my sails. I thought she was going to put up more of a fight.

'Okay, great,' I said, pushing my plate away, passive-aggressively.

Mum gave that shrug which means, 'Fine, have it your way.'

While the waiter returned to take our plates away, we were both silent. A thought started bubbling up in my brain – why is Mum being so (relatively) understanding and not her normal dogged self? Something didn't add up.

'What's going on?' I said, as the waiter left again.

'What do you mean?'

'I don't know – it feels like there's something you're not telling me.'

'Darling, how much has Dad told you?'

'About what?'

She picked up her phone (it's huge, this new one of hers, like a mini iPad).

'Let me call him.'

'Now? Why?'

But Mum had already opened up Skype, and moments later, Dad's face was suddenly looming dangerously large on the screen AS IF THEY'D PLANNED THIS (they had).

'Good morning, Vietnam!'

'Darling, we're both here.'

'Hi, doll!' He waved at me.

'Hi, Dad…?'

'How's the grub?'

'Very pretentious.'

'I guess it's gotta be. You don't want to spend all that money on hamburgers and chips. Did I tell you about the time I was in Thailand, with my mate Tim, and we ordered these two…'

'Matthew, let's focus,' Mum said, leaning Dad against the salt and pepper shakers.

'Sorry I couldn't be there, honey. Your mum decided…'

'We both decided…'

'Yes, we both decided it would be better this way.'

'What would? Guys, this is really creepy.'

'Your father and I have something important we wanted to tell you.'

'What did you say? The line cut out.'

'We have something to tell her, Matthew,' Mum shouted at the phone, which responded by sliding off its rest onto the table.

'Oh yes,' Dad replied, once he'd been righted. 'Who wants to do it?'

Mum rolled her eyes.

'Darling…' she started.

'Doll…' Dad said simultaneously.

There was a pause as they both waited for the other to continue speaking. Honest to God, it was like the worst type of comedy skit.

'Your father and I have been having issues for a while.'

'What sort of issues?' I asked.

'Being able to stand each other – that sort of thing.'

'Matthew! That's not helpful. We love each other a lot, we do – and because of this love, we've decided it would be best to separate.'

Boom. There it was.

'Separate? Where are you going? Who's going?'

'I'm moving back to London, I'll get a flat of my own, and your mum will stay in Brighton.'

'But only temporarily, right?'

'Darling, I know this is hard on you, but we've come a long way in our relationship, and it feels like the best time to start a new journey on different paths. We're planning to get a divorce.'

'A divorce? You just said you were <u>separating</u>. But what about me? (And Lil!)'

'We'll still be there for you, only in a slightly different capacity.'

'Yes, a divorced capacity! Have you tried couples counselling?'

'Darling, we've tried everything. We really have.'

'Dad?'

'We have, hun. This is the kindest thing for everyone involved.'

'How long has this… I don't get it, why now? After everything. After thirty-seven years. Did one of you have an affair?'

'No, no, no, it was just time.'

'We are seeing other people though…'

'Matthew…'

'Well, we are – might as well get it all out in the open.'

'It's not appropriate at this juncture.'

'Why can't we say you're seeing one of your colleagues at the uni?'

'Because it's not what we agreed, Matthew. But, oh well, yes – I'm seeing Trevor, he's a lecturer in physics. And your father has a girlfriend in London.'

'Jesus, guys – I leave the country for five minutes… What about in sickness and in health? Mum, you've always banged on about the sanctity of marriage…'

'I know, but I think that stemmed from fear. Fear of doing anything else with my life, but now you're over here, and Lily doesn't need us…'

'It just felt like the right time, for everyone, doll.'

'You're wrong. This is not the right time for me,' I replied, tears in my eyes.

'We understand, darling, but it's our happiness we have to think about.'

'What about <u>my</u> happiness?'

'You don't want us to be miserable, do you? How would that help anyone?'

'I don't know,' I said sulkily. I felt ganged up on, and I wished you were there. Oh, why weren't you there? You'd have put them both in their place, and started yelling at least. Anger was always your secret weapon. You can't have creativity without anger, you'd say, and I don't know if I believed you, but it sure sounded good. It sounded punk, and dangerous, and cool. And that's you, Lil. Cool under pressure. Cool in the face of adversity. Cool without trying. Like the time that woman in the library said we were of the 'darker persuasion' and you bit her head off. That was rock 'n' roll right there. You would have known exactly what to do in Mum and Dad's ruddy ambush.

As it was, I apologised weepily and stood up (knocking Dad flat on his back again) before leaving my divorcing parents to go back to my flat for a proper cry. With some justification, don't you think? This felt like the last piece of our childhood being forcibly dismantled (after selling the family home too – but at least we know the real reason why). Mum and Dad have been miserable on and off for years, and the past three years have been especially difficult for obvious reasons, but hadn't they gotten over the hump? I thought they were in that magical stage of marriage, where you basically can do no wrong. All your quirks and foibles, if not forgiven, at least accepted. All the fights played out. No? Why the heck does anyone get married at all then?

On reflection – and against my better instinct – I think Mum is slightly right about me. I <u>have</u> been subconsciously trying to get married, because it's what they did – even though Mum and Dad's marriage was flawed, it was STRONG, or so it seemed. And now for them to just relinquish it, like that, after everything… Where does that leave me? Do I even want to get married anymore? Who am I now I don't smoke or drink, now I ride bicycles, and drink smoothies and kiss colleagues and live in Copenhagen? I don't recognise myself half the time. There's a lot of good in there, but I feel unmoored, and I wanted to call Jakob as soon as I got home, but I knew I shouldn't pour all this craziness down the phone and risk him breaking up with me. I wanted to call Robby too, because he knows Mum and Dad, and would be rightly shocked by the news of their divorce. But most of all, I wanted to call you. I would pay all the money in the world for just one phone call. Even for ten minutes. No, even for a minute.

What would you say?

You'd probably laugh, and call them the 'c word', and we'd start remembering all the funny stories – all their stupid fights, and disagreements – and you'd say, 'It's a miracle they stayed together as long as they did,' and we'd agree to never be like them, and not to make the same mistakes. You'd say they were being dramatic anyway, and probably would never go through with it – and I wouldn't believe you, but it would be nice just to hear. That's what you'd say.

Lil, it's too much sometimes. It's just too, too much.

LETTER TWENTY-TWO

Wednesday, 8 August

Well, she's gone again (also, hi, Lil).

I'd like to say I was a grown-up during the rest of Mum's trip, but after the divorce bombshell, I retreated into the most childlike, petulant version of myself. Mum's tactic was to ignore me (a method that held up during our teens) and compensate for my lack of communication by talking for me. I grudgingly accompanied her to a modern art gallery, and to Tivoli (nothing brings out a sulk like an amusement park full of happy people whizzing away on rides and eating candyfloss), and of course, shopping. Boy, can that woman shop (it's up there with her other super power – identifying Iranians in the wild simply by their eyebrows). Without saying a word, and sighing every time I was asked a direct question, I still ended up with a new bra, a dress ('Lily would love this,' she said at one point. No, she wouldn't, Mum – Lil never wore a dress past the age of fourteen) and a top for work that even Greta approved of.

Speaking of Greta, she and Mum got on famously, and again I had that sneaking suspicion that other women quite like Mum. They talked about television shows, and favourite books, with me looking glum the whole time and playing on my phone, sending churlish and passive-aggressive messages to Dad. When I finally packed Mum off to the airport, she took me by the shoulders, and said, 'Darling, you're doing well. Don't get in your own way.' When I rolled my eyes (even though it was nice to hear a compliment), she added, 'You must be doing something right, you've managed two boyfriends here already – one younger, one you work with.' Then she changed tack, 'Your father and I love each other, we're doing this out of love. One day, you'll understand.'

With that, she was gone. I had an unexpected weep in the station, walking around sniffling, with my make-up running, until I caught sight of my reflection and marched myself home.

Over the course of the weekend, I decided I had to let Jakob know what was going on – it was impossible to act normal after such upsetting news. He was very understanding – Jakob's parents divorced when he was fourteen (Denmark has an incredibly high divorce rate apparently), and I felt bad he'd gone through it as a child, while I am a woman well into her fourth decade of life, and so should be more resilient. Still, I didn't smoke a cigarette, or drink an alcoholic beverage, and Greta even allowed me half a teaspoon of honey in my smoothies as a comforter – so that was nice at least.

To take my mind off everything, Jakob decided to take me out on a surprise outing the following weekend. I was slightly concerned, as we are still clandestine at work, and there was the issue of his therapy floating around in my stupid brain (I've pretty much ruled out Jakob being an axe murderer though, and even if he were, he'd take so long choosing exactly the right axe to murder you with, you'd probably have time to escape), and I wondered if it was a great idea to be seen out together in public, but Jakob assured me mysteriously that 'No one will see us where we're going' (actually, that's exactly what an axe murder would say…) so I threw caution to the wind and agreed. I'd finally had enough sulking.

Jakob picked me up at 11 a.m. on Saturday.

'Are you wearing eyeliner?' I asked, when I opened the door.

Jakob smiled his broadest smile, his gorgeous freckle twinkling mischievously on his lower lip.

'It accentuates my eyes,' he said, beaming – and Lil, it did – he looked even more like a boyband member, and I was. Into. It. We made out so much, Jakob had to physically hold me at arm's length.

'We should go,' he said, panting.

'Fine,' I said, lunging at him one last time.

We caught a bus, and then jumped on a train, and I started to notice a lot of the other passengers were dressed up in Scandi-Goth outfits, and I remembered a scary flyer I'd once seen on Jakob's desk for something called CopenHell, and I finally put two and two together.

'We're going to a heavy metal concert?' I asked nervously, because I was definitely not wearing the right clothes if we were.

Jakob winked a smoky eye, and unzipped his jacket to reveal a vintage Iron Maiden T-shirt underneath. Great, I thought, I'm going to stick out in the crowd like Pollyanna – but then he dug around in his bag and produced alcohol-free ciders and a matching Iron Maiden T-shirt. Isn't that CUTE? The cider helped with the nerves (even without any booze content, strangely), and the T-shirt helped me feel like I'd fit in, and his eyeliner was still working on my loins (haha, gross, 'loins') so I was raring to go by the time we arrived at the station. We walked a short way, following the line of people dressed in black and dangling beers. The weather was bright and hot finally, a proper summer's day, and felt very at odds with the macabre, hell-themed attire.

Inside the concert grounds, it was already getting crowded. The festival was to be an all-day event, with three stages, and some big headliners (none of whom I'd heard of before, although I appreciated the names, they were all like, DEATH HOLE, DEMON FISH, HATE PILGRIM, ANARCHY TOAST. Okay, maybe I'm not great at inventing these...).

Buying more drinks and finding a seat at a picnic table in the sunshine, we could hear the grinding roar of the warm-up acts in the nearby tent.

'Jakob,' I said, 'can I ask you something? It's a little embarrassing…' Jakob instantly turned bright red. 'Nothing serious though,' I clarified quickly.

'Okay…'

'What is "hygge"? I think I understand the gist, but perhaps I'm wrong. I mean, does it just mean "cosy"? Because if it does, you guys are really overselling cosy.'

He relaxed immediately.

'Not really. It's hard to explain in English – hygge is about survival. Here, the winters are very long and cold, so you need something to bring happiness. The candles and the hot drinks get you through the bad weather, but hygge is also about what you don't say. You don't talk about politics or religion or anything that might upset the other person.'

Avoidance, huh? I can relate, I thought to myself.

Jakob took a big sip of alcohol-free cider and looked me dead in the eyes (God, those crystal-clear blue eyes, Lil! They'd turn you straight, they're so beautiful. Straight, I tells ya!) and said, 'There's something I need to tell you. And it's not very hygge.'

Of course, my mind went straight to the addiction issue. This is happening, I thought, trying to stay composed.

'I want to be honest with you, Joy – about myself, because I feel a real connection with you. But it's difficult.'

'Because I'm your boss?' I offered.

Jakob smiled. 'That doesn't help.'

'I can promise not to fire you, if you like?'

'That would be nice.'

'And if it makes things easier, I can show you my boobs? That's the least professional thing I can do in the situation, really.'

'You don't have to,' he replied, laughing.

'Maybe just one boob?' I suggested.

Jakob took a big breath. Crikey, this is really hard for him, I thought, and it scared me. What if he was about to tell me something that completely changed my opinion about him? What if it made me want to end things immediately? What if it was really dark? But I couldn't imagine it would be – Jakob seemed so nice and normal. I <u>knew</u> he was nice and normal. I'd seen under the bonnet, at least a little bit, surely? I imagined what you'd do in my situation, with all your social worker training. Nod and make appropriately comforting noises. In work capacity, you were the opposite of regular Lil, really – ha!

'With my last girlfriend…' Jakob began.

You killed her. Accidentally. On Purpose.

'…I had a problem. And things started to get worse to the point that she broke up with me. I've tried very hard to deal with this issue. But I want to be honest with you, because keeping secrets doesn't make anything better.' I placed my hand on his sympathetically, ready to yank it away if he revealed he was the Copenhagen Serial Killer. 'I've had counselling and done a lot of work, and things are starting to improve,' he continued.

It was very surreal to be in a sunny field of thrash-metallers, talking counselling, but at least it was a public space (I kid, I felt safe).

'You can tell me anything,' I said. 'If you want to. When you're ready. No problem, if not – I respect your privacy. But you can totally tell me.'

Jakob took another deep breath.

'I have a problem with…'

Alcohol. Gambling. Serial killing.

'…sucking my thumb.'

I cocked my head to one side.

'What now?'

'Thumb sucking.'

He looked so nervous, Lil.

'Is that a euphemism for some weird sex thing?'

'No,' he shook his head vigorously, 'it means I still suck my thumb. As an adult.'

'Oh,' I said, trying not to sound, disappointed?

'This is hard for me to talk about, but I want you know the real me, Joy. I started sucking my thumb when I was a baby, and when I was five, my parents tried to make me stop – I knew it was wrong and shameful, so I would only do it in secret, all through my childhood and teens. I kept it hidden until I had relationships, and then it started to cause problems. My last girlfriend was disgusted when she found out…'

'Disgusted? That you sucked your <u>thumb</u>?'

'She said I had issues with my mother. It made her feel unwell to see a grown adult with his thumb in his mouth like a baby. So, I went to therapy. But it wasn't enough to save the relationship.'

'Hang on,' I said. 'So just to be clear, in case there's a hilarious language misunderstanding happening here – you mean your addiction is putting your thumb in your mouth, and keeping it there?'

Jakob nodded.

'I had to have braces all through my teens to stop my teeth pushing forward. I still have to wear a retainer at night.'

'I've never seen you wear one…'

'I don't with you because I'm still trying to – you know – be cool,' he said, bashfully. 'Therapy has really helped.'

'Which thumb do you suck?' I wasn't making fun of him, I promise – I was just a bit in shock, I think.

'This one,' Jakob said, showing me his left thumb.

'Huh,' I said, the cogs in my brain still whirring. 'Can you show me? I mean, is that allowed?'

Jakob looked horrified.

'No,' he said, shamefaced, and I realised then he was serious, this wasn't one of his jokes, he was really troubled by this, and

I wanted to smoosh his wonderful face with both hands. 'I haven't…' he said a word in Danish, trying to think of the English translation, 'Used? I haven't used for five days now.'

'That's great,' I said genuinely. 'Oh, is your thumb sucking the reason you used to take so long in the office toilets?'

He nodded solemnly.

'When you first started at the company, I was still sucking my thumb, and I'd go sit for a few minutes, to calm myself.' There I was thinking Jakob was gambling at virtual casinos. Either that, or masturbating. 'Then later, I went to the toilets to do the breathing exercises my therapist taught me, to replace my thumb sucking.'

We sat there, in the gorgeous sun, Jakob watching my expression carefully, staring with his smudgy eyes, while I struggled with what to say next.

'And there's nothing else?' I clarified. 'No heroin, no pyramid schemes, no bestiality?'

Jakob shook his head vigorously.

'Then it makes me like you even more.'

Jakob was so grateful after our talk – that's the only way to describe it – he seemed less heavy, as if a huge burden had been lifted from his shoulders. The light in his beautiful eyes shone brighter. I told him about some of my eating things too – for example, my compulsion for spreadable nut-based butters. Afterwards, we kissed for a long time, and had to stop when we realised we were close to making a public spectacle if we weren't careful, and so we went to see our first band play. They were called Zombie Hamster or something, and the crowd was very young – they all looked so wholesome, like they were cosplaying metallers.

Jakob and I moved towards the front of the stage, not in the mosh pitty bit, but close enough so we could really smell the body odour. We swayed to the aggressive music, holding hands, and drank some more of our non-alcoholic cider, and after a song or two, I felt warmed up enough to give some head nods, and really, when you get into it, dancing to heavy metal is similar to 5 rythums (which I've now been to three times. Yes, you read that correctly. THRICE. Me, Joy – committing to things), and I felt the same connection to a group and to being animal and primal, and throwing our bodies around, and the noise was pretty deafening. At one point a chap in front of us dramatically pretended to cut his wrists with a broken plastic cup, and I asked Jakob what kept whizzing over our heads towards the stage, and he responded cheerfully, 'Oh, bottles of people's urine.'

'Don't they like the music?' I asked, Jakob responding, 'Yes, of course.'

With you-know-what just around the corner – it's less than a week until the anniversary, ugh! – it felt good to shake my body out, to get rid of toxins, and jump around with the other hot, sweaty, smelly monsters in the mud and the dirt and the grass.

Oh, there's one more revelation.

Get this – when I first started, Jakob showed a friend of his my social media because he LIKED me. Then one day, this friend spotted me on the boat in the middle of the canal – he took a photograph and sent it to Jakob, asking, 'Is this Joy?' Jakob was instantly jealous I was on a boat with some guy, and so he asked Nansi if it looked like we were dating, and SHE dobbed me in to management.

Nansi. Wow! Can you believe it? You think you know someone. Maybe she was getting me back for all the times I had to smack her phone out of her hand?

That's all for now.

Love you, my horrible monster.

xxxx Joy

LETTER TWENTY-THREE

16 August

Hi Lil,

~~Okay, how do you want to do this? The hard way or the easy way?~~

~~This is my third attempt.~~

~~Ugh.~~

~~I'll start. I'm really angry at you for not being here. I think it's selfish, ultimately. Leaving me here all alone, the way you did. Not that I wanted to go with you, particularly. I don't know. I just want to pinch your arm so hard it leaves a bruise. Is that fair? I want to hear you squeal with pain. You owe me that much, surely?~~

~~I knew this was going to be difficult, that's why I've been avoiding it. This is like looking directly into the sun.~~

Let me start again.

I miss you. I miss my sister. I miss having a sister.

If you haven't already guessed by now, FaceTime Margaret was the instigator of these letters. She said I was blocked, I needed an outlet, and it would be a healthy way to grieve. I don't know if I've grieved really – I feel like I've almost made you into a cartoon character of yourself, an imaginary sidekick. The real Lil wouldn't put up with my bullshit. She would have told me STOP SENDING THESE GODAWFUL LETTERS. I'M TOO BUSY FOR THIS CRAP. But you can't. Perhaps I'm punishing the imaginary version of you with all this wittering? Maybe my correspondence is an act of vengeance?

But I do miss you. Today, on the anniversary, of course – but I missed you the moment it happened too. Instantly. The second the nurse told me in the hallway. I remembered ten things I wanted to tell you. Not major things. Just a girl's shoes I liked, and this song that was driving me crazy, a new show I thought you should watch. The nurse touched my shoulder, and I think I said, 'Shouldn't I speak to a doctor?' and she did that tight-lipped smile, because really, doctors are all too busy, and you should take kindness when it's presented to you. It doesn't take a PhD to communicate the fact that someone is gone. I kept thinking, she was only supposed to stay the night for observation… They weren't even particularly worried about you, Lil – you were a little dehydrated, and there was some odd stuff with your bloodwork, but keeping you in was only a precaution. I was planning to go into work the next day. That's how much of a non-event it was – I wasn't even co-opting your time in hospital as an excuse to play hooky.

I've never seen Mum look so small. Dad was just… gone. Not there. We kept converging into these weird patterns. Me sitting, Dad standing (when he was around), Mum crying into her hands. Me standing, Dad pacing, Mum on her phone. I'd notice the way we were arranging ourselves, like a play, as if we were trying to make interesting shapes for the audience. We can't all be crying, or both pacing. Dad would stop and collapse into a chair, and I'd find myself standing and walking up and down the corridor as if I was taking over his shift.

There was no humour in that place, none at all, which is weird, because you always absolutely loved gallows humour. You would have found your own death hilarious.

'Did Lily have a significant other or partner?' asked the nurse (I remember thinking, oh – past tense. Did she, not <u>does</u> she).

'You mean a boyfriend?' Mum replied briskly. 'No, she doesn't.'

Present tense. She doesn't have a boyfriend. ~~She~~ You (I still can't talk about you like you're not here) didn't have one for a long time – your last boyfriend was when you were ten, that scrappy-looking kid from down the road. Ian, wasn't it? Ian Grady? Irish? Gap between his front teeth. You used to throw rocks at each other. Not really trying to hit each other, but points for getting close – which is what love is, basically.

You didn't have a girlfriend either. At the time. That I knew of. No, you definitely didn't, you would have told me. I wished you had, maybe I would have been brave enough to say her name in front of Mum. Jasmine! I would have said to the nurse (that's the first female name that popped into my head). Perhaps I still wouldn't have. I'm not sure who it felt less fair on – you, all recently deceased, and already being talked about like you weren't even there, Mum, not knowing the true identity of her youngest daughter, or me and Dad for being so cowardly. The sadness of death trumps everything else. It claims the space. It holds court. You'd think it would make people braver, but actually, it makes you more timid. It made me more timid, at least. I should only speak for myself.

I didn't do any of the things you see in movies. I didn't ask to see you. I didn't drink a Scotch for my nerves. I didn't even cry. I felt like a fraud. I'd been worried my whole life about the 'd' word – and then it happened and I wasn't able to do it properly. I did realise, the moment you were gone, how happy we were with each other, and that I should have appreciated that happiness more, celebrated it even – the times you'd check in with me if I was having a stressful week, all those stupid emojis I'd send if you were a bit down, the heartbreaks and hangovers. It happened so suddenly, you going. There were no parting words, no farewell notes. Poof, and you were gone.

Mum, Dad and I took a taxi home, leaving the car at the hospital. I'd been taking antibiotics for a throat infection, and you're not supposed to skip a day, but the pills were at my flat, and I wasn't going there by myself. It might have been easier, though, not seeing your bedroom so quickly afterwards, with a random exercise bike in it, Mum threatening to turn it into a home gym for years. When we arrived at the house, Mum went straight to bed, while Dad and I sat in the kitchen. Neither of us was hungry and somehow being with another person made it worse – more real – so we said our goodnights. Dad didn't even hug me.

It was worse in the morning, waking up in my bed like it was Christmas morning, but the reverse of Christmas. Instead of glee, there was this feeling of dread, like the biggest freefall on a roller coaster. Mum making calls in the kitchen. Phoning people, letting them know, keeping busy, cancelling things, asking for help. Dad was already gone – the great avoider.

I didn't know what to do. Be helpful? Hide? I knew instinctively I needed a role or otherwise Mum would assign me one – so I thought I could call your friends, the ones Mum didn't know about. Basically, the lesbians. I rang Janey first, but I couldn't get through the conversation. Poor Janey, it must have been horrible for her. You're supposed to deliver that sort of news with an ounce of decorum. From start to finish, I was blubbering on the phone. I messed up the information and Janey had to spend a good twenty minutes kindly extracting the right details from me and waiting patiently as I wailed down the phone. Once the waterworks started, that's all I could do for a while. When you cry for so long, it's like having a cold. You start wiping your tears away with any old piece of tissue paper, and then as your skin gets tender, you move to softer fabric, dabbing and blotting at your face so as not to scratch it. You can't leave the house. My face was so puffy it looked like I was having an allergic reaction.

Dad came home with a whole lot of random food we'd never eat – a mango, a jar of those cheap black olives, egg-fried rice in a pouch, beef jerky – and Mum – well, Mum had her mask on, and was calling family overseas, which kept her busy for another couple of days, a notebook of neatly-written names in front of her, glasses on her forehead, flipping them down when someone picked up. I noticed she never said the actual words, she always delivered it in a roundabout way, painting a picture, and letting the recipient voice it out loud. 'Well, yes – she has,' Mum would say quietly, when they finally pegged. 'She has, yes.'

Robby came over, and I've never been more relieved to see someone. Being in his car was miraculous. 'Can we drive somewhere?' I asked.

'Where would you like to go?'

'I don't know, to the sea?'

Bless him, he drove. He didn't even play any music or put the radio on, and I know that's torture for Robby. He hates silences normally, but I needed there to be quiet.

'Is this really happening?' I asked him when we'd arrived on the coast.

He nodded. 'Yeah, babe. I'm sorry.'

We didn't even get out of the car or open the window. It was a rainy day, windy and cold for the time of year. Seagulls were fighting over some discarded fish and chips, chasing each other, grabbing a chip and flying off. I don't even know which coast we were on – south, I think. Robby drove us back, stopping at a McDonald's on the way. I didn't want anything, but I ended up eating his fries, scavenging them like a bird, swooping in.

When we arrived back, the house was dark, empty. I thought everyone must be out, but as I was packing my things, Mum wandered in, wearing her pyjamas, barefoot – she'd been sleeping.

'Where are you going?' she asked.

'Back to my flat.'

She didn't say anything, she just nodded and padded back to her room. Can you ever remember her simply nodding, and leaving the room? Not making you feel guilty for going? Not loading you up with plastic containers full of food? Not trying to convince you to stay?

I don't know where Dad was.

Being back at my place was both better, and infinitely worse. Robby stayed that night, but he had to go into work the next day. People were calling now, Mum or Dad must have said something on Facebook, and instead of feeling supported, I felt overwhelmed by the attention. I wanted company, but I didn't want anyone else except <u>you</u>. That was the main problem: I wanted to talk about you, to you and only you. But there had been a significant and dramatic reduction in youness on the planet. A definite drought, you might say. I watched films, but I had to be careful which ones. Adam Sandler films worked, because they were terrible. I think I watched 'Grown Ups' three times. I made the mistake of putting 'Punch-Drunk Love' on, but quickly turned it off. Who knew he'd made a good, emotionally engaging film?

That's how it was for a long time. Days? A week? At some point there was a funeral, which was horrible. Sorry, it was. So musty and traditional, you would have hated it. I know funerals are for the living, but it was crap. They used a photo where you still had shoulder-length hair, and none of your piercings. There were even lilies on the coffin. It was all wrong. I failed you there. I'm so sorry, Lil – I was crushed by grief, and everything passed by in a fog.

At some point, I had to go back to work. At some point, people talked to me about normal, everyday things again. At some point, people stopped lowering their voices when I entered the room and started being dicks again. It's amazing how little the world cares, really. Strangers stand on your toes on the tube, your boss still wants you to deliver those reports, Mum still makes comments about that cupcake you're eating.

Every night I think about all the ways I could have saved you (step one: become a specialist virologist), ways I could have been more loving and giving. I wanted to leave London, partly to get away from that voice in my head. I've succeeded to a point. But these letters, I know they're most likely a burden while you're trying to enjoy the afterlife, trying to flirt with the prettier angels, and then 'ding', there's another one in your heaven letterbox – but they've helped me, so thank you, and thanks to FaceTime Margaret too, I suppose. She may not have the best internet connection, but she always calls you right back.

Hope that didn't get too heavy. I hope THE RAMIFICA-TIONS OF YOUR OWN DEATH didn't bum you out too much.

I realise I try not to mention the 'd' word because it ruins the idea I'm actually writing to you. You could be in Brixton, in your cramped little flat around the corner from Costa. The moment I start thinking about you in the past tense… I don't know, I'm not ready yet. It was hard enough when I came and visited you that couple of weeks ago – at the tree where we sprinkled your ashes. Scattered. You scatter ashes, not sprinkle them.

You'll always be my sister. Always. Present tense. So you're going to have to stick around a little longer, even if you're just in my head, and these idiotic letters.

I love you.

I miss you.

I love you.

I miss you.

Joy

LETTER TWENTY-FOUR

Tuesday, 28 August

Oh – hi, Lil,

And there you were, thinking I might have come to my senses about writing these loopy letters, but I'm nothing if not ~~consistent~~ persistent! I've given up so much already (London, cigarettes, booze), I'm still not ready to forgo you as a pen pal, I'm afraid. I could do with sisterly perspective, however limited – and let's be honest, your input so far has been severely limited. It's like you're not even trying…

Something happened. Well, might have happened. Remember that smear test I had, where they found some irregularities, and I was supposed to go back and have another test, just as a formality (or so I thought)? Obviously, I procrastinated about booking the reappointment, until I started waking up in the middle of the night in a sweaty panic. Not because I thought anything was wrong, but because it was medical and official, and of course my mind wanders towards the worst. But it's always okay, right? Until it isn't. Like, well, with you.

To my credit, I did finally go in again, and they swabbed me up (different nurse this time, who didn't grill me on 'Harry P' while she had a hand up my wotsit). Results were irregular again. This was last week. I was still dealing with the emotions of your anniversary, and everything developed into a perfect storm of sadness. I knew it was important I take some action, so I told Greta about the results of the second test, and she marched me to a specialist, where things escalated quickly.

Lil, there's an issue. They don't really know what yet, but it's enough of a problem to make doctors stare at the page for a long time before saying anything. A long time.

I haven't told Jakob about the results yet. We are still trying to stay under the radar at work, although I think Nansi knows something's up, but she's super pregnant and grumpy, and hopefully, she won't get me in trouble a second time. Also, she's going on maternity leave soon. That leaves Hagen, but I don't think he would twig about our covert relationship unless he actually caught Jakob and I bonking on the photocopier.

Just had a panicky thought – what if I can't, you know, do it again? Sex. Ever. I'm scared to Google anything, and Greta's never had an issue. Apparently, she has a textbook-healthy vagina, which is not information I thought I might be privy to until a few weeks ago. So, I need you to be sisterly for a second. Tell me not to be scared. This is a routine procedure. They have amazing doctors here. They found it early. They do this every day.

All the things I told you too, I suppose.

The upside is – if anything happens – I guess I'll see you sooner than expected. Not that I'm likely to get into the Pearly Gates, what with all the one-use plastic I've discarded over the years. I'm imagining they're big on biodegradability up there. Heaven probably smells like old teabags and compost, and that blue bio detergent stuff you get in Portaloos. Oh God, what if heaven is like some wanky festival? That'll be just my luck. You bopping around with glow sticks, off your chops, hugging me all the time and saying we're one soul.

My next appointment is in two days at the hospital. Greta and Sara both say they'll come with me. I haven't told the folks yet either. Maybe I can use this to guilt them into not divorcing? The stress broke my uterus?

I made the mistake of texting Robby. He replied, 'Want me to come over, babe?' like he could pop by, like we were still going out – and the thing is, I knew he would come if I said yes, bless him.

As I might have mentioned earlier, if it's not too much trouble, I'd really like some sisterly support. Could you send me some soothing Angel vibes? Or if you aren't an Angel, but you know one, get them to send me some vibes? Actually, could they fix my womb? Or just the vibes, that's cool too. Whatever's easiest.

Bye,

J xxxx

LETTER TO MUM

Tuesday, 28 August

Hi Mum,

I know it's probably strange to get a letter from me, but I'm not really sure the best way to do this. I'd prefer not to do it over the phone, and I now have Skype PTSD after the stunt you and Dad pulled at the restaurant. I've been writing a lot of letters recently, believe it or not, and I've become used to the format, so I thought I'd give it a whirl. So here we are, whirling.

I have some not-so-great news, I'm afraid: I have a growth in my uterus. I went to the hospital last week, and they took a sample of an abnormality they'd found, and when the lab tested it, they found something wasn't right. Where we are now (I hate that expression, it's what all the doctors use), where we are now is trying to find out what type of ~~cancer~~ growth it is. Again, I'm sorry to dump all this on you, and I'm even sorrier not to do it face-to-face, but things are happening really fast, and I wanted to get the information down and across to you as best I could. If you can let Dad know too, that would be great. He can read this letter as well, if he likes. But tell him, I'm still mad about the Skype thing, ha.

I know this is going to freak you out, but I don't expect you to jump on a plane over here. There's nothing you guys can do right now – I'm still going to work each day, and I have good, supportive people around me. It's better if I just try and behave as normally as possible, because I think otherwise, I might start to unravel.

Jakob is being amazing. I blurted out the news last night while he was cooking me dinner, and afterwards put his arms around me for so long, the gravy bubbled over in the saucepan and went everywhere.

I want you to meet him next time you're over (or hopefully, when we pop across to you once I'm given the all-clear). It's so different heading into a romantic relationship when you've been colleagues and friends before. I feel a connection to him I haven't felt with someone else. Yes, I was worried that I might get fired from my job if our romance was discovered, but apparently, it's quite common for Danes to meet at work, and there's not as much negative stigma around it. When we officially became boyfriend and girlfriend, he simply went to HR, and confessed. They thanked him and said he'd have to move teams but apart from that there was no issue. It's actually for the best, managing someone you're dating is not the healthiest thing in the world – I mean, people get really judgemental when you start making out at team meetings (that's a joke, Mum).

I also want to apologise for the way I handled news about the divorce. I sulked the whole weekend – I ruined your trip. I'm not trying to rationalise my behaviour, but by way of an explanation, I can offer this: I was processing the sadness of not having 'parents' anymore (not true, of course) and also residual emotions about Lil's death, feelings of abandonment and whatnot. Basically, Lil was a pillar in my life, and now she's gone, and you and Dad are a pillar too, and now that's changing, but I know it's not going away. I'm starting to understand the distinction. You always say you want me to be happy – and I want the same for you, genuinely. I know you guys were having problems for years, Lil and I both knew. We talked about your potential divorce all the time when we were teenagers. Sometimes we wished you would. But then we left home, and you guys carried on, and well, I guess we forgot about you, forgot you had lives of your own. You were just 'Mum and Dad', and I focused on my own day-to-day, hoping my eventual happiness would make you happy too – feeling some (healthy) parental pressure, of course, but I never stopped to think I was putting pressure on you guys too. I don't know if I'm at a place where I can totally accept the divorce and give my blessing, but I'm moving in that general direction. If this health scare has done anything, it puts what's important about life into stark relief (I'd be quite happy to not have any more scary medical emergencies though – thanks, Universe, if you're listening).

I guess I've been putting you in a box for a long time, Mum. I thought you wanted me to get married and have children. I felt that pressure quadruple once Lil was gone, because all your hopes were pinned on me, your only child now, and I was fast approaching middle age, but now I can see more clearly you're on your own journey – and when you say you want me to be happy, you mean it. On my terms. But the same goes for you: you want to be happy. If you're happier not being married to Dad, I understand. Or I will understand eventually. Because I want you to be happy too.

And Lil would have told me to get my shit together, I think.
Love you lots, Mum,
xxxx Joy

Notes for final draft:
Definitely, definitely do not use the word 'cancer'.
Probably don't go into the Jakob stuff so much.
Touch on the points that FaceTime Margaret suggested to include, or conveniently ignore them? The second one.
Go to post office before work. Do they have an expedited international mail service in Denmark?

Bring up the thing with Lil? Or not a good time? (It's never a good time though…)
Like, don't fucking swear in the last line.

MUM'S LETTER

Thursday, 30 August

Dearest darling! My precious beloved!

I know we spoke yesterday and this morning, but darling, I just reread your letter and I found some Basildon Bond writing stationery that my cousin Hebden gave me the summer after last, don't you like it? Such beautiful birds, so I thought I'd write you a letter.

I want you to know you are loved, and whatever happens with your father and I, we will always be there for you. We still love each other very much, which is why we can let each other go to the next stage. It was very hard with your sister, a very difficult time, but I couldn't have done it without him. He was more than a rock. He was the only light in a long, dark night, and for that, I will always be truly grateful.

I just spoke to Miriam Fox, who had an issue like yours, and apparently, it's a very simple procedure. If they catch it early, it's very optimistic. Are you sure we can't fly you back here and get it done privately? Please, consider it – I feel so far away from you, I want to hold you, and tell you stories like I did when you were my baby. I would much rather you come here, but I respect your decision too. You have made a life for yourself in Denmark, after all.

Darling, you are doing so well. I know I don't always tell you that, but I think it often in my heart. I'm not sure I have fully recovered from the loss of my other baby, and sometimes I think you are too capable as the older sister, and I don't give you enough praise. It is hard for me. As you know, my mother was not a very emotional person, and she was often very negative and would cut me and my brother down if we were too loud or if we wore the wrong things, heaven forbid. When I was sent to Germany, and then travelled to London by myself, I was very frightened – remember, I was only fifteen – and my English was fine, but people struggled with my accent and that made me shy, so for a long time I didn't have the confidence I saw in you, my two beautiful girls. I have always been in awe of you.

When you decided to move to Denmark without discussing it first, I suppose I was angry. I felt as if Denmark was the promised land in your head, and I knew, after my own experiences, that travelling to another country is wrought with difficulties, and I wanted to save you from that pain. I also felt sad you felt you could only find happiness there and not here with us. What did Denmark have? I cried. But your father told me to let you go – you were choosing your own life, you could come back whenever you wanted. This has been a learning curve for me also.

I am so happy for you and your new beau. Your father wants to know if he is a Viking, but shush now, I tell him.

I am glad you wrote me your letter. I have been able to put down thoughts clearly that I haven't done before. I see so many words with my students now – essays, dissertations – I forget how powerful the written word can be.

My sweet, you are in both our thoughts. Tell us the moment you get the results back, won't you? I will be praying for you.

We love you very much.

Mother and Father

LETTER TWENTY-FIVE

Dear Lil,

Oh, it feels good to write that again. It's been a while, I've missed you. How's the afterlife? A radiant place filled with wonder and happiness, you say? Good. Also, how's the hummus?

I went in for my surgery last Wednesday. I've never actually had a full anaesthetic before – I've always been terrified I'd never wake up again – so I'm happy to report they knocked me out (and revived me again) successfully, and the hospital staff were super nice, especially considering I was such a jumble of nerves. Jakob was with me the whole time too, or pretty much the whole time, he had to go to work occasionally – you know how those Danes are, work, work, work.

I wasn't sure how I should roll things out to Jakob, vagina-wise. Did I want to throw him so thoroughly in the deep end? In those first few weeks and months, the impulse is to show only your best side, your nicest underwear, to present your reproductive organs as relatively cancer-free. The decision was made for me, however, because when Jakob discovered what was happening, he was there, with me. Full. Stop. I'll always be forever grateful to him for that. Greta and Sara were amazing too. They are an extremely unlikely duo – I don't think they'd particularly choose to be each other's friends, but they both enjoy fussing over me and bickering over the best ways to do things. Sara can mostly trump Greta, as she knows more about reproductive issues with all the tests she's had, trying to conceive. Geoff has been wonderful too, throwing presents at me – big bouquets of flowers, chocolates, teddy bears – to the point my bedroom was getting crowded and Sara had to tell him to stop.

Jakob took the day off work for the surgery, and we hung out at my place until we had to head to the hospital for 2 p.m. I wasn't allowed to eat anything beforehand, so I was cranky, and everything Jakob did irritated me, uncharitably. THIS IS WHY I DIDN'T WANT YOU HERE, JAKOB, I thought crankily, but he just shrugged off my irritability (spelling?). At the hospital, the surgeon was very brisk and seemed underwhelmed that the operation wasn't more complex. What, we're not whipping out your uterus? his look seemed to say (okay, okay, I was very hungry at this point, he was probably only concentrating). It was surreal to be in a hospital as a patient this time, rather than on the other side. I thought of you a lot, Lil – how scared you must have been through everything. The term 'PTSD' is banded around willy-nilly (mostly by me), but I might have been experiencing some legitimate post-traumatic, you know, stress. I also felt like, ah – so this is what the Universe has decided to test me on? Just when I've given up smoking and drinking and was feeling even the teeniest bit better, I get thrown this curveball. I only cried twice; once, when they were wheeling me towards the operating theatre, and Jakob wasn't allowed to come any further, and I had to wave goodbye, and Jakob looked so nervous – and once when the anaesthetist was really nice to me, and I knew it was because I was looking petrified, and they were worried I was going to hop off the bed and scarper.

When I woke again, I was in a ward bed by myself. A nurse arrived, and told me Jakob and Sara were outside. My nether regions hurt quite a lot, with a dull faraway ache. The problem was I needed to wee, but I remembered the nurses telling me before the operation they were going to hook me up to a catheter, so I tentatively tried it out – it was slightly uncomfortable, and a very odd sensation, but I finally managed to make it rain (what? That's not how you use that expression?). I quite enjoyed the catheter, actually. Very practical. You know what a small bladder I have – car trips were always such a nightmare.

Maybe it was the surgery drugs, but for a second, I almost believed you'd come bustling in with Jakob and Sara, with some buffoonery worked out to make me laugh, a weird breakdance routine, maybe. The robot. Yes, you'd do the robot, and knock something over, and the nurse would yell at you.

I was allowed to go home a few hours after I'd woken up. Jakob took me back to my flat and settled me in – I was still pretty groggy, but in a relatively upbeat way. It felt so strange to be on painkillers, to be anything other than clear and sober. When you've not had a sip of alcohol for many weeks, it really feels odd to be altered in any way. Interestingly, I prefer my sobriety now, much better.

Jakob stayed the night, which was lovely, but I hoped I wouldn't bleed on him, or wet the bed, so fortunately neither happened. I was quite a bit sorer in the morning, and of course, the drugs had worn off, so I was pleased to have him there, making breakfast, playing death metal songs to help with the pain (it does, surprisingly), and escorting me to the loo. He was supposed to go into work, but he took the day off instead, and we spent the morning playing Monopoly.

A couple of days later, when I was feeling better, I had the loveliest surprise. Sara and Greta had conspired together, and drove me to a secret location.

'We're your Fun Squad,' announced Sara excitedly, when she arrived to pick us up.

'But not too much fun,' Greta interjected. 'We don't want Joy tearing her vaginal stitches.'

A double act for the ages, those two.

I recognised the red brick church first – we'd driven to Viggo's place. You remember, where I first stayed in Copenhagen? Apparently, I'd mentioned to Sara a few (thousand) times that there was a cat living there I had a confusing crush on – and she contacted Viggo to ask if we could pay Minnie a visit. Isn't she great?

It was so strange to be in the flat again. Viggo was sweet, and the three of them waited in the kitchen as I went into the bedroom to find Minnie.

For some reason, as I opened the bedroom door, the image of Jodie Foster visiting Hannibal Lecter in 'Silence of the Lambs' jumped into my head, and I felt nervous. What if Minnie didn't remember me? Or she hissed? There was a lot of pressure suddenly – a kind of performance anxiety began to grow.

Once inside, I realised the bigger challenge would be locating the cat (and ignoring the omnipresent smell of man musk). She was not on the bed, and my lady parts were still delicate, so I had mobility issues trying to see underneath it. No Minnie. I started to panic – maybe after she'd found out I was coming, she hid purposefully? And then I remembered cats don't understand English, or even Danish, and they don't usually have personal grudges – and there she was now, curled up on the sofa. Minnie looked up sleepily, doing that double blink which means 'Yes, human? You woke me?' She yawned, grimacing and poking her weird pink tongue out, pointy teeth like fangs, but she was still very small and cute (when she wasn't yawning). I sat next to Minnie, and reached a tentative hand towards her, afraid she'd bite or scratch, but instead she pushed her warm little head into my hand appreciatively. I stroked her for a long time – the cat hair swirled in the air around us, and later, I found a stray hair in my mouth, which made me gag, but in the moment, I didn't care at all.

'Beautiful Minnie,' I said, as she purred contentedly.

Lil, I think this is where I come out as a cat person. I've been in the closet all my life, but now I want to sing it from the rafters. Me, Joy. I. Love. Pussycat.

While I remember, I've found out more about Dad's new girlfriend. I've stalked her on Facebook – she has two sons, both in their early teens. Dad's brave, throwing himself back into the teenager racket – you think he'd have learned his lesson with us. I feel a bit odd about it, I won't lie. Part of me wants to ring Mum up and bitch about it, but I don't want to take sides. I wonder what Mum's boyfriend Trevor is like? Oh God, the parentals are multiplying, Lil! We'll have a wicked step-mother and evil step-father in no time, just you wait.

Oh, and an update on Jakob's thumb sucking. His therapist says Jakob's making great strides, and I'm a hugely good influence because of my accepting open-mindedness. Jakob even came out of the bathroom the other night wearing his plastic mouthguard retainer thingy. He looks gorgeously dorky in it, and it gives him a slight speech impediment, which for some strange reason I find irresistible. I'm now worried if Jakob and I ever break up, I'll start trawling dentist offices to satisfy my new kink.

Anyway, I get the results from the doctor tomorrow.

Worst-case scenario? It's not worth mentioning.

Best-case scenario? They've discovered oil and I'm a millionaire.

Only time will tell.

Love your chops.

xxxx Joy

LETTER TWENTY-SIX

Later

Me again,

'That time' has been trying to assert itself in my brain, especially right now with everything, especially when I'm trying to sleep. You know the one I mean – I can feel it on the verge of my awareness, as if it's hiding around the next corner waiting to pounce – so I'm going to write it down instead. Face that fear. Maybe not face it – sidle up to it and slap a sticker on its back that reads, 'Kick me'. ~~That'll teach it for killing my sister.~~ No – no stupid jokes.

We were supposed to have dinner in Soho at that Mexican place you like, but you weren't feeling well, so you asked if I could come over to yours instead. I remember thinking, lazy tart – you obviously couldn't be bothered to leave your house. It wasn't the first time you'd pulled this stunt, but giving in to your demands was always better than trying to reschedule, or one of us getting pissy with the other, and not texting for days.

You looked pretty wretched when I arrived. You had a headache and a temperature – well, a fever – you'd get really hot, and have to take off all your clothes except your knickers and bra, and have me fan you with a magazine, and half an hour later, you'd be freezing. We were laughing about it. Mostly. You were like a sweaty beached whale one second, and then buried under sixteen duvets the next. I wanted to call Mum, but you didn't want her getting involved.

'It's a cold, it will pass,' you kept saying. 'I must have caught it off one of those little rotters.'

You probably did catch it from one of the children you worked with. They don't even have to be sick themselves or have symptoms to be carriers of the virus, I found out later. You loved being a social worker, and you were good at it – the kids thought you were amazing, so I find no relief in imagining, what if you had a different job? Would you still be here? You were perfect at it – making the boys feel comfortable and the girls would be in total awe. You were so calm, speaking to them like real people, never patronising or condescending. I remember this look you'd give them, which meant, 'We're going to get on, okay?' and they seemed happy to oblige, even the damaged ones, the really skittish ones, the kids most at risk. I saw it the times I popped into the after-school group you organised – you were everywhere at once; playing basketball, encouraging the shyest ones to join in, and always bossing everyone around – sign in, come again next week, become a volunteer, take these over there, have you had some juice?

It was a cold. A common cold. Sure, every sniffle I've ever had I've blown out of all proportion, but you were different.

We got pizza delivered – you barely touched your vegan feast (which I said was an oxymoron, to which you replied, 'What did you call me?' Vintage dad joke) – and we were watching things, and chatting, and playing on our phones, and I was bloated from the pizza, and lying down with my big pregnant wheat belly, and you were under the duvet at this stage, just your face showing, when you started complaining the lights were too strong. I turned them off, but then the laptop was too bright, and you couldn't even look at your phone. I thought you were overreacting, and it was getting late, and I was tired, and I had work in the morning, and you had to live all the way across London, didn't you?

Anyway, you'd tell me if you were <u>really</u> sick. You probably just needed to sleep. You said as much. I kissed you on your sweaty forehead and told you if you needed anything, I'd come straight back. I could grab an Uber. It would take me forty-five minutes.

Mum texted me the next morning.

'Darling, your sister is very ill.'

She'd said you'd collapsed. Your flatmate had found you and called the ambulance. They were giving you tests at the hospital. I burst into tears at my desk, and everyone thought someone must have died.

When I arrived at the hospital, you were already very far gone. You looked so different from the night before. Your skin was grey. The nurse said you'd been calling out my name. When you saw me, you thought I was Mum – that scared me.

The doctors said you were dehydrated, but you would be stabilised, and they were running more tests. I think meningitis was brought up in the conversation, but I can't be sure. My memories aren't the most trustworthy.

In the evening, I went back to my flat. Mum was with you, I'd been at the hospital all day, there was no place to sleep, and they said you were getting better.

That's why I went home, Lil.

That's why I wasn't there when you left.

LETTER TWENTY-SEVEN

Wednesday, 19 September

Dear Lil,

The good news – it's not the worst news.

Bad news, it's not the best.

On Friday, Jakob came with me to the doctor to get the results. My appointment was at 4.15 p.m. and I'd had a stomach ache for about two days due to stress and overeating slightly from worry (Greta has really let me fall off the wagon, I blame her completely). Mostly, I just wanted to get the appointment over with, so I could dislodge the ball of worry in my gut. Jakob held my hand as we waited for the doctor, and I could feel acid reflux in my throat every time I swallowed.

Finally, we were ushered in. The doctor had his laptop open in front of him, and he scrawled for a long time before he spoke.

'The reassuring news is there's no cancer.'

Jakob punched the air silently, and then went bright red. He's the best.

'Unfortunately, we have found some irregularities with the tissue.'

'But it's not cancer?' I repeated.

'No, no, no. But these irregularities mean it will be very difficult for you to get pregnant.'

'Ooohh,' I said in one long breath. 'Difficult, but not impossible?'

'It is hard to say,' the doctor said over his glasses. I could tell by the way he was breathing that Jakob wanted to retroactively neutralise his fist punch.

'How do we find out?'

'You and your partner can try, of course – the natural way. If that doesn't work, there are fertility measures.'

'That's not terrible then…'

'The issue is not just conception; the walls of your uterus are compromised, which means a much slimmer chance of the foetus coming to full term. I'd say about a 50% success rate. And that's considering the father's sperm is at 100%. Have you been tested?'

Jakob went from vivid red to a hot pink.

'No,' he stammered. 'But I can. Should I book an appointment?'

He looked lovely as he said this. Like a chivalrous beetroot.

'We've just started dating,' I said, squeezing Jakob's hand. 'Babies are some way down the line yet.' Or never.

'The good news is you're healthy. Remember that, it's important.'

As we left the hospital, Jakob said, 'That's a relief,' but both of us knew it wasn't completely, and I think I was in shock, because I didn't feel anything, just numb. We went home and Jakob offered to make me dinner, but I told him I needed some time by myself – he resisted initially, but I gently manoeuvred him towards the door, and he told me to call if I needed anything. After I shut the door, I felt the stillness of the flat. Greta wouldn't be back for another hour. Quickly, I dressed in my cycling gear and went down to borrow her bike.

Once on the road, things were better: I could concentrate on riding, the stopping and starting, the rhythms of the traffic. I felt relief being with other people, an anonymous cyclist. I didn't know where I was going, so I made decisions based on ease of access (I still find turning left scary here, so there are always a lot of right turns when I'm cycling). Copenhagen was beautiful – there was a slight breeze, and it was warm still, and everything had that late summer feeling of idle contentedness. Except I wasn't content. I was whirring along with these wonderful Danes, who were all obeying the rules, and of course, the children caught my attention – three of them bundled into a cart, eating handfuls of gummy worms. A baby sat backwards, staring at me with cool, recriminating eyes. A toddler on the pavement holding his mother's hand, before bending at the waist to pick up something from the ground daintily between finger and thumb, the mother smiling on. Things aren't as scary if you follow the logic, the knowingness of patterns. I'd been following the rules of existence laid out for me since I was a child, but all certainties were suddenly gone. First, you leave. Then Mum chills out considerably or stops caring as much – I'm still not sure which. And now this. I'd lived a life based on the assumption that I'd eventually get married and pregnant. Secretly, I was looking forward to it. I think – ultimately – I did want it even more than Mum. She does only want me to be happy. Happiness for me was replicating the family I grew up in – ironically, considering how much effort I spent trying to break free from its grip.

At some point, I realised where I was cycling to, and I hated myself for it. I knew JP's address, because we'd dropped his bike off in Geoff's car the day of the boat ride. Did I know why I was going there, Lil – really, consciously? Yes, I suppose I did.

When I arrived, I wasn't sure which buzzer was JP's, or if he was even in, and it started to dawn on me I was making a terrible mistake – when one of the windows swung open.

'My English girl,' came JP's voice. I could see his sinewy tattooed arm holding open the window, and I remembered him in the boat with the soggy transparent underwear. 'What are you doing here?'

'I was in the neighbourhood,' I answered lamely.

'Then come up.'

I got scared then, and my impulse was to cycle away, but I'm too English, too polite. I locked up the bicycle, and JP appeared at the door. We chatted small talk in the way that doesn't mean anything but also means a lot. I didn't mention Jakob, and neither did he – there was a hole in our conversation, one we both tiptoed around.

JP's place was exactly as I imagined it – full ashtrays, melted candles, shelves of exotic liquors, and random guitars lying about. He shared the house with six other people, most of whom seemed to be still asleep in their bedrooms. I accepted a glass of water and tried not to look too closely at its cleanliness as we moved to the massive shaggy sofas.

We were still having a perfectly harmless conversation the entire time, all while I was silently assessing whether the flatmates would make a sound to alert us before wandering into the living room. Which underwear was I wearing (horrid ones, of course). I was even preparing for afterwards, how I would make an excuse to leave – Greta needed her bike, something lame like that. I'm telling you all this, Lil, because I know deep down, you'd understand. I felt like I was being controlled by someone else. No, that takes away my culpability – it was as if I wanted to <u>be</u> anyone else, even if that person was a hypocrite and a cheat and about to perform an act of obvious self-harm and sabotage. I wanted to control the pain, make it mine, to take away its power – the hurt of my diagnosis, of losing you, of the inevitable breakup when Jakob found out who I truly was. It made some kind of hysterical sense – be the author of your own tragedy. Bust everything wide open. Banish the light.

Reading this back now, it sounds like absolute tripe.

The chit-chat drew to a close, and we fell silent.

'Joy…' said JP, softly.

It was the first time he'd spoken my actual name, and it gave me a sharp jolt, and I began to come to my senses. Jakob.

Wonderful, lovely Jakob. I imagined us avoiding each other at work, never being able to kiss his freckled lip again, having to go to the doctor without him there to fist pump the air. Unable to hear him talk excitedly about a really great paint thinner he'd discovered. There was a lovely energy to Jakob, an inner glow, which I was actively trying to extinguish.

'…are you okay?'

'I'm fine,' I replied.

JP didn't look convinced.

'I think I came here to sleep with you,' I began – actually out loud. 'I wanted to squash all this sadness down somehow, like in a trash compactor.'

'I think it's normal, natural,' JP replied quietly, shrugging in that cool French way. 'It must be hard to lose your only sister.'

That hit me, because I hadn't told JP about you (sorry), but of course, someone else must have – they always do – Sara maybe, or Geoff, out of kindness. It's this weird badge you wear when someone dies suddenly, a grief pin – some days you think no one can see it, and others, it feels like it's stuck to your forehead.

'My mother died,' JP said, 'In a car accident. I was twelve.'

'That's awful.'

'I started drinking at thirteen. I had my first tattoo at fourteen. Got a girl pregnant when I was fifteen. It was difficult.'

'I just want to be happy again,' I said, starting to cry. 'The way I was before everything happened.'

'That would be nice,' JP replied. 'I would also like that.'

'How can we?' I sniffled.

'Build a time machine.' He made a whistling noise, a machine zipping back to the past.

I nodded. 'Do you miss her, your mum?' Which is of course a stupid question, and one I absolute hate when people ask me about you.

'Every day, there is a moment, yes. I think about what she would be doing, would she like this new band – because she loved music, you know. Silly things, like would she be on Facebook?'

'I know, it's the silly stuff that really gets you.'

I wiped my face, and JP fanned his hands at my eyes to help them dry, and that made me laugh, and I don't know how it happened, Lil, but our faces were slowly moving towards each other, and my life flashed before my eyes – well, all the most self-sabotaging minutes of it – almost snogging boys I shouldn't have (Robby), smoking illicit cigarettes, the hangovers, the blackouts… and I knew I needed to get out of there, that I was heading around in a loop again. I stood up, and made my excuses (poor, lovely JP – he really gets the short end of the stick with me) and rushed downstairs to the bike. And this time it felt even better to be riding again. I wanted to go and go and go. I cycled further than I ever had before, past everything familiar, into the suburbs, with their neat lawns, and wood-framed houses, people walking dogs, and further still, until I was in a forest, with stone bunkers which looked left over from the war.

I kept on cycling, until finally I rushed off my bike, and threw myself into a field full of long grass, or something like grass, and I used the grass to pull me along, towards the centre of the field – fistful of grass after fistful of grass, feeling my body heaving great tears. For the first time in my life I wasn't worried about someone hearing me – usually when I cry, I'm scared the neighbours will hear, so I try and stifle the sounds. In the teary weeks after you'd gone, I'd stick a cushion over my face until it was mottled with stains and wet with snot and I had to throw it out. Here, I was free to release the empty aching feeling inside my breast, the disappointment, and this is going to be a lot – so stick with me, you're really the only person I can tell – but I felt a sadness greater than anything before, because I realised I wanted a child, a baby girl really, so I could keep you alive, so I could teach her about her Aunt Lil. These letters were a way of trying to make you finite in some way, to capture your essence as a legacy – your humour and your courage and your strength, and how much you loved me, and how much I loved you. When the doctor told me the news, I knew the buck stopped with me, and I might be the last person who really knew you. <u>Really</u> knew you.

I was pulling out great fistfuls of grass (sorry, farmer, if you're reading this. Also, how are you reading this?), and convulsing with tears, and I felt your presence, stronger than I ever have before. It was the most wonderful feeling, and also devastating too, because I realised how much I'd been coping without you. I felt you in the ground, in the grass, and the sky, and the clouds. You were everywhere, Lil – and I realised nothing is ever lost, it just changes. In that moment, I was me – but I was also you, and Mum, and Nanna, and weirdly, my daughter. I realise that sounds ridiculous, but I did – I felt her – I WAS her. I know this is super trippy. My hands were a little cut from the grass, but the stinging sensation was good. The stinging meant I was alive. I was so lucky to be alive. I also realised my eating was fine, it was good I had given up alcohol, and cigarettes, but I don't have to be so militant with food – I needed to relax. Greta had been wonderful, but I could find a way of healthy eating for myself, one I can sustain. After all those years of struggling with my eating, all the binges, I'm actually doing okay. I'm so hard on myself! The Universe loves me. I'm trying. It appreciates that. Just chill, Joy – just chill for once in your goddamn life.

The light was fading fast (the sky was a beautiful magenta and blue), and I was getting cold, covered in tears, and bleeding gently from both hands because of the grass cuts.

On my bike again, and pedalling towards home, I realised I had to tell Mum about you. She couldn't live in denial anymore. Your sexuality was an important part of your identity. I know you would have told her if you'd had more time, I felt sure. I've been dithering over it too long. It doesn't honour you, misremembering who you are. Mum needs to know. I can't believe it's taken me so long. There's this big chunk of information she doesn't know about you – really, it's a gift for her to receive.

But then I was scared again. And sad. The feeling of epiphany was leaving faster than I could pedal.

When I got home, I was sooooo tired, more exhausted than I've ever felt in my life, bar the night you left. I washed my hands, put antiseptic cream and plasters on the worst of the cuts, and crashed out. I slept eight hours straight, and now it's 6 a.m. while I'm writing this, even though it's slightly painful holding the pen.

I'm still sad, but it's a manageable sadness.

I keep walking to the window to watch the dawn break.

Love you,

J x

LETTER TWENTY-EIGHT

Tuesday, 25 September

Hej Lil,

Life is slowly returning to normal. I felt odd for days after the field of dreams incident (what I'm calling it) – energised, and strangely happy once I passed the initial sadness. I'm still undecided how I'm going to tell Mum about you (oh, and also – must tell her I might not be able to have children too! Such great conversations I have lined up).

Things at work have obviously taken a back seat due to my health drama, but on Friday, Hagen finally realised Jakob and I are dating. We were sitting next to each other at lunch, Jakob's hand on mine – he gave me a peck on the cheek as he got up to go, and Hagen almost dropped his tray.

'We're going out,' I explained.

Hagen glanced around conspiratorially. 'But you guys don't even like each other?'

'Sometimes that's how it works,' Jakob said, kissing my hand.

'Do _they_ know?' Hagen asked in a whisper, as if we might get hauled away by armed guards at any moment.

'Everyone knows.'

He shook his head, bewildered.

'The world is a crazy place.'

Um, thanks Hagen?

That evening, Jakob borrowed his friend's car and we drove up to the house he's been renovating – about an hour out of Copenhagen – to give me some time away to clear my head. It was quite the build-up obviously, I'd seen all the pictures on Instagram, and heard Jakob talk about it since I first joined the company – the blood, sweat and tears he'd soaked into the property. But Lil, the place was stunning. STUN-NING. For one, it was a big house, on its own land, set in woodland. In my head, it was a tiny holiday cottage, but it actually had two large double bedrooms, and everything was so carefully decorated in the typical Danish neutrals, but with accents of actual colour too – jade greens and deep ocean blues, that made the place feel more masculine, and so beautiful.

My mouth was agog as he took me on the tour. He undersold everything, in a typically Jakob way. 'Wardrobes,' he said, glossing over the fact one of them was WALK-IN (the dream, Lil!), and I had to grab and hold him by the hand so I could savour each moment.

'You did this?' I kept asking. The place had a real sense of calm and tranquillity (even with the midges and plucky mosquitos – there was a lake nearby). The house is not quite finished, which I liked too – I can still be a part of it somehow.

After the tour we went foraging. Yes, you read that right: we foraged. In the forest. WITH OUR HANDS. Maybe it's growing up in London, but it felt very otherworldly – we each took a basket, and Jakob showed me which plants we could pick and the mushrooms and roots we could eat. At home, we washed them, prepared them and ATE them. As if it was the Dark Ages. I liked it, Lil, even though I was scared we'd accidentally eat something poisonous, but at time of writing, I'm still alive.

The interesting thing was, I could see myself in the house, coming back year after year. I really felt settled in a way that was unique during my whole time in Denmark. I turned off my phone and we talked the entire night – we didn't even have any music playing. I thought I might become morose, out in the back of beyond after what had happened, but it felt good. Like I'd turned a corner. I laid out my concerns to Jakob – all the risks about telling Mum about you, that she would yell at me, or worse, cry and get upset.

'Why didn't Lily tell her?' he asked. 'You always made her sound so confident and proud.'

I tried to explain you still had your blind spots – Mum's approval was ingrained in us growing up and was a hard thing to shake. You were building up to telling her about your sexuality, we'd obviously talked about it. Was it my place to tell Mum now, though? Maybe not, but on some level, I felt you wanted her to know.

'There's your answer then,' Jakob said, smiling.

'What if Mum ex-communicates me?'

Jakob shrugged. 'She's only got one daughter left, right? Puts you in a powerful position to negotiate.'

I hadn't thought of that. Clever Jakob.

'Mum isn't particularly religious,' I said, 'but she's not <u>not</u> religious, if you know what I mean. She's religious in all the wrong ways – casually, selectively. I'm scared that if I tell her about Lil's lesbianism, it changes Mum's opinion about where she is…'

'What do you mean?'

'You know, heaven… and the other place.'

'But you don't believe she's in… that place?'

'No… Of course not…'

'Then it's another excuse.'

'Alright, tough love – I get it.' But he was right. It <u>was</u> an excuse. Over dessert, Jakob went on to tell me he'd had his sperm tested. Yes, entirely of his own volition, he'd taken himself off to a fertility clinic. I was speechless.

'I thought it would give you options, you know, if down the line…' he trailed off, bright pink. 'Also, I was interested to find out myself. I'm not saying I want children soon, but…'

I wanted to know everything about the sperm test. Jakob explained it is all very much against the clock – you need to get the semen into the small jar, and back to the nurse as soon as possible so the results can be accurate, but long story short, he has exemplary sperm (also, sorry about all the sperm talk, Lil).

'So, who knows, it might work?' he said with a big grin.

He looked so sweet. I can't say all Danish men are amazing to date, because I don't have a large enough sample, but I know my one is pretty incredible.

'Jakob, I have to tell you something.'

'Did I go too far – getting tested? I didn't mean to put any pressure on you…'

'No, that was lovely, it really was. Masturbation has never been more romantic. I need to tell you about JP.'

Jakob's wonderful brow creased, but he didn't say anything.

'The day of my results,' I continued, 'after you'd gone, I needed to clear my head, so I took Greta's bicycle and…'

'You went to see JP?'

'Yes.'

Jakob shuffled in his chair, folding his arms.

'Did something happen?' he asked, a pause between each word.

'No.'

'Did you kiss?'

'No.'

'But you wanted to?'

I hesitated. I considered explaining there was a hard ball of pain inside me, and whenever it was in the driving seat, in my weakest, darkest moments, it tried its best to screw up every other aspect of my life. Rob me of happiness. Self-destruct. But that didn't sound like taking responsibility for my actions. That sounded like another excuse.

'Yes, I guess I did want to kiss him, initially. Until I realised I was only trying to mask the pain. So, I decided to feel the pain instead. Like I'm doing now.'

'How does that feel?'

'Terrifying.'

Jakob uncrossed his arms and took my hand. It was a small gesture, but it meant the world. It meant, we can talk about this. We're all human. We make mistakes. I still love you. You're safe here.

And we did talk, for hours, and not just about what did or didn't happen with JP, but other things too – Jakob opened up about his childhood, and also about things I don't have the right to commit to paper, so I won't. Suffice to say, it was one of the best nights of my life. It was the night we told each other, 'I love you'.

Seem to have something in my eye, so going to sign off for now.

Miss you.

xxxx J

LETTER TWENTY-NINE

Sunday, 7 October

Dear Lily Vanilli,

Hello. Have I spoken to Mum yet? Well… no.

I've been incredibly busy at work, what with the arrival of replacements for both Jakob and Nansi. We're about to start a new design soon, our last project has gone into production, and early sales are promising, with doctors and patients responding well. Jakob, Nansi and Hagen should take all the credit, of course – they are the wonderfully smart, creative people – and I only held them together like beautiful glue. And just like glue, I got in the way sometimes, and perhaps I stuck a few things together I shouldn't have, and you have to run me under very hot water to get completely rid of me… you get the idea. The replacements are nice, but obviously no match for the originals. I mean, I can't secretly snog either of them. Neither of them is questionably pregnant. They simply turn up to the office and do their work. Boring.

A couple of days ago, Geoff threw a birthday party for Sara. I always love being in their cosy home, so Jakob and I went early. I think I finally understand what 'hygge' is too. It's that moment when you're at a Sunday roast with friends, at a nice pub, and it's raining outside, and you really need a wee, but you're squished in the corner, and everyone will have to stand up to let you out, and Pete is telling a funny story, it's one you've already heard, and the first time was groan-worthy enough, but you wait instead, because you can see your food is about to arrive.

It was great to see Sara. She was so excited to see me, and I felt bad for casting her as a party girl when I first quit drinking (absolutism can make me very preachy).

'I have something I must tell you before everyone arrives,' she began, but then Geoff grabbed her and she was gone.

The rest of the guests started turning up – the woman I'd met at the first dinner, whose name I can't even remember, and JP. He's broken up with his girlfriend, telling us a hilarious story about coming home to find her in a foursome on their bed. It was the final straw, he explained – he'd only just changed the sheets. JP squeezed my shoulder, and I could tell there were no hard feelings between us, and I told him how sorry I was about his girlfriend. 'Oh well,' he said, shrugging, 'but it means I am heading back to France in a couple of weeks.'

'Oh no!' I said. 'You can't leave us, JP.'

'And you? Will you stay?'

I looked over at Jakob, who was flipping through Geoff's record collection. 'Yes, I think I will,' I replied.

'He likes you,' JP said, 'I can tell.' I smiled. 'You English girls, making all the men fall in love with you.'

Greta turned up next, with Hagen.

'What are you doing here?' I blurted at Hagen.

'We are dating,' he said.

'Why didn't you tell me before?'

'You didn't tell me about Jakob…'

Fair enough. Greta and Hagen seemed quite sweet together, despite my misgivings. Who would have thunk it, huh? Not me, that's for sure.

But the surprises didn't end there.

Who turned up next, but Angelo. It was the first time I'd seen him since the breakup and all that social media nonsense – that's what Sara must have been trying to warn me about, I realised. I felt a massive lurch in my stomach the moment Angelo entered the room. He was pretty sheepish – he didn't make eye-contact when he shook my hand, which I actually appreciated – YES, YOU SHOULD FEEL AWKWARD, I thought. Overall though, I was weirdly calm. A lot had happened since the breakup – I was in a very different place. I had Jakob, I was happy. We did some polite chit-chat, and then he moved on to some other people, and we didn't interact again all night, although I caught him casting a few furtive glances towards Jakob.

The final surprise was Geoff's. Once the place was packed, standing room only, he dinged a wine glass, and I yelled 'Speech!' of course (why do I always do that?). He began to wish Sara a wonderful birthday in excellent Danish (show-off! My Danish is still abominable). I remembered then how annoying I'd found Geoff at the language school, and how I would have missed out on all this fun if I hadn't gotten to know the real him. Eventually, the Danes all laughed and clapped, and Geoff started speaking in English, 'Happy birthday to my beautiful wife – not only is it a celebration of <u>her</u> birth…' and I suddenly knew what was about to come out of his mouth… 'but we're also expecting a child of our own.' Everyone clapped ecstatically, and Sara beamed, slightly embarrassed, as Geoff kissed her stomach. She caught my eye, and gave me a 'I should have warned you' look, and I gave her the 'Please, you didn't have to' face, but I wanted to melt into the carpet. If I'm honest, I wasn't quite ready to be brimming with enthusiasm, but I wasn't upset either. I was truly happy for them, I just wasn't in a place to be around a lot of smiling, congratulatory people, especially where babies were concerned, so I locked myself in the toilet, and pretended to use the loo (I went through the whole charade too, sitting on the seat for what seems like the right amount of time, taking off some toilet paper and throwing it in, unused). After I flushed, I was washing my hands when I noticed someone had left a half-full glass of champagne on the sink. I picked it up gingerly. There was a lip imprint on the glass, so I turned that side farthest away, and then I held it, imagining the consequences if I drank some. No one would know. Sure, someone might smell alcohol on my breath – Jakob, maybe – but I could wipe some toothpaste on my tongue afterwards? Totally normal, brushing one's teeth midway through a party.

I sniffed the champagne, and it had the yeasty smell of bread, and the sharp tang of chemicals. I dipped my tongue in, and my taste buds were hit by the acrid sensation of alcohol, and I recoiled, remembering that last hangover after my blackout night, and the shot of vodka that Greta made me drink. I tipped the champagne down the sink, but I didn't feel victorious in any way, and then someone knocked on the door, and I yelped in surprise, flushed the loo again, and rinsed the champagne glass under the hot tap.

Jakob was standing outside the bathroom door.

'Are you okay?' he asked, and I wished I had rubbed toothpaste around my mouth.

'Not really,' I replied truthfully, trying not to breathe on him directly. 'I feel bad for Sara, because it's her big day, but I don't think I'm in the mood for celebrating. Is that unfair?'

Jakob gathered me up in his big DIY arms.

'Shall we go?'

'It wouldn't be very polite.'

'We could spread a rumour, end the party early?'

'What kind of rumour?'

Jakob contemplated this, seriously.

'We could say there are bedbugs?'

'What?'

'Yes, we could explain we saw some. And then we could burn our coats.'

'Why would we burn our coats?'

'Because we think there are bedbugs on them. Everyone is terrified of bedbugs!'

Jakob did a terrified face which made me giggle, and I felt better.

'So, you would ruin someone's birthday and baby announcement just for me?'

'I'd do it for lots of people – but for you too, yes. I also really like the idea of burning the coats.'

Oh God, Lil – remember when I thought he was an arsonist?

'Do you want to know something else?' he asked. 'I saw Greta and Hagen kissing in the bedroom.'

'Not on the coats?'

Jakob nodded. If there was ever a reason to burn clothing that was it (not because of Greta, Greta is my own personal Betty Ford, but Hagan could do with a tad more bathing. And the incineration of his socks).

Together, Jakob and I sort of shuffled back into the party, still hugging each other, and stood in the doorway surveying everyone. Hygge was in full force – there were toddlers, and a puppy, and candles, and lots and lots of cake, and booze, and Danish flags, and more candles. Sara saw us, and darted over, and sort of hugged Jakob and I, so we were like three nesting dolls, me inside the grasp of Jakob, and Jakob in her arms. She asked me again if I was alright, and Jakob said he'd go and get us some more drinks, bless him.

'I'm so happy for you,' I said because I genuinely was.

'Thank you,' Sara replied. 'I feel very close to you, Joy. And I'm going to need you, over the coming months, to keep me sane and remind me about the outside world, okay? I don't want to turn into some boring parent. You have to tell me I chose this – to settle down, and get fat, with a nice man. Remind me, okay?'

'I will,' I said, noticing the slight panic in her eyes. 'Is everything okay?'

'Yes, yes… Just sometimes I am not sure about everything, you know. The situation.'

'But you love Geoff? You guys are so great together.'

'Yes, yes – but life is so long now. Who knows how I am going to feel when I'm fifty? You have to make all these long-term decisions and I don't know what I'm going to feel at the end of the week, let alone the end of the decade. And Geoff is older, what if he dies and leaves me alone with his children?'

And Lil, I knew this type of panic, I'm an expert in it – so I grabbed Sara's hand and I squeezed it really tight, about as hard as you should probably squeeze a pregnant woman's hand, and I looked her dead in the eyes, and said, 'Everything's going to be okay.'

'You'll be here?'

'Yes, I will.'

'Good. You need to help me, okay?'

'Of course,' I promised, and Lil, I meant it. I'll be the best honorary auntie to Sara's baby I can be.

Your blister of a sister,

Joy

LETTER THIRTY

Monday, 15 October

Dearest Lilian,

Oh God, my premonition was right – the flat has become the official love nest of Greta and Hagen! He is in attendance most of the weekend and at least one weeknight now – Greta doesn't like the ambience of his place (not nearly enough white throw cushions, I'm guessing). But, Lil, the noises they make… Not sex noises, per se – although how can you be certain? – but the growling, cooing, giggling, and high-pitched laughter, it's obscene. Prior to Hagen arriving in the flat, I think I heard Greta laugh approximately once – now it's like she's hooked up to laughing gas. What could be so hilarious? I shudder to think. But it's when the laughing stops – that's when you need to be most vigilant, because who knows what they do <u>then</u>?

Nothing puts a dampener on your own romance than close proximity to another couple in lurve…

Two nights ago, Jakob was over as well, and the four of us all milled around the living room and kitchen, trying not to get in each other's way, but failing miserably. Greta lets Hagen off with everything – he's even allowed to wear his horrible boots in the house.

So I now share a flat with <u>three</u> colleagues, one of whom I'm shagging, one who I'm directly responsible for, and one who knows all my deepest secrets. Just brilliant. I really don't want Hagen seeing my tampons – I just don't – so I went around trying to hide anything that made me look unprofessional. This included:

- 'The Dummy's Guide to Team Management'
- A book you gave me, if you remember, called 'The Multi-Orgasmic Woman' as yet untouched (the book, that is)
- All drying undergarments
- Any photos of me on display where I'm drunk, making a weird face or poking my tongue out because I hate photos (so all of them)
- Jakob's rash cream (he had an allergic reaction to one of the paint strippers, and now has red splotches up his arms).

All I need now is for Nansi to move in and start breastfeeding her baby in the bathtub (she's had a boy, by the way – all healthy). Or Norwegian Max from HR to join Hagen and Greta in a polyamorous three-way.

To his credit, Hagen seems to be pretty romantic. He's forever bringing Greta flowers (and more bloody candles), which has triggered Jakob's competitiveness – I've had flowers two weeks in a row, and even the sex has been slightly more frenetic overall, so maybe there are some benefits. And to think, I once considered myself a 'one-and-done gal'…

Of course, with Greta focused so much on Hagen, it means her life counselling has slipped considerably. I'm eating poorly again – crisps have snuck in, I blame Jakob (he's also gotten me addicted to liquorice, it's a national obsession over here). But after the field of dreams experience, I'm trying not to worry about food, and honestly, when you're happy, and someone seems to like your body pretty much as it is, you lose all motivation to eat salad. Take Greta. The other day she ordered A PIZZA. WITH EXTRA CHEESE. But I still haven't smoked or caved when it comes to drinking. It helps that Jakob doesn't drink booze much himself. He's similar to Angelo in that way, but less high and mighty about it. Jakob doesn't like the taste of alcohol, never has, and so when he drinks, it's usually in social settings where he's forced to. I remember that feeling, being forced to drink. Everyone always says, 'Don't you miss alcohol?' and honestly, I don't. Not the hangovers, or the waking up sweating in the middle of the night, remembering (or trying to remember) what an idiot I'd been, and I definitely don't miss the walk of shame to the recycling bins, bags clinking, to tip a skip-load of bottles away.

Jakob and I are still very much in our honeymoon period, even with Greta and Hagen trying to steal our thunder. We can't stop touching each other, and he's sweet and kind of bashful in a way I find absolutely adorable. Love makes a moron of you. We have stupid pet names for each other (nope, I'm never going to share them with you) and we can sometimes spend a whole evening just lying next to each other and talking. I'm so behind in my TV watching. We binge <u>each other</u>. Of course, there are issues too – there are always problems, I don't want to make out it's perfect or anything. I get insecure he'll come to his senses and go off with some Danish girl, and I think he's worried I'll run away back to the UK, and he can go quiet sometimes – thoughtful, he says – but it makes me hypersensitive.

There are also the pitfalls of dating someone else in therapy – therapy talk wars. When we fight, we are equipped with the best possible terminology to try and win, using the most weaponised therapy-speak.

'I hear anger in your voice,' I might say patronisingly.

Or Jakob will ask, condescendingly, 'Is that something you've experienced before?'

What's worse is if someone says, 'Have you talked to your therapist about that?' or the coup de gra (spelling?), 'perhaps you <u>should</u> talk to your therapist' delivered with this smug little smile (okay, maybe only I do that). And EVERYTHING is a projection. But I feel like I'm evolving with him in a proper grown-up relationship for once.

Jakob has helped me with Mum too, gently nudging me to decide on dates and flights (basically calling me on my ineffectiveness every time I'm gormlessly on the web instead of taking action), booking time off work, etc. It just all seemed too daunting. In the end, I decided to take a Monday off, and make it a slightly long weekend. Mum wanted to know the reason for my trip, and I worried she could sense something was up, so I told her as nonchalantly as I could, I was feeling homesick and wanted to see her. I probably shouldn't have added that second part – she acted more suspicious after that. Dad will be in London, and I might not get time to see him, but I can't think about that right now, I just have to focus and achieve this one thing. All I have to do is say, Mum, Lily was a lesbian. Is a lesbian? 'Was' sounds like you were one once, but stopped. You are a lesbian. Even your ghost is lesbian. Mum, Lily is a lesbian. No, sounds like you're alive again. Mum, she had a Robyn haircut. You must have realised she was gay. Gay, Mum. Gay.

Ugh! I feel like the lesbian police will arrest me for speaking out of turn.

Should I let sleeping lesbian dogs lie?

Well, I've paid for the ticket now anyway.

Bon voyage, I suppose.

xxxx Eeyore

P.S. Oh, and Hagen made a stain on the white sofa, and Greta barely batted an eyelid. If I'd done that, I'd have been put into one of those shackles in the town square and pelted with rotten fruit.

LETTER THIRTY-ONE

Sunday, 21 October

Hi Lil,

I'm huddled on the cot in the spare room at Mum Towers (formerly Mum & Dad's place) in Brighton, the room which used to be Dad's workplace for all his furniture sanding, and still smells of sawdust and varnish, even though Mum must have cleaned it seventeen times (sawdust is her nemesis, she hallucinates the stuff now. 'Is that sawdust?' she'll bark at you. No, Mum, it's just regular lint/dandruff/general fluff, Mum, sheesh. She bruised my boobs earlier from her over-forceful brushing of phantom sawdust from my jumper).

I'm so tired, and emotionally drained, but I want to get this down, for you – and for me too, I suppose.

Okay, enough preamble. I'm going to lay it all out as best I can.

My flight was delayed. There was terrible bumpy turbulence when we finally took off, and a crying baby two rows behind me, so I landed in London pretty frazzled, taking the party train to Brighton and arriving just after 10 p.m. Mum was in bed when I arrived. We had a quick cup of decaf tea together before I hit the sack.

Yesterday was strange from the outset. I kept wondering if <u>this</u> should be the moment I talked to her, but it was as if I had stage fright, and then Mum would be off on another tangent (one of her students has reported her at the uni, saying she gives them too much homework and marks them too strictly. Mum is furious). I kept stuttering and spluttering so much, she kept asking, 'Darling, what is it?'

What is it? That was my cue, but nothing. We had lunch together, followed by some light shopping (by Mum's standards), and then we collapsed at home for a quiet night in. We talked about going to the local cinema, but we were both kind of bushed (as Dad would say) and I knew it was now or never.

How do you start a conversation like this?

'Hi Mum, I know this is really none of my business, but remember your youngest daughter, yes that's right – the one who died tragically? Well, guess what? When she was alive, there was something she didn't tell you. She wanted to, but she never found the right moment – or not telling you was an act of rebellion, something you weren't allowed to judge or control. Really, it was her prerogative who to tell and when. Alas, she did us all the disservice of not being alive anymore, and so it's fallen on me, her sister, to impart this important personal fact about her, because I feel I owe it to her, and to you too, of course. I mean, it wasn't the <u>most</u> important thing about her… But if you know about her lesbianism, maybe you'll understand some of her anger, especially directed at you, and the distance she created, and maybe, just maybe, you'll love her more? That's what I'm hoping for at least. That's my gambit. Dad never told you, not even after he said he might, because I think deep down, he's more scared of you than I am. Lil was never scared of you though, because you were so similar. All those epic clashes about ridiculous things, because you'd both decided the sky was a different shade of blue. So yes, in summary, Mum – Lil was gay.'

Maybe I should have written it in a letter and posted it under her door? Oh, why didn't I write a letter? I'm an idiot! The one time my writing skills might have come in useful…

So there I was, Mum yawning and about to get up from the sofa, when I said, 'Mum, wait.' She looked at me, put out because she was just about to start the 'going-to-bed' process. It was late, she was tired.

'What, Joy?' She waited, practically hovering over the sofa in her readiness to go (you can say a lot about Mum, but she has extremely strong haunches).

'I need to talk to you.'

'About?'

About something that's none of my business. Or all of my business now. I still can't decide.

'About Lil.'

At the sound of your name, Mum let herself sink slowly into the sofa with a grunt of resignation.

'I've been meaning to talk to you about your sister,' she started. 'I was planning to wait until tomorrow, but if you...'

'No, Mum. I need to talk, don't hijack my conversation.'

'Darling...'

I had to be firm.

'Mum, I have to tell you something really important about Lil.'

She rolled her eyes dismissively as if to say, 'What could you possibly tell me about my own daughter?' and it was good she did that, because it gave me a flash of angry courage, which spurred me on.

'Did you ever wonder why Lil never brought anyone home?' I asked.

Anyone. Gender neutral.

'What do you mean, darling? She brought people back all the time. Friends.'

Friends. Gender neutral.

'But not a boyfriend?'

Mum looked exasperated, as if I'd asked why we breathe air or why worms wriggle in the ground.

'Lil was young,' she said. 'She was still finding her feet.'

A wave of – pain? tension? – passed over Mum's face and made me falter. Push on, I thought, you've been so close, so many times before… push on…

'She wasn't finding her feet, Mum. She'd found them. Lil knew herself better than most people. She was proud of who she was.'

'What are you talking about?' asked Mum, but I could tell she sensed something was coming, as if she was being backed into a corner.

'Lily wanted to lead by example. She wanted to be visible. It was important to her. But you were her blind spot, Mum. The last hurdle she didn't quite clear in time.'

'Darling, it's late, and you're talking in riddles. Are you feeling well? Maybe you have a temperature?'

'Mum, I'm fine.' And I was, there was a cool collectedness to me now. I was no longer worried about _if_ I should tell her, it was happening – I just had to go with the momentum.

'Lily didn't bring any partners over because she was hiding that part of her life from you.'

'Hiding? What could she possibly have been hiding? I knew everything about my daughter. You can't tell me…'

'But you didn't, Mum. It's not your fault (not completely, at least), but you didn't know one crucial thing about Lil…'

'There is nothing I didn't know!' Mum's voice was loud now, and it surprised me, the intensity of it. 'She was my daughter. _My_ daughter. She came out of my body…'

I tried to stay calm. I tried to do the practice FaceTime Margaret suggests of seeing the other person as frightened, vulnerable – as a scared version of ourselves. I looked at Mum, and she seemed so much like you – there are your cheekbones, Lil, your lashes, your lips.

'Lil loved you,' I started again in a quieter, more serious tone, 'and because she loved you, she didn't want you to know anything that might be… upsetting. Lil was always worried about what you would think. Deep down. So, she kept a part of herself from you. And that part was about who she loved. But more importantly, about who she was…'

Mum reached out then, actually grabbed hold of my wrist and looked me deep in the eyes, and it was such an intense stare that I froze. It was shocking, Lil, the emotion in her face. Again, she reminded me so much of you.

'I know,' she said, her voice a growl.

'No, I…'

'I know,' she repeated, and she squeezed my wrist even harder, and in that moment, I realised she did. She did know. But, Lil, why did she say those things at the hospital, at the funeral?

'How come you've never talked about it?' I stuttered.

Mum let go of my wrist.

'Your sister never spoke to me, and I didn't want to embarrass her. She deserved her privacy.'

'But… but… all those times, after she – at the funeral? With the nurse? About her having a boyfriend?'

'I didn't know those people, the doctors, the funeral arrangers. I didn't want them knowing my daughter's business. They don't deserve to know her inner life. I was protecting her. I would do the same for you – I do! Can you imagine I tell strangers about those years with your eating, how hard it was for you? You think I'm singing this information from the rafters?'

I was still shocked.

'You were okay with Lil being… with her being…?'

Mum shook her head.

'Darling, my approval, my approval! What is this, what really? Do you think I had my mother's approval when I married your father? When I cut off my hair? When I became pregnant with you before I was married…'

'You what?'

'Yes, darling. Shocking, isn't it? You see, we all have our secrets, our inner lives.'

We were getting way off topic. I put a pin in that piece of information. I was so close, I didn't want to be deflected. I needed to hear Mum say the words, otherwise she was liable to slip off to another place and we could never talk about this subject again, because in her mind it was CASE CLOSED. Against every impulse, I pressed on.

'When did you know Lily was a…?'

'Please, darling, do not say that word.'

'Why not? It's how Lil identified.'

'Yes, but I'm her parent, it is not relevant. She was my daughter, that's the only word I need.'

'It's very relevant, Mum. It mattered to her, her sexuality was a big part of who Lil was. She went on marches and sit-ins and she was part of a community that mattered to her. And so that should matter to us.'

'But, darling, she's gone.'

She said this so matter-of-factly, I was caught off guard. <u>She's gone</u>. The words twanged like a wonky harp string, like when you feel a muscle ping in your calf. 'She's gone,' Mum repeated, 'and we're all entitled to our memories of her. I have mine, you have yours.'

Yes, I thought, but your memories are wrong.

It was as if she read my mind.

'Darling, I might not have been invited into that part of Lily's life, but I set the foundations for it – you have to give me that at least. I came here to this country – I survived – I overcame a lot of my own family conditioning. You think it was so easy for me? We weren't allowed to wear trousers. I loved my trousers! Then we were displaced. Your father is from an island. For my parents, that was like coming from the moon. In my first days in London, a man spat at me on the street in Camden, for no reason except that I was different. Lil always knew who she was, that was apparent. Abundantly clear. She and I are alike in that way. Joy, my sweetheart, maybe you don't always know yourself – that's why your sister and I worried about you. You lack a sense of identity we both shared. Who your sister decided to spend her time with was her business. But I knew, I knew! When Lil was two years old, I knew. When she was ten and would only wear a pair of dungarees, I knew. When she was fifteen, and all her friends from school had punky hair and piercings, I knew. But I respected her – she was her own person. I may have felt resistant, because I knew what it was like already to be different, to be an outsider, to receive violence in the streets, and did I want to save her from that pain? Of course! What type of parent would I be, if not?'

'But, Mum…' I was crying now, I think (I know).

'No "but Mum". Hear me out, darling. I loved your sister. Had she lived, she would have gotten through her twenties and undoubtedly, she would have mellowed in her thirties – I know this, because that's what happened to me. We would have sat down, her and I, together. And Lily would have told me things, in her own way, in her own time. Yes, we would have argued and slammed doors, but there would be understanding too. Love. I was waiting for her – out of respect – but we didn't have enough time, darling. That's all. We ran out of time.'

Oh God, Lil. I needed this moment, I realised, to be with Mum in such a clear, focused pain. I also understood: this was all about me. I'm sorry. I'm so sorry I used your sexuality as a subterfuge for my own hurt. I should have opened up to Mum on my own terms, but I don't think I knew any other way to break through by myself. This was the only way in.

Why wasn't there enough time? Mum had our future all mapped out. I had it all mapped out too. We had plans. You ruined them, Lil. You went and left, and it's so unfair of you, because there was so much more. And I do understand what

Mum means, because if you or I had died when we were horrible teenagers, we'd never have come back to each other in our twenties and found ourselves as (slightly nicer) adults. No growing that bond again – it would have been snuffed out forever. Mum was right, who knows who you would have become in your thirties, Lil? Maybe you would have met someone, had a kid? Then you'd have needed Mum, I'd put money on it. She's so good with babies – they get sort of spaced out when she holds them, and Mum can do all of those noises to lull a baby to sleep. She's a freaking baby charmer. Perhaps you would have bonded then? Covered in baby puke? Watching your mother rock your poor sick baby to sleep?

I wiped my face with the backs of my hands, feeling a surge of frustration again.

'What about all that talk of heaven and hell when we were children?' I spluttered, 'All that good versus evil stuff? I was terrified about what would happen when I died. What must it have been like for Lil? That you'd think her… the way she was… it would stop her from going to…'

'No,' Mum said so firmly, pointing her finger at me with such conviction it startled me again. 'My baby is happy, there's only one place for her.'

'But…?'

'No,' and with the tone in her voice, I knew she meant it. 'I know where my baby is. Anyone who says anything else can answer to me.' And I was so glad to hear it, Lil. It's so silly, but we did have God stuff rammed down our throats when we were smaller; at school, by that angry neighbour with the roses you butchered, Mum in her way too, and there was always this niggling question, of what if they were right? I know it's ridiculous, but in my weaker moments, I worried. In my lowest moments, and there have been a lot of those since you left, that's where my brain went. Mum being so adamant, was – I don't know – lovely, reassuring. God didn't stand a chance with our mother scorned, and I felt better in that moment than I have forever, because there was surety – you were good, you were fine, you were somewhere safe. I have Mum to thank for that.

Oh God, I'm crying again, thinking about it. She was brilliant, Lil. She looked as if she'd kick anyone's butt who tried to say otherwise. You'd have been proud of her, Lil, you would. She loves you, she does. I know it was often hard for us to see it, and I wish you guys would have been nicer to each other, but oh man, we could have done much worse for a mother. I'm hard on her, but imagine if I had a ten-year-old daughter now? How much would I be screwing her up?

I hugged Mum then, and she seemed so small, like a child herself, and it felt weird hugging her (she is not always the most natural of huggers – unless she's trying to get sawdust off your back). Eventually, she broke free from my snotty embrace.

'There's something you need to do for me now,' she said, a serious look on her face. Immediately, I thought, 'She's going to ask me to lose weight,' because she felt my love handles and back rolls while she was hugging me, and I start to pre-emptively bristle, but that's not what she says at all.

'Darling, when was the last time you spoke with your father?'

'Dad?' I said. 'Recently…?' But I couldn't remember exactly when. 'Why?' I became worried. 'Is he okay, health-wise?'

'He's fine, but, darling – I think you should go see him.'

'I'm flying tomorrow…?'

'If you get an early train to London, could you see him?'

'Mum, tell me why?'

'I think it's better if you do it face-to-face. Just promise me you'll try. Don't leave it hanging. If your sister has taught us anything, it's that we can't depend on some distant future with these things.'

With that, she went to bed.

I'm now absolutely drained, lying in my cot, but with enough emotional energy still remaining to worry about Dad. He must be alright? We spoke on the phone a couple of weeks ago, I think – he sounded fine. What can Mum have meant? Or is she just being dramatic? You'd think I'd be relieved after that talk, but I feel like I've closed one door and opened up a bigger, scarier one.

I'll text Dad in the morning, and maybe he can meet me at the train station before I head off to the airport? He's fine. Mum's just being silly.

Isn't she?

Ugh!

x Joy

LETTER THIRTY-TWO

Monday, 22 October

Lil, remember this one?

Knock, knock?

Who's there?

Banana?

Banana who?

Knock, knock?

Who's there?

Banana?

Banana who?

Knock, knock?

Dad would go on like this forever, until we were practically squealing for him to stop, begging in fits of giggles.

Then, finally:

Orange.

Orange who?

Orange you glad I didn't say banana?

So bad. Even as a child, I knew it was bad. Such a long joke. Dad really had to commit.

Okay, so I texted him before I went to sleep (after finishing my previous letter). I didn't want it to sound urgent or panicky, but I was in a pretty emotionally raw place, and he texted me back super early, although I slept through the alert. Needless to say, when I finally did wake, Dad was convinced there was something wrong with ME, and I had quite the job of reassuring him I was absolutely fine and Mum had not murdered me for sawdust-related crimes. Dad confirmed he could meet me at the station, but after some gentle grilling on my part, I was none the wiser as to why Mum wanted us to meet – she simply kept repeating, 'I think you should talk to your father.'

'About what?'

'Speak to him and see.'

She is so annoyingly stubborn.

Before I left for the train, Mum hugged me again (a record – twice in two days!), a better hug this time, more relaxed, and maybe that's the trick: you just get out of practice and your muscles don't remember how to technically engage in a hug. If Mum and I hugged every day for a month, we'd be naturals. A small part of me wanted to stay and try that experiment, but then she made a remark about the quality of the cardigan I was wearing, and I was like, I'M OUT OF HERE, OLD WOMAN – BYYYEEEEE!

On the journey back to London, I kept turning over what Mum could have meant about Dad. I mean, he already knew about your lesbianism… Maybe he was getting married to this new girlfriend? Or had knocked her up already? I tried to imagine how I would react to Dad starting a new family, and the answer always came back loud and clear: not well.

When Dad met me at Victoria station, he seemed as nervous as I was. You haven't gone through this, Lil (conveniently) – but when you lose someone in a family, the subsequent members all get pretty skittish and jumpy, reading into everything, and panicking at the drop of a hat.

We started off on the back foot too. When I first arrived, there was something strange to the side of Dad's face – his lip was sort of drooping in a weird way, and so of course, I start screaming, 'Dad, you're having a heart attack!' in the middle of Victoria station, because I once saw a poster in the doctor's office about how a paralysed face was the first sign of one (I was also thinking, maybe Mum really is a witch, and she sent me, knowing he'd be in trouble?). Dad started mumbling incoherently, which made me freak out even more, but to cut a long story short (one which includes a cancelled ambulance, lots of worried onlookers, an aborted attempt at the recovery position, and a free paper cup of water from the nice people at a Caffè Nero), it transpired Dad had needed some emergency dentistry at an out-of-hours clinic that morning, hence why his face was numb.

After we established this fact, Dad was all, 'What's wrong?' (slurring and dribbling) and I was like, 'Nothing, what's wrong with you?' – and absolutely nothing seemed to be wrong – so we realised we had been hoodwinked by Mum into one of her set-ups for no clear reason, so we went to grab a coffee and figure out why the heck she was meddling.

'It's not fair of her,' I complained, 'after everything we've been through with Lil. Mum should just say, "You should visit your dad" instead of turning it into this big scary mystery.'

'She means well,' Dad replied, although it sounded more like, 'Shhminshwell.'

He was dressed in a lilac jumper, and I think he's lost a bit of weight, his eyes were less puffy than the last time I'd seen him. He seemed better, Lil. Healthier. I think he's drinking less.

I then relayed the full story about talking about you to Mum – what she'd said, and how much better it made me feel (because, isn't that what really matters? Joke). I didn't tell him the heaven and hell stuff, because in the cold light of day, I wasn't sure how to repackage that thinking.

'How are you really?' I asked.

'Yeah, good as gold.' ('Gooasgol.')

I mean, at least Mum will talk. She'll talk and talk, and talk if you're not careful, but Dad, unless you get a few drinks into him…

But then I had an idea.

'Do you want to go and see her?' I asked.

'Who?'

'The female Pope. Who do you think? Lil?'

'Now? You've got a plane to catch…'

'It's only a cheap Ryanair ticket, I'll reschedule it or buy another one.' (Yes, spontaneity was very unlike me, but Dad's fake near-death experience had made me reckless.)

'Don't you have work tomorrow?'

I shrugged.

'It's worth it. When was the last time you visited her?'

'A couple of months ago, I think,' said Dad unconvincingly. 'I've been meaning to go again.'

'Let's do it now then.'

'Okay,' but he sounded hesitant. 'I have to make a call first.'

'To your girlfriend?' I asked teasingly, but he went quite shy.

'What's she called?' I asked when he'd finished the call.

'Aroha.'

'Is she kiwi too, then?'

'Yeah, from Hamilton originally.'

This weirded me out a bit. Not that I expected Dad to start dating another Iranian woman, but what if he went back to New Zealand with this Aroha lady? (Ha, that's how Mum and Dad must have felt about me moving to Denmark… A taste of my own medicine.)

'I think I have survivor guilt,' I said to Dad, as we walked to the tube station afterwards, 'with Lil.'

'She'd be very proud of you, doll.'

'Would she? Perhaps she'd think I was being silly all the time?'

'Lil had a lot of what we call in New Zealand "mana" – you know, wisdom. So do you. She looked up to you.'

When we arrived at Brixton, it was as frenetic and loud as ever, and pungent with the smells of popcorn and coffee and spice – the absolute antithesis to Copenhagen's ordered calm (and Denmark's almost exclusively white folk) – and it reminded me so much of you. I had to regularly stop my brain from navigating my feet towards your old flat. Once we'd walked the short distance to Brockwell Park, it took us a long time to find the tree we'd sprinkled your ashes under. To be fair, I spotted the tree straight away, but Dad contested the accuracy, until I eventually won him round (because I was right, plain and simple). We stood, looking up at the leaves – it's called a Maidenhair tree or a Ginkgo Biloba if you're fancy, and it has these fan-shaped leaves, which had all turned an autumnal yellow. The sky was absolutely clear, and I'd missed it, this winter sun – we get so much cloud in Denmark. I realised then we should have brought something, flowers or a ribbon to tie around the trunk? I thought about picking some daisies and making a chain with them, but I could feel the gust of air from your ghostly eye-roll, so we just stood in silence instead. It must have looked strange, two people standing next to each other in front of a tree. I'm sure there were a few odd stares in the park behind us.

After some time, Dad said, 'Remind me again why Lil wanted her ashes here and not at the house?'

'Home was too tied to childhood. Brixton represented who Lil was now – the freedom, the openness, her grit. She also didn't want to be divided up – Mum taking some to Iran, you to New Zealand. Lily wanted to be in one place.'

'She told you all this?'

'Uh-huh. We talked about it all the time, especially after that cousin, the accident, you know… What to do if one of us died. Of course, I never actually thought…' I trailed off.

'I don't feel like I ever got to know Lil properly. I don't just mean the gay stuff. I mean, everything about her.'

I wondered then if I could show Dad these letters, or at least edited parts of them. Because in a way, he's right: he was always excluded to a degree. He was an absentee father a lot of the time, and maybe you and I were a little cliquey in our twenties, but that's what happens when you become an adult, isn't it – 'us' against 'them'?

'Mum said Lil ran out of time.' I was quiet for a moment. 'She loved you, Dad. And I love you too.' I took his hand in mine, and as I did, I could feel him start to cry – big, choking sobs. He was like a boy, a crumpled child allowing his grief to come out finally, and I started crying too – so if we looked weird to people before, we now added heaving and sobbing into the mix.

Dad stood straight again, wiped his face and started speaking in Maori – a chant, low and guttural, and it was beautiful. Often his heritage gets eclipsed by all the louder Persian-ness, but it's a part of us too: you, me and him. It was lovely to hear. He squeezed my hand, and I squeezed back.

'Want to know something else?' I said, wiping my face with my sleeve, trying to lighten the mood. 'Another reason Lil wanted her ashes in Brixton – it's where David Bowie was born, and also, where his ashes are scattered. Only she didn't get her research right, because after Lil died, I found out he's actually scattered in Bali.'

Sorry you have to find out this way, Lil, but it's true.

After saying goodbye to Dad, I was about to head straight to the airport and chance getting on another flight when I had a sudden idea.

Robby picked up on the first ring.

'Joy? Is that you?'

'Hey, Robby. I'm in London and there's something I need to do. Can you come pick me up?'

'I'll be there in twenty minutes.'

'I haven't even told you where I am yet.'

'What did you say, babe? I was putting on my shoes…'

Aw, Robby.

Once he collected me, we drove south-west into the London 'burbs towards Sunbury. On the way, I grilled Robby about Debbie, but she'd moved bars and wasn't returning his calls, so I didn't tease him (much).

We slowed down to a crawl when we reached our house. Well, not <u>our</u> house anymore. The house we grew up in. It looked pretty much the same, except for a strange car in the driveway, and I think new curtains in the living room.

Robby shuffled down in his seat as we approached.

'We're not casing the joint, Robby,' I said. 'But thanks for bringing me. This would have been much weirder in a taxi.'

'What are you going to do now?' he asked.

'I'm not sure. Part of me wants to go meet the new owners. Tell them I used live here. Maybe see Lil's room one last time.'

Really, I wanted to stake a claim on the house – our <u>family</u> house – for longevity somehow. Bury an object of ours in the garden or scratch our initials on the door.

'You know,' Robby said, as if he was reading my mind, 'there's a part of Lil that will always be here.'

'I hope so.'

'I mean dust, right? It's mostly human skin. That means Lil's skin dust is all over the place, in nooks and crannies. You could rinse the whole house with bleach, and she'd still be there, somewhere. In dust form.'

I patted Robby's arm~~, he always knew what to say~~.

'I don't remember Lil's funeral,' I said, shaking my head. 'Isn't that weird? The whole day's a blur. Even the scattering of her ashes is a fog.'

'The food was good,' Robby said, and he was only half-joking, but I laughed gratefully. And then I asked him questions about the service and afterwards, things I half-remembered and worried over, things that only came to me in dreams, and Robby patiently helped fill in all the blanks.

'We should go,' I said, eventually. 'Before we get arrested for kerb-crawling.' I blew my nose. 'Thanks for being there for me, Robby.'

He stroked my shoulder.

'Anytime, babe. I did it for Lil too.'

'She'd have appreciated it.'

'I know,' he said with sad smile.

Robby wanted to drive me to the airport, but he was already late for work (and I wouldn't let him), so he wished me bon voyage and I jumped on the nearest tube. There were no more flights to Copenhagen though, so I had to stay in an airport hotel until the morning. Oh man, are they weird, but it also feels very grown-up too – like, I can afford to stay at the AIRPORT, oooh. And actually, being alone in a sterile hotel room, with the occasional roar of a plane taking off, was just what I needed to decompress.

I missed Jakob. Alone in my room, my separation anxiety crashed over me like an emotional wave made of emotions. I love him, I really do. He'd been sending me text messages the whole weekend without being needy (like Robby was sometimes) or demanding (like Angelo) – Jakob is just the right amount of things. I know it sounds cheesy, but he really HEARS the words I'm saying. I can describe things to him in a way that I can't with anyone else – except when you were here. I don't want to make this a goodbye, because it's not, but I always thought you were the only person who could understand me, really get me, so when you left – no, when you died – I not only lost my sister, but also the greatest connection I had with another human being on the planet. And, Lil, that was just another reason why it felt so devastating. That's why I needed to write these letters, because only you understood. It's early days with Jakob, but it's there, that understanding – I can tell. Not the same way, but close, related. A cousin once removed. And he can't/won't replace you, that's impossible – and who knows? Perhaps you wouldn't like Jakob if you were still here, maybe you'd be jealous, but I'm almost certain you would. I'd bet my life on it, in fact.

I ended up sleeping solidly in the perfectly adequate hotel room bed, and when I woke up, it was very strange to be so close to my terminal, and I was on the early plane and in the sky in record time. I was very calm on the flight – serene even – intermittintly (spelling?) excited about seeing Jakob. I missed him so much on this trip, it was almost a physical pain. I know that sounds dramatic, but it's the truth. I had a window seat and as we came into Copenhagen, I could see the city spread below me, the land jutting out into the water, the Øresund Bridge snaking its way through the sea towards Sweden, the golden glow of the city lights. There was not a cloud in the sky, everything looked freshly smelt.

I thought about Jakob, of course, but also Greta, and Sara, and everyone at work, and I am happier here than I've ever been, Lil (minus the ongoing anguish of missing you, of course) so I've succeeded, haven't I? All I know is, it felt good getting off the plane, and breathing in the Danish air, and there were five funny messages waiting for me from Jakob, and one slightly passive-aggressive one from Greta, asking where I'd left her curlers (I hadn't touched them, honest. Okay, they were in my room).

So, I'm here, Lil. I'm here.

FINAL LETTER

Sunday, 7 May

Dear Lily,

Wow, it's exceptionally strange writing that after so long! It's eight years since I wrote my last letter to you, can you believe it? Maybe you can – I'm not exactly sure how time works over on your side. I imagine you have all those clocks everywhere, like at airports or travel agents (remember those?), with the different time zones. Except the clock shows the date on different planets, so you can keep track of progress. Pretty science fictiony for me, this concept, I know. Science fiction usually gives me a headache. You were always trying to get me into 'Starship Voyager', or whatever it was called. Moody people in spandex with weird rashes on their faces.

The reason I'm writing now, after all this time, is because I found all my other letters in a box in our attic – I must have put them away up there when I moved out of Greta's. I decided to tidy up a bit while Jakob was taking the kids out on a day trip (I know, kids – I have kids! Spoilers!) and instead, I discovered your teddy bear, Harville, and the letters – they were slightly beaten up, lots of the pages had tea stains on them – and I've been reading and reading and reading. Oh my, it was a lot, Lil. A lot. If you hadn't already died, the weight of all my needs and hopes (and the sheer amount of paper) might have crushed you.

Before I update you on all my news, I want to apologise. My letters simply stopped. I know you were never actually reading them, but it became my ritual to keep you in my life, to keep you alive, and it might have seemed like I shrugged you off. It's not what happened at all – I was constantly writing you letters in my head. Constantly. Daily. That hasn't changed. Life got busier, is all. So, so busy.

Oh, Lil, reading through those letters, there's so much of me in them, obviously – warts and bloody all – but there's so much of you too, or the space where you should be. I'm not sure if someone coming to these letters who didn't know you from before would get to know you by reading them – there's a Lil-shaped hole on each page, which I try to fill with all my prattle – but they'd definitely realise how much I loved you. Love you. And miss you. I can feel the pain and sadness of my younger self in every sentence – it's seeped into the paper. As it should be, I suppose.

It's not that I don't miss you any less now, but I'm better at coping with it. I have years of practice. The cost for all this emotional muscle power is that the memories lose their definition. Everything fades. I wish you would come back for five seconds so I could see your face again – just five seconds, that's all I need – to remember the detail, high definition in a three-dimensional space. You wouldn't even have to say anything, you could just pop back, smile, and then zip away again, poof – like on 'I Dream of Jeanie'. Oh no, that actually sounds horrible – one, it would scare me, and two, it would be a torment not to hear your voice again. Okay, you can say three words. No, five. Why am I giving you a limit? Come back for a whole afternoon. That would be heaven, it really would. No kids though. Actually, you'd most likely want to meet them...

I have kids, Lil. Me, 'terrible barren uterus' Joy! Seems that Jakob's sperm were excellent quality, as advertised, and one of his swimmers somehow managed to impregnate me. We were taken off guard by the pregnancy, as you'd expect, but also because we were pretty far down the adoption process. So, that's how we ended up with a newborn baby <u>and</u> a two-year-old child simultaneously. It was touuuuugh going during the first eighteen months. I was really tearing my hair out, and oh wow, I missed you, and Mum came over whenever she could, and Dad was actually a pretty great help too, and Jakob's Mum Clara was a GODSEND. Sara was wonderful too, but do you know who was the real MVP? Greta. She even glances at a crying child and it goes mute. It's eerie. Which might account for the eight she's had of her own (okay, not eight – two with Hagen, and two with her new chap).

Ah, there's so much to tell you. Jakob and I are still together. We never married officially, but over here in Denmark, co-habitation is pretty much the same as marriage. I love him. I love him still. It's been hard work, and I can't say I haven't wanted to pack it all up and move back to England ~~every day~~ numerous times, but we've stuck it through, not just for the kids' sake. He's so patient, and funny, and we can argue like two old mules with sticks up their butts, and he can go silent for days, and I can get stroppy and irritated, but he loves me still, I know he does, and I do too. It's such a different love from those old letters though – now with added war wounds and regret and baby sick. It was strange reading about our first love, feeling the hot flush of it again, as if the words were smouldering. I miss it, and I don't.

We live half an hour out of Copenhagen (it's too expensive to buy in Copenhagen now, even with all the tax breaks and co-op organisations to help you buy – it's crazy). I still work at DMTech – can you believe it? I'm a lifer there practically. I now project manage the other project managers, supporting them all and making sure they have a shoulder to cry on. I'm a project manager manager, you could say. If the Danes hoped I'd integrate completely, I think I've failed, but then I've always felt like a cultural outsider. I'm a bad Persian, worse kiwi, passable Brit and terrible Dane, but hey, it's a living. I barely notice all the Danish flags anymore, they're just white noise to me. That means I've acclimatised a little, right?

Again, I keep burying the lead, the kids! There's Mitchel, he's seven now, and Sammy is nearly five. Sammy is so much like you, except considerably blonder (she's the biological one, although we never make that distinction unless we're having 'real truth' conversations). She is a right tinker, and thinks she owns the world, and you almost want to let her get away with troublemaking too, what with her cheeky grin and rosy little cheeks (almost, but not quite). Mitchel is mixed race too – half Algerian, half Moroccan – with the softest hair, and is much quieter than Sammy. He had some troubles when we first took him in, he was exhibiting some traumatised behaviour, so we had to go pretty softly softly (Jakob was AMAZING), but he's totally blossomed since those early days into a sweet, earnest boy who loves books, and planes, and his new mummy, of course.

After Mitchel arrived, Jakob left DMTech and went back to university to become a children's therapist, which was great for him and the kids, but a bit harder on us financially for a good few years. It put a strain on our relationship too, so I'm pleased he's back in gainful employment. I think that's been tricky, my old patriarchal way of thinking (a man being the provider) has truly been tested – but when we have enough money coming in, and I don't feel panicky that we are basically subsisting on government benefits (although considering all the Danish taxes I've paid over the years, I might as well enjoy it), life is good here.

What else? I still don't drink (okay, maybe a sherry at Christmas like an old granny), and I don't smoke either – I kicked that habit for good. Here's something – Mum and I took a trip to Iran together, just the two of us. It was about seven years ago now, not too long after my last letter. Mum just sort of sprung it on me – she had some holiday coming up, would I like to go? I found myself saying yes before I'd really wrapped my head around the concept, and then you're in Mum's tractor beam, so there's no getting out of it. It was so weird being in Iran, visiting old buildings I remembered as a child, seeing family. It's changed a lot, Lil, and not for the better. There's a suffocating energy about the place, as if everyone is watching everyone else (which of course, they are). Mum took me to the house where she was born (pretty much rubble), and we had dinner with a cousin of hers. Mum was lighter and – I don't know – something really clicks when she's there. It's as if she's running on low fuel in the UK, and I know she would never move back to Iran, but I don't give her enough credit for how tough it was to leave. Oh, and we also went to Brighton Pride! Mum, wrapped in a rainbow flag. She loved the drag queens (and they loved her). It was a revelation!

So, yes, – Mum's good, she's single, I think she dates, but it's all pretty on the down low – she says men her age are all so OLD.

Dad's good too – he did get remarried after all, not to Aroha. Her name is Wendy, she's also a kiwi and I actually quite like her. They moved back to New Zealand three years ago, to Auckland. Dad's always complaining about the house prices and how many people live there now.

What else? Sara and Geoff are great – three kids now, God bless them. Don't know how everyone does it. Two kids are almost more than I can handle.

JP resurfaces on Facebook occasionally – he's a tattoo artist in Paris now.

And Robby, here's the thing about Robby, right? Robby won, like, a million pounds – well, not that much, but a considerable amount on a blinking scratch card, went on a round-the-world trip to celebrate and met the love of his life. Can you bloody believe it? That money, by all rights, should be mine…

How's my Danish? Still pretty cruddy, thanks for asking.

I have an admission to make, Lil. It's a tough one. I've read the first Harry Potter book – I HAD TO. Mitchel wanted to read it, and you can't exactly turn down a child's request to read a book, can you? Believe me, I tried! I didn't enjoy it much – okay, maybe in the moment I did, but it's seeing the joy on those blinking kids' faces. Then they fall asleep, and you secretly read to the end of the chapter by yourself in the other room, just to know what's going to happen. And maybe you stay up all night finishing it… I hated it really! I'm still loyal to our pact, I promise!

Ah, that was a text from Jakob: they'll be back soon. The madness resumes. Better start making the food. That's all you are as a parent really, the dinner lady. Eat this. Drink this. Repeat.

Oh, but you'd like them, Lil. They're funny and dippy and mischievous, and they remind me of you SO MUCH. I think ultimately, way back when, I wanted to write those letters to capture you in some way, bottle your essence, and then I could eventually show them to my kids. After reading them back, that's never going to happen – I'm burning those letters, they're too exposing, ha. Anyway, I don't need to bring you back to life, because you are here already, in them – the kids. Genetics are a wonderful thing, but it's not even that, because Mitchel is a dead ringer for you too sometimes. He can get slightly obsessive like you, loves computer games… Maybe I'm only projecting, as FaceTime Margaret would have said before I eventually cancelled her (also, FaceTime is now called… Oh, actually, why would you care?). But there are moments with the kids, the silliness and the word play, it's – I don't know – it's just you. Only you would get the humour in the same way. I sometimes try and explain it to Jakob, but he only shrugs. And Mum says, 'Yes, yes, Lil is always with us,' but she doesn't get it either. You're here, living on in my small people. They are such fun – when they're not screaming, waking me up, or both simultaneously. Or smearing things. Or eating things they shouldn't. Or doing anything dangerous. Kids are the worst. What have I done, Lil?

Also, we have a cat. Me, Joy – a cat! Mickey is her name (our first cat Minnie was unfortunately flattened under a neighbour's car). Guess what? I still don't really like cats!

Right, I'm going to wrap this up. Part of me doesn't want to finish this letter. It's like I've conjured you back again and I don't want to let you go. I could write more letters, I suppose, but no, I won't. I don't have the time or brain capacity – life is too chaotic these days. But it was the truth when I said I'm forever writing you messages in my head, I am. Hope you get them.

Another long letter. At least I'm consistent after all these years…

I miss you. So much.

I don't want to finish just yet. I'm filibustering this letter. Four more years! Four more years!

But really, I'm good. I'm happy for no reason, often – to paraphrase someone smarter and more spiritual than me (Oprah maybe?) – when I watch my children sleeping, or after a good meal, or when Jakob runs a bath for me, and if that's not joy, pure joy, then I don't know what is.

Bye, my wonderful Lil.

Bye.

Love, Joy

A LETTER FROM DREW

Thank you so much for reading Dear Lily – and accompanying Joy on her journey. If you'd like to know when my next book is out, click on the link below to sign up to my newsletter. I'll only contact you when I have a new book out and I'll never share your email with anyone else.

www.bookouture.com/drew-davies

I lived in Copenhagen on-and-off for several years recently, and so Denmark very kindly became the location for Joy to find her way (Fun fact: my initial title suggestion for this book was *Great Danes, Low Expectations*. It did not make the final selection). If you enjoyed *Dear Lily*, could you please leave a review? Until I became an author, I never realised how important reviews are. Honestly, forget about giving me a birthday present this year, a review is more than enough! (Unless it's a very nice present, then I'll have both, please.)

And I love hearing from you – get in touch via my Facebook page, Twitter, Instagram, Goodreads or my website.

Thanks again, and as the Danes say – *strømpebukser*!

Cheers,
Drew

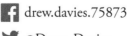 drew.davies.75873

@Drew_Davies

 drewdavieswriter

ACKNOWLEDGEMENTS

Thank you to all my friends and family for your love and support: your messages, your emails, your comments, your patience when I've had deadlines, for suggesting me to your mother's book club in Hereford, and to your Friday knitting group, for taking me to read on holiday, thank you. And to all the new friends who I'm connecting with each week, your feedback and encouragement and reviews and funny one-liners absolutely make my day.

Special thanks to everyone in Denmark – especially Eleni, Mads, Mette, Birgitte and Thiago – you've made me feel so welcome over the years, and brought much hygge into my life. I know Joy is a little tough on Copenhagen, but for me it's another home away from home.

Thank you to my editor, Christina Demosthenous: your patience, enthusiasm and skilful steerage is never less than amazing – and to Alexandra, Ellen, Kim, Alex, Peta, Oliver and all the fabulous team at Bookouture.

Thank you to my agent, Hattie Grunewald, for being such a wonderful sounding board, and the only person I trust to call me 'Bozo' when the need arises – and all the superb team at Blake Friedmann.

Finally, to Marios: thank you for going on this wild writing ride with me, making me porridge when I was sick, and then not minding when I wouldn't eat it because there was too much cinnamon on top. Seriously, though, I could not have done this without you.

Printed in Great Britain
by Amazon